The WRONG Proposal

LEESA BOW

Editing and Proofing by Swish Design & Editing
Proofing by Virginia Tesi Carey
Structural Edits by Lauren at Creating Ink
Cover design by Letitia at RBA Designs

Please join my mailing list to be notified of Leesa's latest releases.

You can sign up and learn more about me on my website at www.leesabow.com

If you're on Facebook, I have a reader group where I chat about books, offer giveaways, and sneak peeks of upcoming books.

To Demi,
You inspired me to write Penny's story.
Your kind soul and thoughtfulness to the environment, your
commitment to a better world, and your love of animals.
You give me so many happiness pennies.

PROLOGUE

PENELOPE

NOT ONE PERSON makes someone happy.

It took me longer than it should for those words to sink in.

Even in high school, I was never without a boyfriend for long, which says more about me than I like to think about.

My parents also emphasize how happiness is about a person's well-being. They link contentment with society and respect for the environment. While I understand it, I'm not as invested as my parents in joy sourced from a relationship with nature. Because it's been six months since the man I imagined spending the rest of my life with shattered my heart, and all the advice to immerse myself in nature hasn't helped. The countless trips to the beach or hiking in the mountains until I fall into bed exhausted fail to heal the gaping chasm in my chest.

This month, my relationship with nature is on hold because she's just *not* doing it for me.

Although the grapes to make wine—tick.

So, I'm sticking with what other almost-thirty single women do on Friday nights—drink wine with my besties until it numbs the pain.

Tonight is my friend Hugh's twenty-ninth birthday. In typical Hugh style, he has booked birthday celebrations every day for the next week.

September is perfect in LA to enjoy the warm nights, and tonight Hugh chose a restaurant to begin festivities. Otium is fabulous, although I feel uneasy being here because it's where my ex and I came on regular dates. The food is to die for, so I'm not letting stupid memories ruin my fun, and I've wasted no time downing a few glasses of white wine.

"So how do I ask her?" A muscle tics in Hugh's jaw as he looks between our other close friend, Zara, and me. He lounges back in his chair, and the ridiculously expensive yet surprisingly tiny cocktail in front of him is yet to be touched. "There are a hundred scenarios, and I want it to be smooth yet romantic. If it's complicated, I'll freeze and mess up."

Hugh has been in a relationship for two years, and I didn't see a proposal coming.

"Mess up like say the wrong thing or not ask her at all?" Zara rolls her eyes as though asking someone to marry you should be the simplest thing for anyone.

"Yeah. The last thing I want is to be at an expensive restaurant wearing a suit and surrounded by other people, witnessing..." He changes direction, "What if she says—"

"She won't," Zara and I say in tune.

"She loves you. She only wants you. You'll be fine," Zara almost sings.

Hugh's nervous eyes dart and lock on me before staring at his hands.

"Hugh." I wait for him to give me his attention. "Bernard

was a dick. Don't compare your love to us." No one should compare their relationship to my ex and me, especially me, because I always pick the guy destined to break my heart.

Hugh is in love.

Bernard was not in love with me.

And I wish it didn't take five years for me to realize that fact.

His gaze turns to understanding. "Thanks, Pen."

I smile then catch the faint outline of my reflection lost in the city lights in the floor-to-ceiling glass window at our side. Bernard and I used to flirt in the glass, catching fleeting glimpses of the other's reflection. A year ago, I misinterpreted his expression. His pained eyes were not from a stressful week that came with being the CEO of a construction firm. Over the prior twelve months, I'd become acquainted with tension on a Friday night. Only this time, Bernard stumbled to find the 'right words.' I saved him the embarrassment and left the relationship myself—a learned skill to *read between the lines.*

Two weeks later, I resigned as an interior decorator.

His company's head interior decorator.

"Pen, you're the creative one of all of us." Hugh forks the gnocchi seasoned with black truffle in his mouth and groans. "I could live on this."

"You say that every time." Zara shakes her head.

"You should try it just once."

She straightens her back. "You know I don't eat pasta. Too many carbs."

"You used to eat pasta," I remind Zara. We grew up together, and both left San Diego to go to college in LA. That's where we met Hugh.

"When I was a teenager." She rolls her eyes.

Hugh shakes his head. "Anyway, where should it happen?"

"I still think a restaurant," Zara says. "Just make it intimate."

Hugh stares at her deadpan. "I'd rather dine at my place. I want to arrive and have a setting that's relaxed, alone, and neither of us has to do anything."

I take a sip of my wine. "Relaxed? What about the beach?"

"Yes." Zara's brown eyes round. "Take a picnic basket and a blanket. That's simple and romantic."

Hugh's shoulders rise and fall with a long sigh. "But how do I set it up?" he asks quietly.

"Have someone set it up for you." I shrug. "It's an easy solution."

"Set what?" he prompts.

I tap my fingers on the table. "The blanket. But it needs to be modern and not just a basic picnic blanket. A small table. Cushions to sit on. Flowers set on a side table. A candle burning with a backdrop of the sunset and ocean."

"And in the basket is wine, glasses, and appetizers ready to serve." Zara grins at Hugh as though we have it worked out for him.

"And a sign in the sand with her name on it or the question already written for you." I wink at him.

Hugh gives me his attention. "You're so good at this... romantic ideas."

I smile at Hugh. "It's something I've always enjoyed... planning dates." I planned so many fun dates for Bernard and me during our time together.

Hugh scratches at the five o'clock shadow along his jawline. "Could you set something like that up at Santa Monica Beach?"

"Me?" I choke on a piece of chicken. "There are companies who specialize in proposals."

"But they don't know me like you, Pen. You could

personalize it for us. You know Sienna, and you've known me forever."

For months, I have distanced myself from anything remotely romantic. "Anyone but me," I murmur.

"I'll pay you three hundred dollars and cover the cost of any props." He doesn't plead yet with the way he stares at me, he could soon be on his knees.

"Maybe I..."

"Yes." Hugh smacks his hands on the table. "What about next Friday around five? I'll take Sienna to the beach. After a short walk, we'll casually stroll up to your amazing setup."

I let out a long sigh. "Fine. But I want to source everything, and the weather must be ideal. Otherwise, you'll need to postpone it."

Zara bumps my shoulder. "Pen, you should consider a side business with your artistic flair."

Sealing a couple's fate with artistic skills is not on my radar since I've managed to mess up every relationship I've been in since high school.

Now, I hope my bad luck doesn't rub off on Hugh.

As fate has it, the following Friday is nothing but blue skies and a faint breeze. Every prop is packed in the car.

When I arrive at Santa Monica Beach, I transfer everything to a small cart and wheel it down to a location away from the crowd. After unrolling the beige blanket, a color to blend with the soft sand, I give it a shake and allow it to float down like a cloud falling from the sky. A wooden table is centered on the blanket, and a round oak table is positioned in the sand by its side. Both are knee-high. I position the peonies and lilies—Sienna's favorite—with strawberry-scented candles on the side table. Then, I place a string of pearls over a large clam shell on the corner of the blanket. Two large cushions are located on either side of the table for the couple to relax. I pitch a macrame half tent behind the table for an intimate feel. And a *Will you be my forever?* sign is on a long metal prong I push into the sand near the side table. I set the table for two, then place the picnic basket holding the food and drinks behind the table in the macrame tent backdrop. Dropping tiny candles in small glasses, I create a path leading from the table to the water. After I finish lighting the candles, I pull out my camera, capture the setting, and send a picture to Hugh with the caption, *Ready when you are. Good luck!!*

Now, to wait nearby to ensure no one else decides to claim the picnic.

"Did you do this?"

I jump at hearing a deep, gravelly voice from behind me. Despite the man's serious expression, the most gorgeous dark brown eyes stare back at me.

Is he a ranger?

"Am I in trouble?"

"What? No. I'm curious."

The handsome man is dressed in a white shirt and black tie and could easily be someone important. Holding my gaze, he runs a hand through unruly brown hair. It's windswept despite there being barely a breeze.

He pulls out his wallet—it's only now I notice his rolled-up trousers and how out of place he is dressed like this—and starts counting his money.

"What are you doing?"

He glances up at me and keeps counting. Then he shoves a wad of cash toward me. "Same place. Tomorrow night."

I hold up my hands to halt him. "I'm sorry if I gave you

the wrong idea. This is for a friend." A friend who will be walking toward us any minute.

He raises his eyebrows. "I have a thousand dollars. Can you do it or not?"

No, and it's not about the money because if he is proposing tomorrow and hasn't thought about it until now, he might regret it, and I don't want that on me.

Wait. A thousand dollars.

Why is he so desperate?

"I could just take your money and run."

"You won't."

"You don't know me."

"I've been watching you for the past five minutes. You're passionate about perfection. You won't run."

"And you can tell that by looking at me?" I fold my arms defiantly. "I'm more than meets the eye."

His eyes lower, taking in my bare legs in denim shorts. Every inch of me feels the heat where his eyes invisibly trace along my skin. When his eyes meet mine again, a slow grin spreads across his face. "I'm sure you are."

I narrow my eyes at him. "Your offer is no longer appealing."

He closes his eyes and slowly opens them again. "Please. What you created here is romantic," he pleads, holding out the money.

In the distance, I make out Hugh and Sienna walking toward us. "We have to go," I say quickly, grabbing his hand to pull him along. I drop it quickly when the heat from his skin seeps into mine. *Not what I expected.* We head up toward the path leading off the beach.

"Here." He shoves the money in my hand. "I'll double it tomorrow night."

"I don't want anymore," I shoot back.

He strides ahead of me. Aware I'm on a public beach, I

shove the cash in my pocket before I'm mugged, then turn to watch Hugh lead Sienna along the candle-lit path.

Even from here, I can see her joy. She touches the sign, and when she turns, Hugh is on one knee. She throws her arms around him, and they kiss. He slides the ring on her finger and then leads her to a cushion. They sit at the table, and Hugh serves the appetizers and the non-alcoholic champagne.

Happy birthday, Hugh.

And just like that, happiness pennies fill my emotional jar.

When I head to the car, the mystery man is gone. Still, I'm smiling as I drive to get a taco, wait until Hugh sends a text to tell me they're leaving, and return to pack up my romantic setup.

The first step of a happy ever after thrills me, even if it's not mine.

THE FOLLOWING AFTERNOON, I'M PREPPING THE SAME SETTING for a couple I don't know.

What is his girlfriend's favorite scent? To be safe, I use vanilla-scented candles. *What flowers does she like?* I decided I couldn't go wrong with red roses. And appetizers—*is she allergic? Gluten or dairy intolerant?*

I've been stressed all morning trying to make an imperfect situation perfect because he has one chance to impress the love of his life, yet he's acted on instinct by liking what I did. Nothing is personalized to them as a couple.

After I finish setting up, I leave a mixture of foods with

labels on packets so the couple can read the ingredients used. Then, at a safe distance, I roll out a towel, sit, and wait.

I scroll on my cell phone and sneak glances like a shepherd protecting her sheep.

A half-hour passes.

Ugh. Did I do this for nothing?

He paid me well—too well. I catch a glimpse of a couple holding hands, walking close to the water's edge. The woman is wearing a cocktail dress, her strappy heels in her hand. Sunlight shines from the diamonds around her neck, light reflecting like shards of glass as it moves back and forth. Mr. Handsome is wearing a suit jacket, white shirt, dark tie, and his trousers are rolled to his knees. His dress shoes are in his other hand.

Why did he pick the beach and not a fancy restaurant?

I shake sand from the towel before retreating to my car.

I recline in my seat and close my eyes.

Maybe Hugh is right.

Making other people happy could be my side hustle.

MY CELL BEEPS WITH A MESSAGE, WAKING ME. THE SUN IS lower in the sky, and the filtered light through the clouds is enough to lull me into a deeper sleep than I wanted.

I open the message from Zara.

How did the suit guy go?

> I fell asleep longer than I should have.
> Heading down to the beach to pack
> up now.

With my cart in tow, I head back down to the beach as the sunlight fades.

Seagulls have gathered near my setting. I rush over and shoo them away from the food left on the table. Despite the birds, I don't have a good feeling. The wooden sign is lying flat in the sand. Hardly any of the food has been touched, and the candles are out.

Shit. I messed up.

His fiancée hated it.

Then I see the note in the basket with more cash.

> *Thank you for creating something wonderful.*
> *I waited for you, but I had to leave.*
> *F.H.*

He waited for me?

I told him I didn't want any more money.

I turn and search the beach.

There is no one as interesting as him in sight.

F.H.

I don't even know his name.

Yet I can't help feeling disappointed that I'll never see him again.

1

FRANKLIN

Two years later...

Every year, Thanksgiving with my family is... interesting. We all come together regardless of how difficult it is since my mother expects us to be a family. Dad takes the opportunity to ask the uncomfortable questions to my younger siblings to keep check on their antics and ensure work outweighs play in the work-slash-play ratio. The longer hours per day you spend in the office, the greater my father's commendation and respect.

"How was London?" Mom asks while Dad is conversing with my younger brother about the current real estate market.

I take a swig of whiskey before answering, "Cold and wet. The sun didn't appear at all, not that I could have enjoyed it from inside the office walls."

Her eyes turn gentle. "I hope you managed to rest some this week." She places her delicate hand over mine.

"Stop worrying about me." I pat her hand. "I'll rest after I close this deal."

She glances at her husband and then at me. I know what she's thinking—she doesn't want me to become my father.

My younger brother, Jobe, is making millions with the real estate company he convinced my father to develop for him. He parties equally as hard as he works, but my father turns a blind eye, allowing Jobe to escape the Thanksgiving interrogation because of the dollars in his bank account.

"In mere months, I assume you'll take your place alongside your brother." Dad scrutinizes my youngest brother, Byron. "Your college revelry days are coming to an end."

Jesus, not this conversation.

Byron stops eating and places his fork on the table.

Mom gives my father a stern look. "Can we at least wait until after dessert to discuss this." It's a directive rather than a question.

Byron remains calm. "It's okay, Mom. This conversation has been a long time coming."

Mom's gentle blue eyes narrow at my father. "You better not ruin our meal, Carson."

My father takes a sip of whiskey from his glass and rolls the ice slowly as though he is pondering his next words.

Byron clears his throat. "I want to go pro."

Silence falls around the table.

Even my mother's azure eyes widen.

"I guess it's a shock as you rarely attend my games, and you refuse to acknowledge the write-ups about us making the finals and how I'm always named as one of the best players." He straightens his broad shoulders. "We expect to go all the way this year."

"All the way?" My father places his glass on the table and ogles my brother. "What the hell does that even mean?"

"Finals. Final Four. March Madness. Premierships. Does it mean nothing to you?" my brother scoffs.

"Mind your attitude, son." The lines between my father's brows deepen. "What has meaning for me is how basketball will enhance our family businesses?"

"As I said, *I* want to go pro. It's *my* dream. I can't see a future as a hedge fund analyst or taking the same path as Franklin."

"Neither do I," I mutter. I love my brother, but I would be riding him hard if he came to work for Hendricks Capital Management.

Charlotte snorts and then apologizes. "Sorry, Dad, but I fail to see future Byron in a suit every day and working in an office." My sister's eyes meet mine. "You're a natural-born CEO, but Byron would rather work out in a gym than flex his power in an office."

The virtual dinner-table tennis match begins.

"In another two years, we'll be having the same conversation, Charlotte." Dad raises his brow at her in warning.

"What if we don't want to work for you, Dad? It's boring to me."

"Boredom comes from laziness," Dad retorts.

I moan. "I dream of being bored," I tell her. "Hold that thought. I never dream because sleep is overrated when you're running a company." I shake my head. My younger siblings are living the party life, whereas my career was etched into rock the moment I was born. As the eldest son, the expectation fell on me to take over the company my grandfather founded. "My college results were perfect as I studied every spare minute to make the dean's list." I was never distracted from my goals. "I chose the hard path, so while I sound frustrated, if I had my time again, I'd take the time to enjoy those years more than I did."

Charlotte smiles at me. "See, Dad. Franklin thinks I'm on the right path."

It's not what I said, but laughter sounds around the table, and Mom's eyes soften. It's how Mom wants Thanksgiving to be.

Joyful memories.

Lola steps into the room, balancing a pumpkin pie in one hand and a pecan pie in the other.

"Thank you, Lola." Mom clears a space. "I'll cut the pie, and hopefully, it will silence the tongues."

"It does smell good." I nod at Mom. Her gentle eyes meet mine, and she flashes her smile. The family together and enjoying a special meal gives her more happiness than my siblings realize.

My father takes another swig of his whiskey. "Before the pie is served, enlighten me on how a basketball career will benefit the family. I understand you can earn millions as a player, but how does that benefit the Hendricks' name? Not forgetting the NBA is not the NCAA, so what is your plan B? We all know dreams can disintegrate quickly."

"You could always buy the team, Dad." My sister shrugs. "And you could offer players to invest their salary with your company before blowing their money on drugs, women, and booze. Is it possible without somehow being a conflict of interest?"

Dad grunts. "Easily earned money is wasted and not respected."

"Easily earned?" My brother raises his voice. "Do you have any idea the extent of training and the physical hardship along with the mental health that is required to be the best?"

"Carson, did you hear what your daughter said?" My mother always ensures the women are heard in this family.

Dad's gaze flicks to my mother and then to Charlotte while he backtracks rather than firing his next response to Byron. "From our investor's point of view, buying a sports team is a distraction. I'm not willing to risk our reputation."

"You're a genius, Lottie," I whisper. She deflected the attention away from my brother. I turn to my father. "Could be an investment worth researching." We've taken larger risks.

Dad pauses. *Is he considering Charlotte's idea?*

"Now..." Mom interjects, "... pass your plates so we can all enjoy pie."

2

FRANKLIN

THE FOLLOWING MORNING, I'm up early to swim a few miles in the Olympic-size pool before showering. I jog down the stairs feeling invigorated even after hours of devising a plan to present to my father the certainties in investing in ownership of an NBA basketball team. Last night, I sent emails to my employees and learned the Los Angeles professional basketball team, the LA Sharks, needs a new sponsor and a huge overhaul to stay afloat. When Jobe wakes, I want to discuss sponsorship prospects with his real estate company to have more fingers in the pie, so to speak. Despite not having the time to deal with this, I refuse to allow an opportunity to pass, especially when it's about timing and because it means helping my brother.

"Morning, Serg," I say to our family's chef. Bacon sizzles on the stove while he stirs the scrambled eggs with a spoon. Sergio has been part of our family for the past fifteen years, and I have spent many a day sitting here on the kitchen island watching him cook. It's therapeutic.

"You're cheerful this morning, Franklin."

I laugh. "I slept well," I lie. My excitement for this new prospect resulted in barely any sleep. "I'm just going to make a quick smoothie."

After blending fruits and green leaves, I pour the smoothie into a glass and head into the dining room, where my father drinks an Americano in his usual clear glass.

"Morning. You're just the man I want to talk to."

He peers up from his iPad. "Morning." He nods to the chair beside him as though he needs me to sit so we can talk, yet I sense we are not on the same page. "Daphne has made the news."

The sound of her name cuts through the air like a knife. Only I feel the knife continue into my gut. For two years, I have tried to forget the botched experience of proposing to her.

She was insulted by my lame beach arrangement.

A casual proposal with cheap cushions and a handmade *Will you be my forever?* sign emphasized how I really didn't know her. Everything about that night was a fuckup—an impulsive moment and my biggest regret.

Daphne deserved more.

A few weeks later, I thought we could continue as we were and when the timing was right, I could counteract my pathetic attempt and make her mine in a way she desired. But Daphne offered no second chance. I blew the one opportunity. She ended us, knowing my work always came first. She reminded me of how I'm so busy I couldn't even arrange the proposal myself and had to get someone else to do it. She even suggested my PA would have organized something special and not some random person on the beach.

And I have regretted it every day since.

Dad angles his iPad so I can see the image on the screen. "Zenith is branching into Italy and France. A move overseas was imminent to oversee the company's growth in the European market."

I absorb what he is telling me.

"She wasn't the one for you."

I meet his gaze, thump my chest, and cough.

"Since you're my son, I assume your ego and fear of failing at something is more important than love."

"No. I loved her. Still do."

"If she'd said *yes,* where would you be now?"

I frown at my father. "We'd be together."

My father scratches the side of his cheek. "Daphne needed more than what you could offer. She wants everything, and so do you. Who would compromise their career for the other? Both your egos and drive to be successful would clash, and neither of you would step back to allow the other to thrive."

I rub at my temple. "In hindsight, I would have done anything."

"That's a lie." My father stands from the table and pours himself some juice from the cart Lola had wheeled in without us noticing.

"How so?"

"You loved the idea of being with Daphne. Infatuation is not love."

"Six years together is hardly infatuation."

"Would you have moved to Milan?"

I hesitate, wanting to say yes. "No."

"Our family has no business in Milan. You are not second fiddle. And the few million she earns is not worth giving up your life for."

I close my eyes, imagining a life in Italy with the love of my life. Only I can't picture it. I try to imagine the dream.

My father observes me. "When the time is right, you'll see."

"See what?"

"The perfect person for you."

I shake my head. "Not when you're not looking."

"The unexpected is when everything falls into place."

"Is that how you met Mom?"

"Are you talking about me?" Mom asks as she comes to join us.

"Good morning." I stand and kiss her cheek. "So, was it love at first sight?"

Mom chuckles. "More despise at first sight."

My father fakes disbelief. "Sophia couldn't keep her eyes off me."

"Carson, really?" she mutters as she sits on the opposite side of the table.

I hold back a smirk.

Mom raises her glass to her lips. "There are two sides to this story, and my version of the truth is more believable than your father's." She ignores his reaction while sipping freshly squeezed juice.

I check the time on my cell. "I would like nothing more than to listen to your story, but I'm afraid I must fly to San Diego for a meeting." Standing, I kiss my mother again, then shake my father's hand. "See you next week. When everyone wakes, tell them I'm eager to see them at Christmas."

Mom holds my hand for a bit longer. "Don't work too hard, darling."

Dad raises a hand. "What did you want to talk about before?"

I lift my gaze to my father. "I emailed you the proposal we can put forward to buy the Sharks."

Dad gives me an approving nod. "I'll read over it today."

Mom glances back at me. "Why don't you spend some time at your Malibu house? Relax by the beach."

"I plan to... soon." I don't mention that I'm burdened by it since it's another thing Daphne despised in a long list of...

What do I hate the most?

3

FRANKLIN

It's the week before Christmas.

Instead of closing deals before the holidays, I'm at a friend's engagement party at a quaint winery in southern Oregon—a full weekend of festivities. Snow-covered rolling hills beyond the vineyard are a picturesque backdrop. My time here will be spent by the open fire and near the bar when I'm not in my room working. I respect Noah, but why do we need an entire weekend to celebrate?

Daphne and her Italian boyfriend are expected to attend.

It's not surprising since we share mutual college friends.

I have a need to see Daphne again and view how she's moved on while my life is unchanged so I can punish myself for messing up our lives. When I look into her eyes, I'll know if there's a chance to ignite what we had and if I stand a chance against her Italian boyfriend. My father's words come back to me. *The family business has always come first.*

Daphne and I are both driven and hungry for the win. I know Dad believes she is not the one for me, and for two solid years, I have ignored every instinct to be with her. Tonight, my feelings will be tested the moment our eyes meet.

I check into my room, freshen up, then head downstairs to the bar. Everyone is gathering before dinner. I weave through the crowd—the weather has forced everyone inside. After meandering to the farthest point of the curved bar, I find a stool and raise a finger to catch the bartender's attention. I shrug off my suit jacket and drape it over the back of the stool. Observing the room, I see no familiar faces. Noah and Olivia have yet to make an appearance. I raise my finger again for service. How long do I have to wait for a freaking drink?

A woman serves me first. "Mr. Hendricks, what can I get you?" I raise a brow. "I'm Melanie, a friend of the couple, and this is my family's winery. I'm helping serve as the snow has blocked some of the roads."

I thrum my knuckles on the counter. "It's made for a busy weekend for you."

"Not when you're celebrating a friend's happiness." She winks at me. "When the roads clear, it will be easier for our staff to get here. I hope the snowstorm continues east and not south."

"Cheers to that." The last place I want to be stranded is in the middle of freaking nowhere.

I peruse the bar's selection of whiskey and stop on the unmistakable bottle with a statue of a horse on the lid. My night just got better.

The woman follows my gaze. "Guess the happy couple knew you were coming with a request of Blanton's. Everyone else is happy to drink the wine from our vineyard. Not to blow our own trumpet, but I highly recommend our cab sauv."

"Yet you just did." I smile. "I'll start with a double on ice and try the red later."

"I'll hold you to that." She grins as she pours my whiskey.

I raise my glass to cheer her when the crowd applauds behind me. "Reserve my seat. I'll be back after I offer my regards to the happy couple." I slide off the stool and leave my coat over the black leather while I search for Noah and Olivia.

Noah is six foot five, so I easily find him by the log fire with Olivia tucked under his arm, smiling nervously, no doubt from all the attention. He pushes red strands from her eyes as she peers up at him.

"Franklin, we're glad you could make it." Noah shakes my hand and pulls me in for a hug.

"Wild horses couldn't keep me away." I lean to kiss Olivia on the cheek. "Congratulations."

Noah steps to the side while Olivia chats with her friends, ogling the large diamond on her finger.

"How are you?" Noah rests a hand on my shoulder. "I see you found the Blanton's."

I raise my glass. "I appreciate the welcoming."

"I'm sorry I haven't called. Between changing jobs, moving houses, and now building a new home in the country, time has flown."

"I understand. Emails work for me anyway. Work has—"

"You don't need to explain. It's good to see you, Franklin. After all the formalities, we should have a quiet drink together."

"I'd like that." I turn to Olivia. "I'm happy to be here and celebrate with you both."

"About that." He takes a step back and leans close to my

ear. "Would you be my best man? I wanted to ask you in person."

I clink my glass against his wine glass. "I'd be honored. Do you have any idea of a date?"

Noah turns as though we are in a huddle. "It's difficult for everyone to get time off work, especially Daph and you." My chest tightens at mentioning our names in the same sentence as though we are still a couple. "So we decided to have a surprise wedding tomorrow."

I cough. "What?"

He smirks, clearly liking the fact he caught me off guard. "Everyone important to us RSVP'd to the engagement, and we didn't like risking not having our friends at the wedding, so we decided to make it a surprise."

"No bachelor party? Hardly fair."

He chuckles. "I'd rather have a quiet drink with you and use the money on a fine bottle of whiskey." He winks. "There is another bottle in the cellar."

It reminds me of our days in college. While everyone partied, Noah and I discussed our life goals while drinking the most expensive bottle of bourbon. We didn't like mingling except when it came to girls, and even then, there was never anyone regular since relationships were not part of our plans. Both of us focused on our careers. Noah worked two jobs, and I offered him free rent to house share off-campus with me. No one but Noah understood my father's expectations.

"You packed a bow tie, right?"

I laugh. "Please. I like options."

"Thankfully, Olivia likes to simplify everything. Less pressure."

"Does she have a sister?"

He laughs. "No, but there are four bridesmaids."

"Four? Am I the only groomsman?"

"Think you can handle four of them?"

I raise a brow.

"Right." He lands a hand on my shoulder. "I invited Damien and Kimberley."

He has my attention. "I haven't spoken to Kimberley in a while," I admit.

"Damien's on antibiotics, and she doesn't want to risk traveling."

I understand what he's saying. Our friend's disability has stopped him from living a normal life. The day he fell sick was a day I'll never forget.

"Kimberley wanted to come but was afraid to leave him."

I blow out air. "His mom is an angel."

Noah hits my shoulder again. "We'll chat more later," he says before more guests close in on us.

The sound of Daphne's laughter carries over the crowd. Every part of me wants to turn and catch a glimpse of her beauty. Instead, I clink my glass with his and meander through the crowd in the opposite direction toward the corner of the bar where my stool awaits me. I'm not yet ready for the pain. Attending to emails while drinking fine whiskey is the best distraction from what is happening around me.

4

PENELOPE

HUGH's first cousin is having a surprise wedding—only a handful of family members know—and when Sienna couldn't make it, he had already responded with two in attendance. For catering purposes, he invited me to join him. A few days away with my friend is always fun, and since he's been engaged, those fun times are few and far between. When we heard Daphne Wright would be in attendance, it made my decision easy. For the past two years, I've been studying part-time while working at Style Line Designs alongside Hugh. Interior remodeling for high-end residential is vastly different than the commercial remodeling I was used to while working for Bernard.

"There she is." Hugh nods in the direction of his idol. Her long blonde hair falls perfectly over her shoulders. The crowd parts, and I manage to catch a glimpse of her champagne-colored dress that appears to be sewn onto her petite figure. Her main accessory is a dark-haired man with an olive complexion. His gaze wanders over the crowd and meets mine. He flashes a knowing grin. The man is so handsome he demands equal attention as Daphne.

"Do you want to go and talk to her?"

I panic a little and take a sip of the red wine. "There is no way I could spark up a conversation with her. I'll just sit and admire while drinking all the wine."

He chuckles. "A little liquid courage is all you need."

"I will need a truckload, and by then, I'll be smashed and say the wrong thing."

"Do you have an elevator pitch ready to impress? I mean, there might be a chance you bump into her in the ladies' room and have thirty seconds to convince her to hire you."

"I'll need thirty years. Besides, you're the one who dreams of working for her." I drain my wine glass and stand. "Can I get you another?"

He shakes his head. "Take your time. I'm going to chat with my relatives, and you don't want to be bored with conversations about harvesting grapes."

I giggle and squeeze past other guests until I get to the bar. As I wait for the bartender, I notice a handsome dark-haired man in a suit with his head lowered, staring into a glass of whiskey. Even from here, I can see how ridiculously handsome he is. He oozes class, and yet he angles himself away from the crowd as though he has the weight of the world on his shoulders. Maybe he does.

The woman beside me moves away from the bar, so I ease my rear up onto the stool. A glass of wine is placed in front of me. I sip it slowly while watching him. Every now and then, his back stiffens. He takes a swig of his whiskey and continues to stare into the glass until his shoulders relax. I finish my wine, and the bartender holds the bottle over the glass and hesitates until I nod. She fills my glass, and with a sudden burst of courage to make a stranger smile, I meander around the bar toward Mr. Sad Face because I'm curious why someone like him is not enjoying themselves.

What do I have to lose?

I push between him and the guy on another stool by his side. "Hi." I give him my best smile.

He glances up at me and frowns. "I think you have mistaken me for someone else."

"No mistaking those sad eyes." I take a sip of my wine. "I thought we're all excited to celebrate the happy couple?"

His eyes dart over my face. Then he frowns again, narrowing his eyes. "Do I know you?"

"Nope." I smirk as though it is a guessing game, but the more I stare at his beautiful face, there is something familiar about him.

"I must know you through Noah because there is something about your face. I wouldn't forget yours."

I flutter my lashes playfully. "I don't know the couple at all, but I like the wine." My words sound disrespectful. "I mean... I'm here as a plus one with a friend."

His brow furrows. "For a moment, I thought you were a gate-crasher."

"No. My friend's fiancé couldn't make it. He's a cousin to the bride." I tilt my head to the side. "What about you? How do you know the happy couple?"

"I'm a close friend of Noah's..." He rolls his hand as though waiting for me to fill in the blanks.

"Penny," I supply. "What's your name?"

This time, his lips part into a smile. "You really don't know?"

"Well, I'm not privy to the guest list." I roll my eyes.

He chuckles. "Franklin." He holds out a hand.

"To be Frank, Frank, I thought you'd be happier for your friend."

"I see what you did there. I *am* extremely happy for my friend. And I'll be telling him later when we're alone."

"Oh, I see. You're not a people person."

"Penny, you have known me for all of five minutes. You know nothing."

"I like this game, though. Am I right?"

"I like doing business with people. Here? There are too many people in a small space."

"And you don't know half of them and retreat to a corner so you don't have to meet them."

"I have some things on my mind, and I'm waiting for an email. That's why I'm here alone."

Only now do I see his cell phone on the bar and his email list open. "Working at a function? Stop being boring and have some fun."

His dark eyes turn on me, and, in that moment, familiarity dawns on me.

Double shit.

It's Mr. Brown Eyes from the beach.

Holy fuck on a stick.

F.H.

Right now, it stands for *Fucking Hell* as in *get me out of here*!

"Fun," he says in a dark, sexy voice. "What sort of fun are you implying?"

He smiles darkly as though his words have spooked me, but I've just failed to hide the horror on my face of knowing exactly where we've met.

The tapping of a microphone sounds through the speakers.

"Thank you for joining us to celebrate Noah and Olivia. Everyone, please move into the dining room and find your assigned seat at the table. A seating map is near the restaurant door."

"Nice to meet you, Franklin. I hope you enjoy the night," I say quickly before grabbing my wine glass and push past other guests until I find Hugh in the hallway.

"There you are," he says.

"I have to leave," I tell him in a low voice. "I can't be here."

Hugh frowns at me. "How much wine have you consumed, Pen?"

I shake my head. "I'm not drunk," I whisper. "But right now, I wish I was."

Hugh scans my face. "Is Bernard here?"

"No. God, do I really look that scared?"

"Yes, now slow down and take a few deep breaths." The crowd moves around us, herding us toward the restaurant. "I'm sure it will be fine." He places a protective arm around my waist.

"Don't let me drink any more wine," I tell him.

"Why?"

"Do you remember the handsome guy I created the beach setting for after I did the one for you and Sienna?"

"Yeah, you were really bummed when it didn't work out for him."

"Right." I look around me, relieved when Mr. Brown Eyes is nowhere to be seen.

"But he paid you well, and the woman's rejection had nothing to do with you," he emphasizes.

"I was just talking to him, only I didn't know it was him until he said something, and... those eyes... I'll never forget those eyes."

"You were just chatting at the bar? And at first, you didn't know it was him?"

"Yes."

"Did he recognize you?"

"No, but his name is Franklin."

"Pen..." Hugh stalls. "Franklin Hendricks?"

I shrug and lift my arms into the air. "Maybe." Shit, F.H. "Yes, it's him. Oh, dear God, kill me now."

Hugh's eyes widen, and his mouth falls open. "Jesus, if you happen to meet Daphne Wright in the ladies' room, do not mention his name."

"Why would I?"

"Because she hated the setting you created for Franklin's proposal to her."

"*He* proposed to *her,* and she *hated* it? Are you sure?"

He shakes his head. "I know from social media his proposal insulted her."

Shit. Shit. Shit. Can the world swallow me up now?

"You'll be fine. Just don't say anything else. No one here knows anything, so enjoy the night."

Right. How can I when my proposal idea was the trigger to the end of their relationship?

Hugh and I find our places and are seated with his relatives at a round table near the wall. There are ten tables with eight guests at each, and Hugh mentions more guests are arriving tomorrow. I'm feeling safe tucked away in the corner of the room until my gaze fixes on Franklin, positioned two tables away, and he is staring directly at me. Oh God, the heat in his eyes makes my heart thump hard.

"Change of plans," I whisper to Hugh. "I'm going to need *all the wine* just to get through dinner."

"Relax, Pen. What's the worst that can happen?"

"*He* is eye fucking me."

Hugh chokes on a mouthful of wine.

"You need to make sure I don't go anywhere near him for the remainder of the weekend."

"Don't trust yourself?" His expression is curious.

"It's been a year since I, you know..."

Hugh chokes again. "Okay, don't share the same stories

with me as you would with Zara. I'm not that sort of friend. But seriously, a year? What about those dates?"

"None of them did it for me."

"Pick someone else and not the most powerful man here, please. Unless you want a fun night with no strings attached?"

In the past year, it's exactly what I've avoided. The two-year journey to discover me, find all the things I like, and not be influenced by a boyfriend is a growing list. One-night stands were added to that list because, after Bernard and a string of one-nighters, I realized random men on top of me made me feel worse about myself. So, I promised no sex until date five. Everyone Hugh set up for me never got past the second date.

But maybe this time might be different.

It feels dangerous to be anywhere near him, and yet my stomach is in knots with curiosity when I imagine what it would be like to spend one night with *Franklin*. I say his name in my head. I imagine those brown eyes peering down at me as his muscular biceps cage my face. *Is he muscular?* I can't tell, but he does look mighty fine in a suit.

And now I want to know.

5

PENELOPE

After dinner, Noah makes a brief speech, thanking everyone for attending, and they are excited for more celebrations tomorrow.

Hugh and I swapped seats with his aunt and uncle as they couldn't see the main table. With my back to the stage, I pull out my cell while keeping it on my lap. Without Franklin's sexual gaze enchanting my mind, I've had time to realize flirting with him is a bad idea.

What if he remembers who I am? How will he react? If who created the setting is leaked to social media, it might influence how people view my work. It could possibly be very damaging.

I stop thinking of the worst outcome and distract myself on my cell, scrolling through notifications. There is a text from my mother asking about Christmas. Another from a client in San Francisco. I've been waiting all week for this email, and now they think late on Friday night is okay.

Popping my cell in my bra, I excuse myself and head to the restroom.

When I exit, I find an oversized white leather chair against the wall. I lean back, enjoying the comfort. Retrieving my cell from my bra, I send a text to my mother and tell her I'll call her when I get home, and I read over the email from the client.

"Why the serious face?"

I glance up at the brown eyes that threaten to undo my demeanor.

"Because these emails are stopping me from having fun." That puts a smile on his gorgeous face. "You should do that more." I push up and go to step around him, only to find his warm hand wrapping around my wrist.

"What's that?"

"Smile. It's why I started talking to you at the bar, because you appeared sad. When you *do*, your whole face brightens."

His lips curl up, but his eyes are serious. "I have something in mind that would make both of us smile."

"I bet you do." I roll my eyes and look away as it's safer than staring into his brown eyes that have the power to mesmerize me. "I'm done with this game."

"Yet you're the one who approached me at the bar earlier. I'm ready to play, Penny. Tonight."

I yank my hand from his. I'm coming to understand what Hugh meant by Franklin being the most powerful man in the room if his bossy attitude is anything to go by. I cross my arms and glare at him to prove I'm not someone he can control. "And what's in it for me?"

He leans down and whispers in my ear, "The best fucking orgasm you've ever had." I close my eyes with him this close. Every part of me wants to grab hold of his tie and keep him near so I can inhale his woody scent. Suddenly, my thoughts whip me into the forest, and I'm lying on soft leaves, and Franklin's mouth is all over me.

God, I could come just by smelling him.

I press my thighs together to stop the ache. "A fucking orgasm?" I murmur.

"Fucking is usually involved," he says in a low, sexy voice. The intensity in his eyes tells me he already knows my answer. His hand rests on my lower back as though I'm already his.

No. no. NO.

I inhale a sharp breath. Is there harm in one night? It's not like I'll ever see him again. Since I first saw him on the beach, I've wondered what's under that suit. "Come closer," I whisper.

He frowns then leans in so his face is inches from mine.

"What do you want?"

His eyes darken. "To make *you* smile." His words are deep and breathy, and the air from his lips wafts around my face. I inhale it as though it's a life force. He then adds, "I want you, Penny."

My knees buckle, and my sex throbs with need. Even the back of my neck tingles as lust rips through my body. No one has said those words to me in a Very. Long. Time. And certainly not the sexiest man in the room.

"You're wrong," I murmur, then trace a finger over my lips. "I almost came hearing my name on your lips. No fucking required." Now I'm thinking of all the things his mouth could do to me.

His eyes widen then lower, and I feel the heat of his gaze on my body. A low growl sounds from his throat. "You're killing me, Penny."

I'm so turned on just speaking to him. "There's some sort of magic in the grapes they use in the wine."

He raises a single brow, cups my chin with his hand,

leans closer, and softly kisses me. I cup his handsome face and hold his lips to mine. He tastes like whiskey and a hint of mint. His tongue entangles around mine, and I let out a moan.

He pulls away, putting space between us. It's probably a good idea since we are standing in the foyer for everyone to see.

"Not magic." His sexy eyes hold mine captive. "This is all me. To answer your question, it's room 208."

"I didn't ask," I whisper as I watch his sexy ass walk out of the foyer toward the staircase. My fingers touch my tingling lips. Why did he have to taste so good? I do everything not to follow him and force myself to return to the restaurant.

"I was about to come find you," Hugh says when I sit beside him.

Now that I'm here, I regret not following Franklin. My sex throbs as though I have denied us a potentially life-changing orgasm. Overdramatic, but it's been so long my sex is no longer in drought. The rain is officially here. I'm so wet for Franklin, I can't think of anything else. I don't look at Hugh because I'm about to tell a lie, and he'll see straight through me.

"I'm not feeling well. Too much wine." I lean down and pick up my purse. "I'll see you in the morning for breakfast."

He touches my arm. "Do you want me to walk you up? My aunt's conversation is hardly stimulating."

"No, I'm good. I want to rest for the big day tomorrow," I whisper.

I stride out of the restaurant and rush up the stairs to the second floor. Before I take a guess at going left or right, I slow, seeing him leaning on the wall with one leg bent, his foot resting on the skirting, his arms crossed.

He smirks at me. "It took you long enough."

6

PENELOPE

HE TAKES my hand and leads me along the hallway, and I count numbers on doors like a time bomb in my head.

200.

202.

204.

206.

I know what this is, but I'm so freaking anxious.

Damn him for kissing me in a way that I want more.

We stop at room 208.

I stop breathing.

He glances down at me. "Nervous?"

"Very."

He keeps hold of my hand while he swipes a keycard with the other. "Don't be. We can just chat since you were determined to cheer me up at the beginning of the night. I was glad to get out of there after all the questions about..."

He trails off and doesn't finish his sentence, although I

sense what he was going to say since his ex is here. If he mentions her name, I'll probably blurt out sorry and say something about the proposal, and then he'll know I ruined his relationship. I know I wasn't the sole reason, but I can't help feeling partly responsible.

Franklin holds the door open for me to step inside his hotel room, and I stop thinking about everything else when I see the size of his bed.

King-size.

I force myself to look anywhere but the bed because my thoughts race, and I'm thinking of us naked when he said we could just chat. There's a small refrigerator and a minibar. A lounge chair and desk are in the corner, with an office chair against the opposite wall. A table lamp provides the only lighting. The wall behind the bed is wallpapered in a green and red geometric pattern. I nod to it. "Woah."

He grins. "I wouldn't hire their decorator to style my home."

I giggle. "I feel like I'm turning cross-eyed."

He chuckles. "That would be the effect of the wine." He points to the lounge. "Take a seat." He opens the refrigerator, retrieves two bottles of water, and then hands one to me. "Can I get you anything else?"

I shake my head.

We fall silent for a moment, and I appreciate him being a gentleman and giving me space as though I'm going to change my mind. The sensible part of me is yelling to get out of here. My hormones argue otherwise.

"Are you sure we haven't met somewhere, Penny?" He sits on the desk chair and swivels so he's directly facing me. "There's something about you." He hesitates. "It's a feeling I never get when I first meet someone. In my line of work, I don't lower my guard *if* I don't know someone."

And he's lowering his guard for me. I guzzle a few

mouthfuls of water. "You seem as though you're a man who would never forget a face."

He eyes me carefully. "This is true. Why did you make it your mission if you didn't know who I was?"

"I spotted you from the other side of the room and thought, why is he so sad? Sometimes, I react on instinct, and it's not always the wisest decision."

He tips his bottle of water to me. "Some decisions require instinct to make quick decisions. Your gut can steer you in the right direction, and tonight, I think it was a good choice."

"Yet you didn't tell me why you were sad." Guilt fills me, knowing why, and I'm keeping it from him.

"You interrupted me while responding to emails." I know he won't be smiling while working, only I know the real reason. Franklin leans back in the chair and rubs his chin. "I didn't tell you that my ex is here."

I sit forward, shocked at his admission. "We were together for a long time and split two years ago. We've barely spoken since, and it hurts because she was also my friend."

My guard lowers at the way he says she *was* my friend. "You're a better person than me. I despise my ex."

He stares at me for too long.

I'm not interested in expanding this conversation. "Let's make a pact not to talk about our exes tonight." I stand and stare out the window at the light snow fall shining from the pathway lights. "Or how we could be stuck in this place if there's a snowstorm." I turn to him.

"I overheard you talking to your friend about San Fran. Is that where you live?"

"Are you spying on me, Franklin?" I like that he's interested. "No, I live in LA. We hope to work with a client in San Fran."

"In what line of work?" He crosses his legs, assessing me. "Or am I being intrusive?"

"Not intrusive." I flop back onto the lounge. "I have a career in making people smile." I grin at him. "First, I get tipsy and then annoy them at bars."

"You could make millions..." His eyes darken and travel down my body to my bare legs, where my cocktail dress ends and then to my feet in red heels to match my dress. Despite the freezing weather outside, it's warm and toasty inside, and the temperature in this room is about to reach boiling point. "The pay isn't great, so I also have a job on the side working for an interior remodeling and decorating company. I guess by the time I finish with people's homes, they are smiling, so it's not a lie."

Franklin's smirk is slow and deliberate, and he doesn't take his eyes off me.

"See? My work here is done." I go to stand, and Franklin snags my hand before I take the first step.

"May I have your business card before you leave?"

I stick out my chin. "You couldn't afford me."

And for the first time, he laughs, and it reaches his eyes. "I'm willing to pay in other ways."

"A bit ahead of yourself, aren't you?"

He stands. I step backward, one, then another. I'm gazing into those heated eyes.

He takes a step.

I move back.

Our lips are only inches away.

His hands are by his sides.

And then my legs hit the edge of the bed.

I'm so aroused all common sense is lost.

"Are you leaving, Penny?" He kicks off his shoes, undoes his belt, and then his shirt buttons.

Yes, I'm leaving.

The words don't get a chance to pass my lips because his shirt is tossed to the chair, and I'm staring at his tanned, muscled chest and a freaking thirty-pack of abs. Holy mother of fucks. Franklin is gorgeous.

"I decided to stay," I manage before slowly lowering my ass to the bed.

His eyes are fixed on me as he slides his trousers down his athletic thighs, his erection bobbing against the band of his underwear.

I swallow, unable to look away. Franklin has the king of dicks if there is a king of dicks.

Do I wait for him to undress me, or do I start to undress myself?

He's about to remove his underwear, so I peer down to my shoes to unbuckle the straps because I'm weirding myself out by staring at him.

"Penny." His voice is demanding. "Do not touch your shoes. Look at me."

I meet his eyes and watch without looking directly at his crotch as he slides his briefs down his thighs and kicks them to the side. With his hands on his hips, he stares at me as though he's waiting for me to lower my gaze. He caresses his dick as though it's a trophy. In a way, it is.

"Do you want this?"

My gaze lowers, and I'm staring, really staring, at his thick, beautiful cock. I nod and lick my lips. I'm ready. Straightening my back, I look at Franklin and spread my legs. Franklin comes to stand between my thighs. Before he has a chance to touch me, I take charge and guide his cock to my mouth. Sliding my lips around him, I start slowly, and as I build, he moves with me, not forcing me to take all of him in.

"Is this how it's going to be, Penny?" His hands are in my

hair, and with a slight tug, my head tilts so I'm staring into those sexy eyes, giving him the pleasure he seeks.

He thrusts gently, slowly speeding up, and I move my head in sync with his actions. His audible breaths tell me he is building, and I celebrate internally because I'm the one who will give him the first orgasm. It's a small win.

More moans escape him as I move my tongue around his cock, tickling the end as he withdraws. One hand rests on my shoulder, and the other is in my hair, wrapping it around his fist.

"Penny," he moans. "I'm going to come."

He's letting me know, but I'm going all the way like a freaking pro. It's been too long, and I'm back on the horse, riding it to the finish line. I suck him harder and faster until he comes, his body jerking with a final thrust. I swallow him, close my eyes, and keep swallowing. There's another tug on my hair, and my eyes flash open. He slides his cock out of my mouth, falls to his knees, and kisses me. He is all over my lips, and then his tongue glides over mine, and I feel a sense of kink that he is tasting himself inside my mouth. Our kiss is hotter than the one in the foyer, and I am ready for this. My clothes are an unwanted barrier, so I slide my dress over my shoulders, needing to get naked now.

"Penny," he growls against my lips. "Stop." He positions me in the middle of the bed. "We have all night."

Being out of practice, I am not going to last much longer. He takes my leg, lifts it, and removes one stiletto. He dots kisses from my ankle along my calf, and I flop back on the mattress, covering my eyes with my arm. A shiver rolls over me when his lips reach the inside of my thigh. His fingers trace a line ahead of his kiss, caressing my skin. He kisses my sex, and I thrust my hips ever so lightly.

Forget the other leg, I want to beg.

He lifts his face and smirks. Oh yes, I'm putty in his

hands. I could just flick my heels into the corner of the room. On the other hand, it's been too long since a man adored my body like this, and it might be the last time for many months. When his lips reach my inner thigh, I place a hand gently on the back of his head.

He stops kissing and lifts his gaze. "Do I need to tie up your fucking hands, Penny?" he growls. He takes my wrists and places them beside my head. "Relax. I've got this."

"I can't relax," I snap. "I want you inside me. *Now*."

He hovers, kissing my neck. His nose nudges my ear. "There is only room for one CEO in this bed, and I'm it. Trust in allowing me to pleasure you."

"I do trust you," I say, all breathy. "But in my last relationship, the sex would be over by now, and I'd be going to sleep," I blurt out.

"What?" Franklin's expression is set as he considers my words. Disapproval gleams in his eyes.

I wince. "Yeah, sex was quick, and let's say I never finished first. But my vibrator is a godsend."

"That's the last time I ever want to hear you talk about your ex since he's not worth thinking about. And after this weekend, you'll want to throw your vibrator in the trash."

I giggle. "Then get to it." I open my legs for him.

"Stop rushing me." He pulls me up by my hand. Kissing my shoulder, he slides one strap of my dress down, then the other. The zipper sounds, and I wiggle my ass as he slides the fitted material over my hips, along with my thong and throws both aside. My bra is unclipped and joins my dress on the floor. He holds my hand and leans back as if to peruse my body. His eyes trail over every inch of me, and heat prickles my skin in a wake from his gaze.

"You're a beautiful woman, Penny."

I allow myself to take in his hard, angular physique—his

broad shoulders, masculine square chest, rock-hard arms, and taut waist, and then my eyes lower to his hard cock.

"How long can you hold a squat?"

I have no idea what he's thinking, but after a few drinks, I can exaggerate the truth. I love the gym, albeit I haven't been for a few months since work became busy, but I maintain decent leg strength, thanks to throwing myself into hardcore workouts after Bernard dumped me.

"An easy five minutes. Maybe more."

"Perfect."

I'm getting more praise tonight than I did in school.

He rolls onto his back. "Stand over me."

I stand, peer down at him, and it feels like a shift in the power. He is giving me a minute. With an overbearing need, I drop onto my knees and kiss him. For a few moments, his mouth on mine is all I'm aware of until he breaks the kiss. "Lift, Penny." I stand as he wants. Sliding down the bed, he stares directly into my sex.

"Straddle my face."

I do as I'm told.

"Slowly lower yourself on me."

"Onto your face?"

"Yes, Penny. I want you on my face so I can eat you."

My insides flip, and my sex throbs hard.

I fall forward and start to giggle as I lower myself. I can't help it. The wine is mixing with my overexcited hormones, and I'm higher on joy than if I'd smoked weed.

"You won't be laughing in a minute."

I silence him with my sex as I line up my clit with his lips. His hands cup my ass with a light smack.

A little squeal escapes my throat, only to be silenced when his tongue brings my dormant clit back to life. He alternates kisses and little sucks with that tongue sliding through my sex, sucking hard, kissing lightly. I'm panting, shaking, my knees weaken as my thighs go limp, and my arms tremble. "Oh God," I cry out as I come for the first time.

He doesn't stop, and I feel myself building again.

"Frank..." I moan loudly, my clit throbbing with pleasure. My head falls forward onto the bed while my ass is away from his mouth and up in the air. I can't take anymore. He moves from under me, and I don't care. I need a minute. Then my ass is pulled higher.

"Stay like this." I hear the sound of foil ripping.

Two fingers push inside me, and my head jerks up. "Oh." From behind me, he circles and pumps his fingers in and out of my sex. "Ohhh. Yes." I circle my ass with another orgasm building. "Yes. *Yes.*"

He smacks my rear, removes his fingers, and I want to cuss, but I'm silent as his thick hard cock pushes inside me. I squeal a little and clench my sex.

"Easy, Pen. Let me in. I want to be completely inside you."

I try to relax as he thrusts gently, slowly. It's a beautiful pain. My body relaxes, taking him in. The squelch of us fucking as his thrusts speed up is such a turn-on.

"Yes, yes!" I moan. "More." I lift my elbows so I'm on all fours as Franklin slams into me from behind. Harder. Faster. My head is bouncing forward with the force as he pounds me from behind. I build fast and come faster than a Hexie bullet train.

God, I need to catch my breath. So I lower my head. How long do couples usually have sex? More to the point, how many orgasms are normal because another builds while the pounding continues? His hips circle, and one hand finds my swollen, sensitive clit. I move my hips with his, pleasure and pain blurred. Then he fires his dick into me at a piston pace, and I hold still to take everything he is giving me.

Breathe.

I focus on taking deeper breaths to stop myself from panting before I pass out from hyperventilating.

He wraps both hands beneath me as he rests his chest on my back, opens my legs, and drives himself harder inside me.

Holy mother of fucks. I face-plant onto the bed, my ass high in the air and his for the taking. Another orgasm rips through me. "Fraaank," I whimper. My arms are limp by my side, and my face is squashed into the linen. I'm floating. Light-headed.

"Penny." My name rolls off his lips, and it's the most beautiful sound. He thrusts hard and jerks, emptying himself inside me. He pulls out as my fatigued body falls onto the bed. Then he moves beside me and lies on his side, facing me. I am exhausted. Fucked. Literally.

"Hey." His breath is hot on my face, his breathing still rapid.

"Hey," I murmur.

"Ready for round two?"

I can't move. All the blood has drained from my brain to my throbbing pussy.

Franklin moves the hair away from my eyes. "I want to see you."

I could stare at his handsome face all day.

His brown eyes are so gentle and caring when he asks, "Do you want a drink? Can I get you anything?"

"Water." But it sounds more like *orta* because my lips are still squashed into the sheets. He laughs, and I decide it's my new favorite sound. Scrap that. My name on his lips when he comes inside me is my new favorite sound.

He scoops me and rolls me over, and I moan as he hands me a bottle of water. "You're rather dramatic."

"So would you be after a sexual drought."

He chokes on his water.

I unscrew the lid and guzzle the cold liquid. The way he's staring at me changes the vibe in the room. His heavy brow isn't an expression of judgment but more of concentration, as if he is deep in thought. His eyes flick over my face.

"Okay, Mr. CEO, stop the assessment." I glance away and sip more water while observing the room. My panties are in one corner, my dress in the other, and my shoes yards apart. *Where is my purse and cell?*

He opens the bar refrigerator, and I stop searching, focusing on the sexiest ass I have ever seen. Could this man be any more perfect? "How often do you work out?"

He turns, holding two ice cubes, and hands me one. "Um... is this for my water?"

"Every day, and no. Suck the ice to numb your snarky tongue. Now lie back. I wasn't kidding when I said that was round one."

What?

"I should go."

"Why?" He sits on the bed beside me. "Is someone waiting for you?"

"You're making me nervous."

"In a good way?" Franklin stands and starts to stroke his cock, slowly and deliberately.

"Oh. I..." I'm tingling inside. Only my pussy is madly throbbing from round one. "I'm not sure I'm up to it."

"You will be."

Why do I believe him?

"Lie back, and for once, let me do my job."

I pop the ice in my mouth and suck. I get a bit of a brain freeze then inhale the sharpest breath when ice is rubbed over my pussy and clit. I keep sucking on the ice to stop myself from saying anything.

"Finally, she learns."

"Okay, Frankie."

"Penny," he warns. "My grandmother was the last person to call me by that name and I was eight-years-old."

Frankie, I mouth, because I have totally lost my mind with nerves, excitement, and arousal mingled with pain surging through me. I'm a delirious mess, drunk on sex.

He pushes the ice inside of me, and I gasp loudly, reaching to grab his hair.

"I'm going to have to gag you and tie your hands to your ankles."

I sit up on my elbows. "Is that a thing for you? Tying up your partners."

"If it's what they like." With one finger on the ice cube, he guides it around my sex to soothe the folds. It's erotic as well as freezing, and I drop my head back and moan. "What do you like, Penny?"

"Whatever you do to me," I say, sounding ridiculously coy.

He moves off the bed and into the bathroom. There's the hiss of running water before he returns with a wet hand towel. He places it across my chest to cover my nipples. He opens the freezer door and takes out another piece of ice. "Your pussy is so hot the ice is melting before I have my fun." He pops the ice between his teeth and lowers his face. With the ice on his tongue, he caresses my sex.

I cover my eyes with the back of my hands. "This is pleasure and torture."

He pushes the ice into my pussy with one finger and licks my folds. He sucks lightly, and I buck my hips.

"Do that again, and I *will* tie you down. You almost broke my nose."

I snort a laugh.

"You have the strangest sense of humor."

I giggle.

He places a hand over my stomach to stop me from perhaps giving him a bloody nose because I can barely stop my hips from bouncing uncontrollably. Seriously, what does he expect with his mouth licking and sucking and his finger inside me with ice swirling around my pussy? It is sensory freaking overload.

"Franklin," I moan his name in warning. "I can't."

"Can't what, Penny?"

"Keep still."

Lifting his head, he removes the warm towel and tucks it over my sex. Wow, my pussy is now an athlete receiving hot and cold therapy on recovery day.

He pulls me to sit, and I'm eyeballing his erect cock.

"Squeeze your tits together."

"Like this?" I lean forward like I'm talking into his dick as if it's a microphone. "Testing 123." Laughter bursts from me.

He lifts my chin and stares down at me. "Do you take anything seriously?"

"I'm sorry. I've never been drunk on sex. It's messing with my brain." Doing what he asked, I push my ample tits together.

He pushes that Adonis cock between my boobs with slow thrusts. "Perfect!" He moans. Franklin lifts my chin so my head is tilted, and I'm staring into those dark, sexy eyes, watching him lose himself while he fucks my boobs.

"You have great tits, Penny," he says.

"I know." I grin. It's the one thing Bernard liked about me—not that I am thinking about him. Not when I have the most beautiful man wanting to pleasure me. Out of everyone there, he wanted me to be sexually satisfied when all I wanted was to make that sad, handsome man at the bar happy.

Well, my mission is accomplished.

But that's not all true.

Before coming to his room, I knew who he is and that I helped to ruin his proposal.

I have to tell him.

He moans my name. "Penny," he says, all breathy. "Look at me."

My conscience is overtaking my thoughts, but I'll ruin everything if I tell him now. I let go of my boobs and grab his cock and shove it in my mouth before I say something I will instantly regret ruining our night.

He is so close it only takes my mouth a few pumps. My lips squeeze his shaft, and then he jerks with a final thrust deep in my throat. I swallow him, trying not to gag because he has pushed deeper than he did the first time. I may have taken over, but his thick cock has silenced me.

He eases his dick out of my mouth. I have a front-row seat with nowhere to look except at his cock as it softens. His muscled abs move in and out while he catches his breath.

"You can't help yourself, can you?" he murmurs. "I wanted to finish inside you."

"Sorry, not sorry."

He lifts my chin with a finger, and I grin. "You. Were. Warned." He goes to his suitcase and pulls out several ties. "There's a reason I packed this many ties. It wasn't indecision. The universe knew I was meeting Penny Sassy Mouth."

I laugh, he turns, and his dark, sexy eyes silence me.

I gape at him. "Are you shoving them in my mouth?"

"As much as I should, no. My cock is going to leave you speechless. Now lie on your back, open your legs, and hold your ankles."

I roll back and do as I'm told, my thoughts racing ahead.

He wraps one navy tie around my ankle and wrist. Wow! Then he wraps a gray tie around my other ankle and wrist.

"This isn't working for me. I'm not color coordinated."

Darkness crosses his face.

Oh shit. It was a bit funny.

He sits back on the desk chair and links his fingers, seeming to assess me. "This is your last chance to voice how you want me to pleasure you?"

My head falls back onto the bed. "You already have," I say, exasperated. I close my eyes slowly and open them again. I'm going to regret ever talking to this man at the bar.

Franklin kneels at the end of the bed and stares at my pussy, open and ready for him. "Your pussy is sexy as fuck."

"Well, that's what it's designed for."

When he eyes me, I shut my mouth.

Franklin lowers his gaze and strokes himself. It doesn't take long for his dick to thicken. God, I want to know his thoughts while he's staring at my pussy.

He rolls on a condom and then lines himself up at my entrance. He pushes himself all the way inside me, and I want to scream with the pain and pressure. He positions his arms so they are straight and above my shoulders. He eases out slowly and lines his hips up with my tilted ass. He spreads his thighs to slip deeper.

Holy fucking hell. "Slower," I plead.

A dent forms between his brows. "For once, trust me."

I take a breath but say nothing.

He moves in and out slowly, deeper and deeper. My pussy must be in heaven as I'm getting wetter. He's slipping in and out easily, and it's a green light. I've never felt anything like it. I can't touch him or move. All I can do is receive his expertise swirling through every part of my body. It's borderline pain, with excitement overriding everything else. His balls are smacking my ass, and the noise of hard fucking and heavy breathing fills my ears.

"Are you sure we don't know each other?" He moans as if he's close to coming.

I shake my head, unable to talk.

Franklin's cock silenced me without it being in my mouth.

His eyes fixate on me.

"Oh God!" I moan, ready for the beautiful explosion of ecstasy. "Ahhh..." The biggest orgasm rips through my body. "Untie me. Untie me now."

Franklin pulls out of me, his dick bobbing toward the ceiling, thick and strong. He pulls the ties off me, pushes inside, and stills. Color fills my thoughts as I need a moment to absorb the joy while my body is limp. Franklin doesn't move, giving me the time needed. Our bodies are mashed together with most of his weight on his elbows. With a light touch, he slides my hair away from my face and kisses my lips, cheeks, and neck.

I'm staring at the ceiling, aware his dick is going limp inside me. This is not about him but me—the pleasure all mine.

I close my eyes, needing to rest.

I OPEN MY EYES SOMETIME LATER.

My bedside lamp remains on while Franklin sleeps beside me, his dark hair tousled after a night of sex. With his strong arm draped over my stomach, I can't move, but I'm busting for the bathroom. *Jesus, I'm still sore, so it's going to burn like fire.*

I lift his arm and gently lower it to the bed.

Now is the time to sneak out quietly without any 'thanks for the orgasms.' So I gather my things and creep to the bathroom.

I dress, take my heels in my hand, and slip out the door. The hallway is thankfully empty, though the elevator dings behind me as I hurry back to my room.

After finding the key, I unlock the door and flop on the bed, exhausted. No doubt I could sleep for a week. Only my alarm is set for seven so I can meet Hugh and head down to the restaurant for breakfast. My hand goes between my legs to ease the throbbing.

When I see Franklin tomorrow, as I inevitably will, should I act like nothing happened?

7

FRANKLIN

IT'S BEEN over an hour of mingling with guests while the bride and groom dress in secret. I stand out like blood in snow, wearing a bow tie and tux. They didn't indicate a time for the ceremony, though I expect Noah to appear soon.

I weave through the crowd to find staff who might know the schedule when an arm reaches out and halts me.

Daphne.

"Frank." She shoots that killer smile. I inhale a sharp breath, ready for my body to react to her touch. *Nothing.* And that confuses me for a moment. "Did you have a good night?" she purrs.

All morning I've been thinking about last night. An image of Penny lying on the bed, her legs spread wide, comes to mind. "It was enjoyable." I smile internally at the memory. "How was yours?"

"Fine. Although Stephano talked for hours in the bar, we headed to bed about four o'clock this morning."

At first, I avoided Daphne's eyes, afraid of what I might see or feel. Ironically, Penny is the one who has helped me through this weekend. The very person Daphne criticized about my proposal setup.

Penny wasn't to blame. I was. And Daphne knows it too, which is fair. But the ugly words she spat at me at the time about the novice setting stayed with me. She didn't watch Penny on the beach like I did, considering every detail to make the experience memorable for another couple. While the beach scene didn't drizzle money, it did have a romantic element with privacy, which is what attracted me to watch Penny work, all to make someone else happy.

I take a long look at Daphne. My brain expects me to weaken after being so anxious in the bar last night. Instead, I notice her bloodshot eyes—an assessment void of emotion. Daphne is not a fan of late nights. She is a workaholic like me and demands her beauty sleep as we both used to start work at the crack of dawn.

I want to say the bar offered us something different since it's where Penny decided to make me smile.

What were the chances I would see Penny again after my disastrous proposal? To be honest, I would have said none. But last night, it took me a few minutes to recognize her again, but I have never forgotten her beautiful, innocent face. That day on the beach intrigued me, and last night, my curiosity shifted to thinking about *her* happiness.

Instead, I say, "Perhaps you could take a power nap after lunch?"

"You might need a power nap yourself?" She eyes me suspiciously. "Did I see a woman leave your room early this morning?"

If only she knew the truth.

It's ironic, really.

I lean in close to her diamond-studded ear. "If someone did leave my room, it's no longer your concern."

Her face drops. "I regret it every day."

I take a step back. "Don't do this. Not here."

"When? I need to talk to you," she pleads.

I shake my head. Not today when tension is high with the wedding and work. I've been checking notifications every freaking minute, waiting for an email from my assistant, who is expecting a call so we can get the ball rolling for my father to take ownership of the basketball team.

I scan the room, hoping Noah will appear when my gaze meets Penny. *Fuck! That woman steals my breath away.* She sees who I'm talking to and turns away before moving through the crowd until I no longer see her. I don't usually care about a woman I was with for one night, but I do care about Penny for some reason.

Lowering my voice, I say, "You did the right thing ending us. We were too focused on our careers." *My father was right.* "I'm not the right person for you, Daph." Needing space, I walk toward the bar without looking back at Daphne's expression.

I check my watch for the time.

Is midday too early to drink?

After the bartender pours a whiskey on ice, I swirl the gold liquid before taking the first mouthful.

"Ready?" Noah's hand lands on my shoulder.

I turn to him, dressed in a navy tux with a gold bow tie. "You scrub up well."

He hits my shoulder several times. "Let's do this."

I down the drink and shake my head with the burn at the back of my throat.

The staff scurries past, carrying an arch covered with flowers, and positions it at the front of the room.

Tap. Tap. Tap. The microphone is tested.

Plastic chairs are carried out, stacked in threes, and pulled apart. About fifty chairs are lined and divided by an aisle. The crowd is buzzing, and a few whispers have struck up as some guests begin to guess what this party is really for.

"Ladies and gentlemen..." A woman in black trousers, red shirt, and matching suit jacket holds the microphone. "Please join us in celebrating the love between Noah and Olivia."

A hum of excited chatter rises above the crowd.

"Are they?"

"No."

There are many questions and statements as some guests take their seats. Noah and I are standing back. His cell pings with a message, and he signals to the guy in front of the sound desk at the side of the room.

"All of Me" by John Legend sounds over the speaker.

Noah and I take our places by the arch of flowers. The woman in the red jacket opens a booklet and grips it like a priest holding the bible in church. I imagine much happened behind the scenes to surprise the guests, yet everything is falling into place with simplicity and ease.

Daphne would have never settled for such an easy and low-key wedding.

I sigh out a long breath of relief.

In a short time, my mindset has shifted. It's what I say to my clients. Keep an open mind and be pleasantly surprised by the prospect of investment. Forget everything you thought you knew until you hear all the options.

Loud, audible gasps and sighs sound over the crowd as the first bridesmaid appears at the top of the stairs. The ladies take each step gracefully.

Noah thought I might spark an interest in one.

There is only one woman I'm interested in this weekend, and I can't find her in the crowd.

I glance up the staircase at Olivia, who's stunning in a long, white, satin gown. She's holding flowers and smiling down at her future husband. A weird feeling twists in my stomach. My friend is getting married, and for some reason, I'm hit with a sense of loss and relief.

I think about what my father told me about the battle of two successful people in power careers. I'm sure many survive, yet my father saw through Daphne and knew we had outgrown the relationship.

Why did he wait two years to tell me?

Would I have believed him if he'd said something earlier?

I turn and skim over the crowd, searching for Penny. When I don't see her, I turn my attention to Olivia walking down the stairs.

Why did I search for Penny? She's impulsive, and I am struggling to find a reason not to see her again tonight.

My cell vibrates in my pocket. It's the call I've been waiting for. Immediately after the ceremony, I will head to my room to work before the dinner. It's the *reason* I do not have a permanent woman in my life.

Vows are swapped, and the happy couple kiss.

Everyone cheers, and Noah takes Olivia's hand before they walk down the small aisle between the chairs. Olivia holds her flowers in the air while the crowd applauds.

I follow. The first bridesmaid links her arm through mine as we head toward another room.

"Please stay for appetizers and drinks while the happy couple sign on the dotted line and take photographs."

Something green catches my eye. To my right, Penny stands near the wall, talking to guests. She looks sexy in green just as she did last night in a red dress. Her smile ignites something inside of me, and I have to force my gaze away.

My cell buzzes again, and it's enough to distract me from the weird sensation in my gut.

As soon as we're in a private room, I excuse myself and walk to the side of the room to read the messages on my cell.

Five missed calls.

Seven text messages.

I fire off the same messages to my assistant and brother, telling them to give me ten minutes.

As soon as I witness the signatures and pose for a few photographs, Noah and Olivia are whisked away for a series of photographs on their own. The weather has eased, so with a coat around Olivia's shoulders, they set out into the snow-covered vineyard to have photographs with a backdrop of white-tipped mountains.

I stride toward the stairs. After a dozen steps, I stop, turn, and lock eyes with Penny. She glances up from her conversation with a guy and gives me a few seconds of her attention before turning to continue chatting. She doesn't acknowledge me.

There is seriousness in her expression I didn't witness last night.

I push away thoughts of Penny and pull out my cell, tapping my assistant's name, then wait for her to answer. "How long do we have?" I ask while walking away from the crowd.

"There are three other offers, and you have until close of business tomorrow."

What was I thinking, taking days off midweek? "Have Paul draw up another offer. Add ten million. Our final offer. Any problems, call me back."

"Will do." My assistant clears her throat. "So, you were the best man. How did that surprise go down?"

"Surprisingly well."

"Great. This trip has been good for you. Relax and have fun. Talk to you later, Franklin."

I end the call before tapping on Jobe's name. "What's the offer?"

For the next half hour, I make calls back and forth about this damn basketball team until I receive a text saying the bridal group is about to make an entrance, so I make my way back to the foyer.

The guests are already seated in the dining area.

The music starts, and the bridesmaids walk ahead of me through the doors to clapping and cheering. Noah and Olivia follow, and the music is barely heard above the applause.

I turn to where Penny sat yesterday. Her friend is in the same seat, but there's no Penny. Immediately, a pang of disappointment hits me. Only days ago, I would have been searching for Daphne, not a stranger who has made me smile.

Noah is seated on my left. "You're up first for the best man's speech."

"Right." I pull out a note of bullet points I thought of when I woke this morning after the disappointment of not waking beside Penny.

There's a small podium, so I tap the mic. "Welcome to the celebration of love for Noah and Olivia. I'm Franklin Hendricks, and I have known Noah since college..."

Penny strolls into the room with a drink in her hand, and some guy is behind her. They whisper before returning to their seats. I'm watching her as she walks, annoyed that she's late and is with a guy. She squeezes past Daphne's chair, and Daphne turns, no doubt to see who I'm ogling.

I clear my throat to continue and glance over at Noah and Olivia, smiling as I talk about our college days. Olivia smacks Noah's thigh in jest after one story, and he points a finger at me in warning. I would never cross a line because there's a limit to the humor I will use to get a reaction from the audience.

I finish with how proud I am of my friend, saying I'm glad he found happiness with Olivia as she's proven to be his forever love.

Olivia holds her hand over her heart and blows me a kiss.

When I take a seat, Noah taps my back in appreciation.

I stand along with Noah and Olivia. "Here's to the bride and groom." I raise my glass, the crowd responds, and drinks to salute my friends.

The entrée is served, and the guests' glasses are refilled. It's a chance to sneak a glance at Penny. She is staring at me with a serious, unreadable expression. If anyone should be pissed with the other, it's me for not being truthful. I recognized her first and didn't say anything.

Before the main meal is served, the bridesmaids speak on behalf of Olivia.

Plates of chicken and steak are served.

As I finish the last mouthful, my cell vibrates in my jacket pocket—a message from Hayley.

"I have to pop out for a while," I tell Noah.

He rests a hand on my shoulder. "I understand, man. We all appreciate how busy you are, and I'm grateful you could be my best man."

"My pleasure, my friend."

"Just hang for another fifteen minutes or so." He scans the crowd. "Have you spoken to Daph? Did she mention how miserable she is in Italy?"

"Yeah, but we only spoke briefly." My jaw ticks, thinking about what she said to me. Now that I've seen her, I won't simply fall at her feet. "I don't recall her saying anything about being unhappy." Indecisiveness is not being unhappy. She only mentioned regret.

"I hoped you two could be friends again. To be honest, I didn't know how it would go with you both in the same room for the first time in years."

"Same. I thought it would mess me up, yet it did the opposite. Seeing her helped me realize she was right to break off the relationship. I'm not the right man for her." I take a sip of red wine and scan the room for Penny. She is sitting on the opposite side of the room. Her big, beautiful eyes meet mine, and for a second, there is a connection between us before she turns away.

"And you came to that realization in one night. It didn't have anything to do with last night and a young lady in a red dress?"

"What?"

Noah smirks at me. "Daphne mentioned perhaps a little late-night tête-à-tête with her."

"Daphne knows nothing."

Olivia leans over and tells Noah it's time.

The music plays, and I witness the bride and groom take their first dance as husband and wife. I take the first bridesmaid, Ella, out onto the floor and join in. The song finishes, and another guy asks to dance with Ella.

Now's the chance for me to leave and attend to the long list of messages, only I stop and weave around the tables to where Penny is seated. "May I have this dance, Penny?" I hold out my hand. Her friend Hugh's eyes round wider than the white dinner plates.

So, she didn't mention our night to him.

Penny stands, takes my hand, and we silently move to the dance floor. It's a slow waltz, so I hold her close and inhale her sweet floral perfume. The sweet scent suits her— beautiful yet alluring. "You look stunning, Penny."

She leans back and stares at me as though I've said something offensive. "I'm surprised you noticed."

"How could I not? Green is your color. It brings out your eyes."

She rolls those beautiful eyes. "What do you want, Franklin?" she murmurs. "Is it the end of the night, and now you speak to me, hoping I'll come back to your room?"

"Am I talking to the same girl as last night?" I whisper in her ear. "You were determined to make me smile. We had fun."

"Yes, we did. Too much. I don't think it's right to hook up again."

What? "Everything about last night was *right*."

Her back stiffens under the palm of my hand. "I feel the same, and now I want to know more about you, and that feels wrong since we'll never see each other again."

"Do you want to see each other beyond tonight?"

Penny nods, then shakes her head. She peers down at her feet just as the song finishes. Something is holding her back. It's probably for the best. "Thank you for the dance. It was lovely to meet you, Penny. I hope you enjoy the rest of the night. Unfortunately, I have emails requiring my attention, so I'm heading to my room to work."

Penny looks up and into my eyes. Her earnest expression shouts she has so much more to say to me.

"If you want to chat, you know where to find me." I lean in and kiss her cheek, perhaps for the last time.

8

PENNY

AFTER DANCING for a solid hour and having a few more glasses of wine with Hugh, I told him I was tired and heading to my room.

Not a lie since I'm still recovering from last night, except the thought of leaving tomorrow and not speaking to Franklin feels all kinds of wrong. I need to tell him what freaked me out. Tell him he did give me the best orgasms of my life, and maybe, just maybe, we were meant to meet this weekend. Officially meet, unlike the first time.

And there's the... *I don't want to be a number because no girl wants to feel cheap.*

Knock. Knock.

Nothing.

Maybe he is already asleep.

Knock. Knock.

I wait and listen.

Just when I turn to walk away, the door opens slightly. He has a towel wrapped around his waist.

What if he is with someone?

This is such a dumb idea.

Franklin opens it all the way. "Penny." He runs a hand over tousled wet hair.

"Are you expecting anyone?"

He raises a brow and turns, leaving the door ajar. I follow him inside, locking the door behind me. Laptop screens glow at the back of the room. Scribbled notes on paper are scattered on the desk alongside a whiskey bottle.

Instinct tells me to stop. "Am I intruding?"

His cells buzzes, and he holds up a finger while he answers, "Tell me some good news."

A slow grin creeps across his face. His hand rests over his stomach as though it's relieving pain. "About fucking time. I'll wrap this up tomorrow when I'm back in the office. Get some sleep."

He ends the call and glances up with a relieved expression. For a change, there is no dent between his dark brows.

"It seems I have something to celebrate. Answering your question, no, you are not intruding. In fact, your being here is perfect timing. I don't want to celebrate alone."

"You could go downstairs. They'll be partying for a few more hours."

He takes a step closer to me. "As could you, but you chose to come to my room because..."

I let out a sigh. "I needed to see you again and say goodbye."

Ever so lightly, his fingertips dust over my cheek. The heat radiates through me as though there is magic in those fingers. He can excite me sexually and give me the best damn orgasms of my life, but the warmth of his hands reminds me of Reiki. He could heal me with a light touch thanks to the heat emanating from him to me.

"Do you need more of last night?" he asks.

I scan his beautiful face.

Is that what he thinks? I'm here for sex?

His eyes darken as though remembering all the things we did. I shake my head to dispel the thought of us together as though it was what we both needed to mend our hearts. Maybe it was. Until last night, I didn't know what I'd been missing in the bedroom. He made my body sing like a freaking opera singer.

Do I want another night like that?

"I just wanted to see *you*," I reply softly.

He lifts one eyebrow, and I sense those brows have a personality of their own. In just two nights, I'm reading his expression. It's giving me clues as to what is going on behind those beautiful brown hues.

I walk to his window and stare out at the snow coating the ground. I should be grateful the storm passed farther north, and we can get home without interruption. Yet the thought of Franklin and me stuck in a hotel together for another day or so sounds perfect, and I'm disappointed we can catch our flights on time.

"Are you happy for us to part ways and not see each other again?" The words trip out of my mouth, and I stare at the glass showing his reflection behind me.

I expect him to rub the back of his neck or chest and flinch to show he is uncomfortable with the question. Those dark eyes meet mine in the reflective glass. His feet are planted on the carpet, and there is no rocking back on his heels. His poker face is set so I spin around.

"You have your business-like expression on."

His brow flinches.

"And this is *not* a business proposition." I sigh. I'm ogling his broad chest, those rounded biceps, and—

I swallow.

Take a deep breath.

Do not fall under his spell.

He comes to me and takes my hands in his. "Pen."

Oh shit. I know what this is—another it's-not-you-it's-me-scenario. I keep my sights firmly fixed on the door.

"Are we being honest here?" His voice cracks. His tone is... different. He guides my shoulders to turn so I'm facing him. His palms glide to the side of my shoulders as though he's securing me to the spot. Those brown eyes lock with mine, and I'm caught in his gaze.

I nod once, unsure where this is going.

"This isn't the first time we have met, is it, Penny?" His poker face is back.

I reach out for a chair—anything to hold to regain my balance, only nothing is close. "I... I... what do you mean?"

"Honesty."

He hasn't blinked or flinched.

"Not really..."

"Not really?" Pulling the chair away from the desk, he sits and leans back, waiting.

I clear my throat. "It's not clear."

"When did you realize who I was?"

"When did you realize?" I raise my voice because this is beginning to feel like a stupid game of interrogation. "Have you pretended not to know who I was this entire time?"

He runs a hand along the side of his jaw, the first sign he is uncomfortable.

"I thought it was something you said to girls to make them..." I shrug, "... feel memorable. Were you playing *me*?"

He pushes up from the chair and takes a step toward me.

"Lies and pretense cause more harm than good. I asked to see if I could trust you. At the bar, there was a moment when recognition crossed your face, and I assumed you remembered how we met. Your face dropped, and you almost ran away."

"But you didn't let me. You could have told me from the beginning that you knew me. Honesty goes both ways."

He reaches and takes my hand. "It does. It's why we're having this conversation. You have made a potentially bad weekend a surprisingly memorable one. Thank you for making me smile." His lips curl up before he leans in to kiss my cheek. "It wasn't your fault."

"What?" I say, all breathy with emotion.

"Your setting on the beach. It was beautiful. Only it wasn't right for Daphne. She wanted the glamour, fine dining, and expensive champagne while being proposed to. I underestimated her worth... her words, not mine. I blamed myself for our breakup. I now understand we weren't right for each other. Because if she loved me as much as she professed, then she would have understood that it is not where, but just that it was me who asked." He pauses a moment, but I'm unable to say anything. "I don't believe any man is sure his partner will say yes. There is always a snippet of doubt, and I believe sensitive times require privacy."

"Right." I take a step backward. "You don't need to explain anything to me." Another step. "Well, it was great to meet you. I had fun," I say awkwardly.

He sits on the bed, giving me space.

Way to go to distract me because I'm back ogling his bare skin and those rippling muscles.

"Penny." His eyes meet mine, full of earnestness. "Rambling is the best way to tell if I'm rattled." He pats the side of the bed.

"You're rattled?"

"For the first time in a long while, I want to try with you."

I lower myself next to him on the bed and take a deep breath. "I sense there is a big but..."

His hand reaches out and takes mine. For a moment, he stares at our linked fingers. "You wouldn't like being with me. You would be forever lonely waiting for me to come home. Waiting for you to mean more to me than my business."

I understand what he's telling me. "And you don't think that will ever happen?"

"Since we're sticking to honesty, then I'm afraid not. It's why things didn't work out between me and Daph. Jumping forward another five years, things between us could be different."

"I understand." I push up off the bed because it feels weird to stay. I'm wise enough to leave on good terms.

He takes my hand and gently pulls so I'm standing between his thighs. "Yet... I want you to stay."

I lean down and kiss him because I could stay, but I break the kiss and step away. "If you ever want to chat about life over a coffee..." I smile and walk away.

9

FRANKLIN

AFTER A FEW DAYS in New York meeting with clients and potential investors, I board our private jet. It's been a hell of a week since the wedding, and I'm keen to head back to LA.

The one thing I love about New York is the amazing view from my penthouse. Although late December is all about gray clouds as snow dusts over the city. The blizzard forecast hit Chicago, so I got out before it traveled farther east. It's making for a difficult Christmas for some, and warnings are being broadcast about driving only if necessary. A dull ache forms in my gut, remembering my college years and how a friend died on the road by not heeding the warning, wanting to get back to his family a day early.

One Christmas forfeited for a lifetime is a deal no one should risk.

I signal to Heidi for a whiskey.

Turning to the window, I stare at the darkening sky and the storm clouds below us.

Heidi places a glass of gold liquid on my table. "Anything else, Mr. Hendricks?"

"That is all, thank you, Heidi." I down the contents of the glass in one hit before opening my laptop. Scrolling through my emails, I find one from the caretakers of my Malibu property.

Dear Mr. Hendricks,

All preparations for your stay are in order.

I do want to point out there is a broken rail on the internal staircase.

Enjoy the holidays.

Yours sincerely,

Clancy,

Beachside Home Services

Malibu is where I can relax.

It's the one place Daphne never visited. She didn't like the beach, so it's still in the original condition from when I purchased it. Daphne handled the interior décor of my penthouses in LA and New York. She said she would arrange renovations to the beachside property when she had time and couldn't imagine doing any interior remodeling before the renovations.

Yet, it's a place where I find peace.

It's not about the inside of the house.

Sitting on the front balcony, staring at the ocean, creates a sense of calm to my unsettled thoughts. Although, if I am preparing to sell it for a substantial profit, it's time to plan a remodel of the home.

Suddenly, I find myself smiling, knowing the perfect person for the job.

My mother has a tradition of us spending Christmas Eve in the family home. I helped Charlotte and Mom decorate the tree since my brothers hadn't arrived yet. It's the first chance I get to catch my breath, so I head to bed at a reasonable time.

I wake refreshed.

After showering, I head downstairs to an empty dining room.

A few minutes later, Dad walks in wearing dark trousers and a white button-up shirt. "Merry Christmas, son." He comes to me and holds out a hand. As I shake it, he places his other hand over mine.

"Merry Christmas. Are you ready for everything Mom has planned?"

He chuckles. "No one is ready for that."

I grin because we've all suffered through Mom's extensive holiday planning ever since we were children. It's her day, and Dad knows better than to interfere.

"She has matching sweaters for us all," he says with a poker face. I know he begrudges it, yet the joy it gives her means we all play along with one rule—no pictures uploaded to social media.

"Are the colors brighter than last year?"

He shakes his head as he pours his orange juice. "I'm not privy to see. Did your brothers wake you last night?"

"No. What time did they get in?"

"Jobe arrived before midnight. His work Christmas party

kicked on without him. And Byron arrived around ten with Brandon."

"The Aussie stayed in LA for another Christmas?"

Dad nods. "It appears we may be signing two rookies."

"Who knew they would become friends when those two met at college as teammates and almost enemies to vie for court time as freshmen?"

"Brandon has more patience than I have with my son."

I laugh. "Byron wants another trip to Australia and to stay with Brandon's family. You know he loves the laidback lifestyle and how Aussies love their sport."

My father shakes his head. "That boy... I can't wait for a woman who can make him settle down."

Byron has plenty of women. "You think a woman will help him see the light of not playing ball and work for you?"

My father grunts.

I don't see it happening anytime soon.

"What time did everyone get to bed?"

"No idea, but your mother woke me when she came to bed around two."

"True?"

"She is excited to have everyone together at home."

It's the small things that give my mother the most joy.

Brandon wanders into the room with his curly hair, a tangled mess. He is wearing a navy college T-shirt and gray sweatpants. My father's poker face hides his thoughts, yet I know exactly what he's thinking.

Sweatpants should only be worn to the gym.

"Morning, Brandon." I stand to shake his hand. "Merry Christmas. It's good to see you again."

He offers a firm handshake. "Morning. Merry Christmas to you both." He turns and shakes my father's hand. "Thank you for your kind hospitality for another holiday season."

"Merry Christmas, and you're welcome. You're up early." Dad checks behind him. "Is Byron awake?"

"No, sir, not yet."

"Have you spoken to your parents?" Dad asks.

"Yes, I just finished FaceTiming before they went to bed. Christmas is done and dusted, and Mum is tipsy and wanted to say goodnight. She misses me. It's the fourth Christmas I haven't returned home, but with a serious training regime leading up to finals, I can't afford the lethargy that comes with jetlag."

"Perhaps next year your family could have Christmas here," I offer.

A smile spreads across Brandon's face. "I would like that because I hope to go pro after college, and games are played on Christmas Day. They would get to see me play."

Dad shoots me a serious expression. "Your mother will not be happy about this."

"Not Christmas Eve," Brandon adds. "Players get that time with their families."

Dad's expression is one where he seems to absorb his words. "There is much for me to learn about this game."

Brandon grins. "Congratulations on your new sports executive position as controlling owner of the Sharks."

"Thank you, Brandon. I officially take over at the end of the season, and it won't be announced until then so the news doesn't distract the players or have the staff worrying about future roles."

"Yeah, Byron said it's on the hush." He pours himself an orange juice. "May I sit with you?"

Dad points to a chair opposite me. "Take a seat. Also, I want you to know there is no guarantee I will recruit my son." Brandon's eyes widen. "He'll need to prove himself to the coaches and be a good fit for the team. Acquiring this team is a business decision and will be treated as that with no favors given."

Bullshit. My father is doing this for his son.

"Merry Christmas, my darlings." My mother waltzes into the room, and the air shifts immediately. She is the happiest woman I know, and her smile could power the city at night. She is classy as ever, wearing a navy and white elegant dress.

Then I notice what's in her arms.

Green sweaters.

"I got you the same size as Byron." Mom beams her smile at Brandon.

Brandon springs from his chair. "This is cool, ma'am. Our family has never worn matching Christmas sweaters or pajamas, especially since it's usually hot."

"Extremely hot from what I've heard." She hands him his sweater. "Where are the others?" Mom asks.

"Sophia." Dad arches his brow. "It's only six thirty. I'm surprised you're awake after the late night."

But when my mother is awake, everyone is awake.

My cell buzzes with an incoming call. I retrieve it from my trousers pocket. It's David, who manages my nightclub, and I wasn't expecting a call from him.

Mom pouts at me. "Please, not on Christmas Day, Franklin."

I give her an apologetic look. "Sorry, I need to take this."

"Sophia, if someone is calling on Christmas Day, it's important," Dad emphasizes.

Before I answer, I catch Mom shaking her head at my father. She has made it clear she doesn't want me to turn out like him.

I stand to leave the room. "Merry Christmas, David."

"Merry Christmas, Franklin. Sorry to call, but you should know what's happening at the club."

I leave the dining room and step inside the sitting room, closing the door behind me. "Do I want to know?" I bought Dricks nightclub as an investment, and it has grown in popularity after some smart marketing. Now, we struggle to accommodate the hundreds of patrons who line up to get in almost every night when it is already at capacity. We hired one of the best DJs in the city, and after renovating the building so the circular upper floors have a bird's-eye view of a central dance floor and large screens that flash from the stage to the dance floor, you are not disadvantaged no matter what level you are on. It's proved to be one of my best personal investments.

"We have a problem. We have limited supplies of liquor for tomorrow night."

"How the hell did this happen?"

"A miscalculation. Our beverage manager was off work sick, and no one followed up on the order. We've all been run off our feet. To make matters worse, one of the newer staff got pinged with drugs on the property while taking a food delivery. After the delivery, the basement roller door was open, and he was observed by an undercover cop snorting lines."

"For fuck's sake. Who does the screening on employment? And was it a miscalculation or theft?"

"I'm looking into it. I didn't want to bother you, but thought you needed to be kept in the loop."

"Appreciate it, especially if someone is arrested. Thanks for sorting it out. I'll be in later in the week after the holidays." I end the call and lean my shoulder on the wall. I need a moment to process the pile of shit that has gone down.

"Everything okay?" Jobe's voice comes from behind me.

Turning around, I reach out and shake his hand. "It will be." His bloodshot eyes from partying last night give away he's not ready for today, even though he has showered and smells fresh. "Merry Christmas."

"You got a minute?"

Something people ask when they really mean, do you have an hour to sort out their problems? "Sure."

Jobe strokes the stubble on the side of his jaw. "The basketball sponsorship. I've had a couple of big names pull out. I wanted to discuss it with Dad, but I need you to be there."

"Why did they pull out?"

"They heard of a new takeover and said it made the club fragile with an uncertain future."

"How many?"

His eyes lower. "Almost all of them."

I let out a long sigh. *Merry fucking Christmas.* "Give me their names, emails, and cell numbers, and I'll take it from here."

10

PENELOPE

THE DAY AFTER CHRISTMAS, I wake in my childhood bed.

After I moved away at eighteen to go to college, I come back to stay a few times a year, yet with every year, I wish Mom would let me redecorate it.

With my contacts, I could do it on the cheap. Only Mom doesn't throw anything away. Why change something if there is nothing wrong with it? She took my advice and painted the walls with environmentally friendly paint because if it's good for the environment, then she'll always say yes.

After showering, I head downstairs to say goodbye.

"Did you sleep well?" Mom asks as she blends me a healthy smoothie.

"Always."

"I think Poppy is lying," Dad says with a grin. He has always called me Poppy in an affectionate way. Sitting at the kitchen table, Dad has a mug in hand. "Lacey, our daughter is sleeping in a bed she has outgrown. I bet she wants to redecorate her room as well." He glances at me. "Am I right?" He then sips his coffee, waiting for me to agree.

I shrug. "I could if you want me to."

"There is nothing wrong with the room." Mom's tone is blasé.

"Poppy is a designer. Let her do it as it will always be her room."

"I've thought about it," I say quickly. "Only I know you love the memories that come with the room."

"We keep the memories up here." Dad taps the side of his head.

"What do you want to change?" Mom stops blending and pours the pink liquid into glasses.

"It doesn't matter, Mom. But if you want my input, I'd style in a natural palette." Holding onto things means it's more than just protecting the environment from unnecessary trash piles. It's preserving a memory, and I don't want to take that from her. We didn't have much money growing up, and my parents raised me not to be wasteful. I was happy and never asked for more than they could give. I started working in the mall while still at school and worked hard on my grades to get a scholarship to college. But now I can help them, though it's hard not to offend Mom.

Mom hands me the glass. "We can talk about this next time you're here."

"We can." I take a sip. "This tastes good, thank you."

She smiles lovingly at me. "I know how much you love it. Did I tell you there is a trunk of things in the garage for you to go through?" Mom limps to the table. It's worse this morning than yesterday. She did fuss after me on Christmas

Day. "We haven't thrown anything away in case you wanted it."

I sit for a moment. "I can next time." I down the smoothie in one go. "I wish you would go and see someone about your leg pain."

"I'm fine." She straightens her back as though she is feeling strong. "Nothing a swim in the ocean won't fix."

Why is she so stubborn? "Thank you again for a wonderful Christmas." I check the time. I don't want to make my parents late for church after they missed it at Christmas time last year during the COVID-19 outbreak.

My dad stands and holds his arms out wide. I stride over to him, and he gives me a bear hug. "Don't be a stranger, Poppy."

"I won't." I squeeze Mom tightly, and then Dad comes to join us in a group hug. "I love you both very much."

They follow me to the front door. "Please keep it locked," I remind them.

I sprint to my car to avoid the chill in the wind.

The weather will supposedly warm by lunchtime, a pleasant temperature for winter, and nothing like the weather I experienced in Oregon.

Every time I remember my night with Franklin, warmth surrounds me.

We had one hell of a night together, and I'll never forget it.

Before starting the engine, I call Zara. "Hey, I'm on my way."

"Great. We'll get coffee first. Do we have time to stop at the OB Pier? The tide might be low, and we can just—"

"Of course." As teenagers, we used to hang out at the pier or Cabrillo to view the tide pools. Coming home is like being in a Twilight Zone, and I am thrown back into it every time I return. I love seeing my parents, but everything is the same. Yet sometimes, Zara and I need a familiar place to reflect. The tidepools are a place that grounds us before we hit the busy city again.

Two months later...

On Friday afternoon, I'm tidying my desk and thinking about sleeping for the entire weekend. It's been a hectic week, and I've been working ten-hour days and then heading home to finalize documentation on some projects. Hugh and I have been coworking on commercial projects, and I have been handling some of the residential clients with smaller remodeling plans. The more experienced staff works with high-end residential clients.

Hugh comes to stand at my desk.

"Oh, no. What is it?" *Please don't ask me to stay back.*

"Sienna's flight was canceled."

"Oh shit. I saw the blizzard warnings. I thought of her and hoped it didn't affect New York."

"Yeah. At least she has somewhere to stay."

I nod. Sienna is from New York and often visits her parents when she is there for work.

"So, since she is out of town, maybe Zara and the two of us could go dancing. The DJ at Dricks is fabulous."

"Why do you love dancing more than me? Seriously, you're the only guy our age I know who wants to spend every weekend at a different club."

He edges his rear onto my desk. "Because I can dance.

You are possibly the most uncoordinated female on the planet."

I pout at him. "So maybe you don't want me to come with you."

"Girl, I am not leaving you to sit home another Friday night and listen to your roommate and her boyfriend go at it like rabbits."

I laugh. "I'm used to it. Besides, I was gifted the best orgasm not so long ago."

"You deserve to have an orgasm every night." He shakes his head. "You can't go a lifetime without sex by remembering one good fuck."

"It wasn't once." I pull a face.

"Anyway, there is plenty of fish out there. You don't live in an aquarium. It's LA, baby."

"Ugh. I have no interest when I'm this tired."

He springs off the desk. "Meet at mine by eight. I'll text Zara."

When I arrive at Hugh and Sienna's place, the television is on full volume in the background.

"Sorry." He mutes it. "I was listening for updates on the East Coast weather while I dressed."

"Your entire apartment block could hear it."

He eyes me up and down and ignores me. "Well, don't you look hot?"

I run my hands over my tight red dress. "It's too clingy."

"Trust me, it's not. I sense an incoming orgasm."

"Stop it. That's not why I'm wearing it. I haven't been to the laundromat in weeks, and I'm running out of clothes."

Changing the subject, I notice there's a bag in the corner of the living room. "What's this?"

"Trash. Sienna and I cleaned out cabinets."

I pick up a glass candle. "These are new."

"Yeah. Sienna hates the scent."

Focus is printed on it in cursive. I take a sniff, and it smells amazing to me. I pick up another and another—all new yet different scented candles.

"Do you mind if I take some?"

"Girl, you can have them all." He shakes his head. "You know you can throw stuff out and not feel guilty. It's a personal choice if you want something or not."

"I know, but these are yours, and I have an idea to—"

"Penny, I don't care if you take them and throw them away next week. If you *need* to take it to make something..." he makes a circle with his hand around his chest, "... or whatever it is in your heart that motivates you to save everything, I won't stop you."

"I don't do it to everyone." I pick up some wooden beads and some string. "Your stuff is sentimental."

Hugh chuckles. Then his eyes dart to the television, and he stills.

"What is it?" I turn, hoping it's not bad news for Sienna, only there is an image of a middle-aged man with dark hair and streaks of gray. His dark eyes are familiar. "Who is he?"

"Your boyfriend's father." Hugh turns up the volume.

"Huh?"

"There is a rumor Carson Hendricks will be the new owner of the LA Sharks NBA team. Is there anything that family doesn't have a finger in?"

"Is that a bad thing?"

"Of course not." Hugh stares at me. "Do you really have no understanding of their wealth?"

I shake my head. "Should I?"

His intercom buzzes with someone downstairs at the door. Hugh presses the touchpad, and the camera flashes onto Zara's face. "Just letting you in, babe." Hugh turns to me. "Are you going to fuck him again?"

God, I want to... a thousand more times.

But given the last words spoken between us, it won't happen, so I answer with, "No."

11

FRANKLIN

INSIDE DRICKS NIGHTCLUB is a room with a viewing window opposite the VIP private rooms on the second level.

I'm here on a Friday night for business matters, not pleasure. These past few weeks are the closest I've come to losing my mind. Hendricks Capital Management lost clients, and after those incidents, I'm hoping the media doesn't get wind of the nightclub's latest problems, especially since someone leaked the Sharks' ownership to the press. It's all unwanted attention.

A private waitress enters the room and refills my whiskey glass.

David is chatting about protocols and the accounts. Most of the problems have been actioned, and it offers me some relief before heading to Malibu for the weekend.

Standing by the glass window, I observe the crowd. Barely any of the wood floor is visible between the bodies dancing. I'm fixated on a dark-haired woman in a red dress. She moves in a familiar manner.

Surely not...

She leaves her friends and moves away from the dance floor.

I have to find out for sure.

"Excuse me a minute."

David follows my gaze to the dance floor. "Is something wrong?"

I don't want to make a big deal about this. "It's someone I know."

His expression slides into a frown. "Do you need security to accompany you?"

"No. I'll be fine."

Standing at the top of the stairs, I glance down at the patrons enjoying the club. I've lost sight of Penny, and I'm frantically scanning the crowd, searching for her. I descend each step slowly. My heart flutters, catching sight of her sitting in a booth in a dimly lit corner of the club, talking to a female. The thump of the bass reverberates through my chest—I'm nervous, and I haven't felt like this in years.

Moving through the crowd is harder than it appeared from upstairs, but eventually, I reach her table. "Penny." She doesn't turn around, seemingly lost in a conversation with her friend. "Penny," I try again.

We pay the DJ a lot of money, but the loud music makes it hard to hear.

I lean closer. "*Penny.*"

Her eyes widen. "Franklin?" Heavy makeup outlines her eyes and highlights her lashes.

Is she on a date?

"What are you doing here? I mean... I didn't think this is somewhere you'd hang out?"

"It's a work thing." I glance at her friend beside her.

"Work as in your team is here?"

"No. I..." A cough stops me from finishing the sentence.

"Sorry, take a seat," she shouts and slides closer to her friend.

Her friend holds out her hand. "I'm Zara. I've heard quite a bit about you."

"Not all bad, I hope." I shake her hand. "Nice to meet you."

"No, not all bad." Zara winks at Penny. "I'll get us drinks," she says quickly and slides out the other side of the booth.

"Allow me." I pull out my cell. "What are you both drinking?" I tap on the number to the bar only a few of us are privy to.

Zara smiles. "I'm drinking champagne, thank you."

Penny shrugs. "Same."

"A bottle of Dom Pérignon and two glasses and a whisky, please." I place my cell on the table. "Your drinks should be here soon."

"Can I have that number?" Zara jokes. "No, seriously, but can I?"

"I'm afraid not."

Penny rolls her eyes at her friend.

"Does that make you a VIP here? Are you a regular?"

"Yes and no. Any other questions, Zara?"

"Yes. Memorable orgasms. Do you..." Penny jabs her with an elbow. "*Ouch.*"

"So, you're not a regular, Franklin. Is it a coincidence we've bumped into each other?"

"I'd say it's luck. Can we circle back to Zara's question?"

The waiter arrives and places my whiskey on the table. Then he pops the champagne and fills two glasses, leaving the bottle in an ice bucket on the table. "Thank you."

"Absolutely not." Penny glances at me over the rim of

her crystal flute. "I feel like there's a reason why we're having a conversation?"

I swirl the ice in my glass, hoping to come across as relaxed. "To offer you a contract to remodel one of my homes."

I had played out how I would ask her in my head, and not expecting to see her tonight has thrown me off-kilter. She is beautiful, but she hasn't dressed like this for me.

"One of your homes? Like your apartment that maybe happens to be close to here, and you want me to perhaps check it out tonight?" Her expression feigns shock.

Zara downs her drink. "I need the restroom, so I'll leave you two to sort out your differences." She eyes Penny. "Don't let them take my glass." Penny nods, and Zara slides out of the booth.

"Not my penthouse. That's already been decorated, although it could be refreshed." I stop myself from speaking of Daphne. "It's my beach house. It's somewhere I go for short breaks."

"I'm good at reviving certain styles when a client no longer appreciates the current design." She considers me. "Or if they want to forget it."

"A change is like a vacation, so they say," I shout over the music.

"Especially for busy men who never take vacations."

"Got me there." I swirl my ice before taking another swig of the whiskey.

"You should go on more trips. It might motivate you on ways to decorate your home. Europe inspires me. One day, I hope to travel for coastal inspiration like the Maldives and the Bahamas."

"I like the sound of it."

"For remodeling?"

"No, the vacation. Do you take your clients with you?"

Penny pouts. "No, but I'd never say never."

I take another swig. "What if a client paid for your vacation?"

"It would depend on the business contract. Remodeling-wise, I imagine you to be a marble and brass kind of guy. All high-end quality and not the relaxed feel of a coastal makeover."

"I'm open to suggestions."

"Have you taken a vacation to simply relax? Do what you want?" With her elbow on the table, Penny rests her chin in her hand. "Lay on the beach all day drinking cocktails under a palm tree or in a hammock."

"It sounds idyllic."

She sits upright. "I think you would struggle."

"Why?"

"C'mon, Franklin. Relaxing for say... one week and not working *at all*. It would send a workaholic like you nuts."

"No calls?"

"Nope. I know a place you're not even allowed to wear shoes."

"That's ridiculous."

She giggles. "All sand and the water. It revives your senses."

She is right. I cannot imagine myself taking a week off. One day is difficult. I need to know what the market is doing every day and be reachable for my traders, clients, and analysts.

With Penny...

"Shoes or no shoes, I think I could take a week off. Except for calls, of course." I take another sip of my whiskey. "I don't think calls count."

"They absolutely do. People like you can spend hours on your cell and get caught up in problems, become stressed, and that defeats the purpose as to why you're there."

"Rhetorically, what if I'm on a business trip with a client and not a vacation?"

Penny shakes her head gently from side to side as if I have exasperated her.

"And why are we talking about vacations?"

"Because you mentioned this house is where you go for short breaks, and I'm curious why you don't take longer breaks, aka vacations? My first thought..." she has my interest, "... you would be incapable of not working on a vacation, and you proved my instinct to be correct."

I chuckle. "Capable or not, I'm interested in your coastal remodeling. The house is in its original condition. It was built in the seventies, and I bought it five years ago. It's not bad... just dated. I would like to spend more time there and hoped you might be interested in giving me some advice on decorating and remodeling."

"Why me?" Her forehead creases.

"I don't have time to research anything." Her eyes search mine. "And I trust you."

For a moment, Penny's expression falls. She picks up her glass and downs all the champagne.

"Would you like some more?" I lift the bottle of Dom from the ice bucket and wipe off the condensation.

She nods. "Yes, because I need some courage for what I'm about to say."

"I'm not twisting your arm," I reply gently. "Perhaps your friend, Hugh, is interested since he is also in the remodeling business?"

"No," she snaps. "I can do it. Though I'd need to see the house beforehand to be convinced I'm the right person for the job."

I'm hit with a rush of relief and excitement. "Are you free sometime over the weekend?"

She swallows the last of her glass. "I'm ready now."

It takes me a moment to register what she's saying.

"Or tomorrow... maybe."

"No, now is perfect," I add while standing, and she stands beside me as I tap out a message to David.

> I'm not coming back upstairs. If other business matters occur, email me the details.

I turn to Penny and say, "Just give me a moment to speak with my driver." I dial his number and he answers immediately. "Royce."

"Mr. Hendricks."

"Bring the car around to the side entrance."

"Coming now, sir."

I place my hand on her back. "Shall we go?"

"Are you leaving?" Zara slides into the booth and pours herself a champagne. "Because I doubt you're heading to the dance floor."

Penny giggles. "Not dancing." She blows her friend a kiss. "See you tomorrow."

"We talked about this," Zara calls out. "Am I supposed to stop you?"

"It's only business."

Zara smiles at me. "Right..."

"I'll get her home safe." I nod at Zara. "It's nice you look out for Penny."

"Oh, I didn't tell you that Hugh left ten minutes ago. I saw him on the dance floor, and he came over to me when he received a message about the change in flights. Sienna arrives in another hour." Zara tips the glass to her lips. "I might as well head home, but I'm not leaving this expensive champagne."

I wave my hand at Zara. "Bring it with you. I can give you a ride."

Penny tilts her head. "I appreciate you doing this for Zara."

I wait for Zara to finish her drink. "I would feel better knowing you're not standing out on the pavement waiting for a ride to turn up."

"He's right." Zara walks past and taps my chest. "It's the gentlemanly thing to do. Lead the way, *big boy*."

What?

I lean close to Penny's ear. "Has someone been sharing details?"

Penny covers her eyes with her hand momentarily and I chuckle. Penny can call me *big boy* to her friends any time, especially if I was the one to give her a memorable orgasm.

And I'm happy to offer *that* service again.

12

PENELOPE

FRANKLIN'S DRIVER, Royce, pulls up at Zara's apartment. A short, loud blast of a car horn sounds behind us.

"Do I have to get out? I love this car."

"Yes," Franklin and I say in sync.

Royce jumps out and opens the door for her.

She groans, and I wait for Zara to reach her front door. She punches in a code, and the glass door closes behind her.

"Malibu, please, Royce." He reaches over and takes my hand in his warm one. We don't speak until we're on the Pacific Coast Highway.

"So, what is the story with Royce? Is he available for when you've had a few drinks?"

"A few drinks? No, he's my driver."

"All the time?"

"All the time."

"Is this your car?"

"Yes."

"You pay Royce to drive you around in *your* car?"

"That's what drivers do, Penny."

"Do you have a license?"

"Of course I do."

"So, you're lazy?" I can't contain a smirk.

"No one has ever called me lazy." He kisses my knuckles. "You know from experience I'm anything but lazy."

My cheeks heat as I remember our night together.

He. Was. *Not.* Lazy.

I stare out the window at the lights flashing by. On one side are canyons and mountains, with homes built into the landform. On the ocean side is a single row of houses with their own private beach. My thoughts race ahead, wondering what Franklin's home is like and why he doesn't go there.

Is this home high in the hills with a panoramic view or on the shoreline?

Sitting in his luxurious black Bentley, I imagine his home to be as classy as his car. We slow as we pass the Malibu Barefoot Bar.

I grin at Franklin. "Your local hangout?"

"I've never been in there."

"You should. Even I've been with friends after they surfed, and we hung out all afternoon. It's fun."

"Don't start with being barefoot again."

We stop, and a garage door slides up as we veer into the short driveway, waiting for the door to fully open.

Beachside.

My heart races thinking about being inside Franklin's home, even if it is for business.

Inside the garage, we park beside another black car—a freaking Lamborghini. Shelves on the side walls are stacked with supplies for an earthquake. My thoughts run away, imagining being stuck somewhere with only Franklin.

Not after an earthquake.

Jesus, what is wrong with me?

But stuck in a cabin or an isolated island on the beach?

Only Franklin would not cope, especially without internet or cell service.

Royce opens the door for me.

Franklin slides out behind me. "Thanks, Royce. I'll see you in the morning."

I must have frowned because Franklin places a hand on my shoulder. "I can drive you home after you have assessed my remodeling needs and if you want the contract." He bites my ear. "Don't call me lazy again, or I might need to remind you of the last time I showed you my room." He takes my hand and punches a code into the door. "After you."

I step inside, and lights automatically illuminate a hallway. Beige-painted walls need a fresh coat and a change from this dull color.

The hall leads to an open kitchen and living room. There's a balcony out front, and I can already hear the waves crashing. The lights come on with so many recessed lights that the room is lit like Times Square at night.

"Do these have a dimmer?"

Franklin turns half the lights off from a wall switch. "I'd like to access controls from an app. Clancy turns on every switch while she's here. She informed me there is enough food in the fridge for a week."

Of course, he has a housekeeper.

"Wait. You're staying for a week? I thought you didn't like to stay here?"

"It's in case I do decide to stay."

I go to him and take both his hands in mine. "It is a beautiful home, and hopefully, you can relax somewhat because I'm no therapist, but I bet if you had one, she would tell you to take a vacation."

"You sound like my masseuse." French doors open to a wide balcony. Franklin holds the door open for me. "I still need something other than a chair to keep it ajar. Otherwise, it will slam."

"Ever thought about internal cavity sliding doors?"

His fingers tuck the flyaway hair behind my ears from blowing over my face. There's a beautiful cool breeze, and I inhale the crisp ocean air. "There is much to love, Franklin."

It's a home on the oceanfront, dated but still beautiful, and I don't understand why he is troubled by staying here.

He's studying my face in a way that sends goose bumps along my arms. "I'm glad you came. I knew you would find the beauty in this home."

I turn back to the ocean. It's black, and yet I find it soothing. "The ocean reminds me of home." I close my eyes and inhale the salted air, willing my heart to slow.

"Where do you call home?" He places a hand on my lower back and turns to stare at the sea. We are side by side, staring at the moody ocean as though it offers us answers.

"San Diego. I left to go to college and decided I needed a new adventure. I thought about New York, but you can't beat our climate. Perfect for swimming."

"I haven't swum here for some time."

"What?" I turn to him. "You have your own private swimming pool right here. The ocean is amazing for your soul."

He pulls a face and glances down at his knuckles tightening over the railing. "Why did it take me so long to meet you?"

I'm tingling all over. He pretends not to be romantic, yet that sounded sweet to me. "Because you were never on the beach. It's where I hang out a lot."

He pulls me into him. Those dark eyes flick over my face, searching for something.

I place a hand on his chest. "Though, we did meet on a beach when I saw a man, oddly dressed in a suit, walking along the shoreline."

He grins and glances at the night sky. His eyes meet mine, and I see a twinkle of fun in them. This is the Franklin I like most.

"When I first saw you, I was mesmerized watching you set the cushions and tableware. You had an eye for detail and fussed about every little thing to make it perfect. You kept bending over in those tiny, ripped shorts, and my dick liked it.. a lot. There's no harm in observing, and the more I looked, the more I liked. You were creating a happy ending for someone else, and it sparked my interest."

It's my turn to look away. I always wanted to know, but I'm not sure if I want the truth. "Why did Daphne hate the setup?" I shrug. "It's not as though I've done engagement setups since, but I want to know if I did something wrong?"

"*You* did nothing wrong." He kisses my forehead. "She expected more, that's all."

"More? How?" It's none of my business, but Hugh and I did fan over her work. She was an icon we wanted to meet.

Franklin blankly stares out to the ocean as though he is reminiscing about the past. "A trip to Dubai. An arranged scene by an event manager with all our friends present for the *surprise* proposal."

"An arranged surprise? Weird."

"I didn't do much with Daphne that wasn't premeditated," he says in a somber voice. "With you, it's easy."

I frown at him.

"You're not easy. When I'm with you, I don't have to think about what I'm saying. It comes naturally. It's like you get me, even though we barely know each other. I like being with you. It's..." he pauses for a moment, "... calming."

I snort out my nose. "The night we had was anything but calm."

He chuckles and wraps his arms around me, so I'm huddled into his hard chest. "Fucking is never calm, Penny."

His eyes pull me in. I could easily get lost in him, but he doesn't want a relationship. I need to make light of the moment before I do something stupid and ask him to date me. "Let's go for a skinny dip."

Franklin's eyes round. "Now?"

I nod.

He laughs with a hint of nervousness. "Perhaps I'll build up to it."

"Deal." I hold out my hand to shake his, when his cell vibrates in his pocket loud enough for me to notice.

He shakes my hand. "Deal." Then he retrieves his cell from his pocket, and his signature frown is back. "Sorry. I need to take this. Why don't you look around the rest of the house?"

As I move away from the railing, he says, "Bill, this better be good."

Silence.

I begin to take photographs of his furniture and the current layout with ideas coming to me fast.

"Fuck. You're killing me. What rate?"

To distract myself I make notes on my cell.

"Jesus. A four-percent drop?"

I jump when he raises his voice.

"Short sell. Do it now. Give me a moment to get into my office." Franklin strides past as though I'm a ghost and heads to a door off the living room—an office. I catch a glimpse of a large mahogany desk and three computer screens before the door closes.

Time to get back to business.

I open all the drawers in search of a tape measure. What am I thinking? Franklin doesn't need to measure anything. He's not a handyman. The thought of him wearing a tool belt—shirtless—I'll keep to myself.

Counting my steps as though each is a yard length, I make notes on my cell. I have great ideas to bring this kitchen to life, and the focus is on the main player—the ocean.

Next, I move to the living room. The open fireplace needs a revamp, and all walls need a coat of paint. The terracotta floor tiles... I tap my fingers on my chin. *Gone*. I don't like waste, but I could use them outside for crazy paving.

I take the stairs and make more notes.

New railing.

New floating stairs and not these dark wooden ones where the stain has faded in places. As I reach the top of the stairs, more recessed lights illuminate another nook—a sitting area. Bookcases line the walls like a mini library. I go to the shelves and run my finger over all the spines— historical fiction, memoirs, crime novels. Not a romance book in sight.

I make a note.

Add some of my favorites to his collection.

The only time I can manage this project will be on weekends.

Upstairs has old beige carpet that flows into a living area, leading to a balcony. I walk past a bedroom, another bedroom, another, and another. The last one is the primary. It has a huge four-poster bed with the same dark mahogany wood that is throughout the house. A mottled cover is spread over the mattress, and matching bedside tables have black lamps on top. It's depressing how dark everything is for a coastal home.

There is a large bathroom to the side with a huge window near the bath where you can bathe and relax while enjoying the view. Ugh, the tiles are deep maroon. The house is almost colonial in styling. He did say he got this house at a bargain. But why when he could have bought any place already remodeled to perfection?

I have a lot to do, and if he's serious about my remodeling ideas, then this will be a month or two of work.

I finish off my notes and close my cell. Ready to tell him my ideas, I skip down the stairs. Only the study door remains closed. He is speaking to someone and heated words are exchanged. I lift a hand to knock, then change my mind.

I'm hungry.

I open the refrigerator. It's loaded with food—fruit, eggs, juice, milk, almond milk, cheese, and sourdough. I take out the sourdough. To the side, there's a walk-in pantry with dated shelves in need of replacing. I add it to my notes. I find peanut butter and spread it over a piece of sourdough. I open all the cupboards until I find a glass, fill it with cold water from the refrigerator, and sit on a stool at the kitchen island.

Being with me is easy.

I mull over Franklin's words in my head.

Should I be more of a puzzle? Did Bernard tire of me because I was predictable and boring? I bury any thoughts of Bernard and focus on why I'm here.

This home is not what I'd expected. It has beauty, not luxurious like his cars, and I can't wait to bring it back to life.

I finish eating and place my plate in the empty dishwasher. This home has had no love for years. My fingertips glide over the tiled countertops while taking in the feel of the room.

Franklin's voice echoes around the house.

Shit. He is angry.

There's another door I missed to my left—a bathroom. I add it to my notes.

After washing my hands, I contemplate leaving. I could call a cab since I've finished inspecting his home. After all, it is technically why I'm here. For a good ten seconds, I stare at the study door. I'm not going to leave without telling him.

There is no way I'm knocking on that door when he's like that.

I wait.

The books.

I head upstairs to the reading nook.

As I run my fingers over the books, I choose one set in the seventeenth century.

Why would Franklin be interested in this?

I take the throw draped over the back of the chair and the book and take a seat.

After a while, my neck begins to ache. With the sound of the ocean too good to ignore, I head to the bedroom closest to the library. I open the balcony door a fraction so I can hear and smell the ocean.

Kicking my shoes into a corner, I curl up on the bed with the book and only a bedside light illuminating the room. I am mesmerized by the ocean outside the glass and find myself reading the same sentence over and over, struggling to keep my eyes open.

13

FRANKLIN

SCRAPING my fingertips down my cheeks, I open and close my eyes, trying to stay awake. The glare from three screens on my desk burns like laser beams to my eyes. My wristwatch reads four in the morning.

Fuck.

Penny.

After numerous calls to clients and investors, my COO, Bill, and I have managed minimal loss at HCM by selling international stock—fast. Thank fuck, Bill is watching figures and has a team of staff who work through the night ready to alert us if anything turns rotten. There are companies wanting HCM to fail, and occasionally, we slip up after one has managed to set us up with a shady deal.

We didn't lose clients or investors.

Despite the monetary loss, I'm taking it as a win.

Hopefully, I can get some sleep if I can get rid of the sour taste in my mouth.

Penny.

Is she here, or did she leave?

I don't blame her for leaving if she overheard my heated calls.

The kitchen lights are on, so I switch them off and head up the stairs. The house is so quiet, I hear every creak with each step. The light is on in the reading nook, so I turn that off too, while I quietly head to my room. Only out of the corner of my eye, I see a figure lying on the bed in the bedroom on my left—the one with the balcony.

Penny assessed the house, and she chose this room.

Not mine.

I let that process for a few seconds.

The door is ajar with the sound of the ocean and a cool breeze blowing into the room. I close it as it's freezing in here, and she only has a throw to keep her warm. I get a warmer blanket from the cupboard and drape it over her before heading to my room.

I strip out of my clothes and slide under the sheets. Tonight, the bed appears bigger than usual. I toss and turn, count backward, and try anything for another hour to relax my mind. I even imagine beachscapes because Penny has put that thought into my head. I sit on the side of the bed, and for a few minutes, I stare out at the dark ocean, the sound telling a story, yet not one compelling enough to send me to sleep. After closing the drapes, I stand and pace the hallway.

Penny is lying on her side, facing the ocean. I slide in under the blanket, shuffle close but not too close it could make her uncomfortable, and close my eyes.

THE LIGHT IS BLINDING.

I force an eye open and attempt to get up.

Did I forget to close the drapes?

An arm rests over my stomach.

I am not in my room.

Even after five years, I become disorientated as I rarely stay here.

Penny lays beside me.

For the first time, this place feels homey.

Her dark hair falls over her face and is splashed over the pillow. I lift her arm and roll onto my side so I can watch Penny sleep.

Her eyes flutter open.

"Morning," I whisper. "Sorry, I was a shit host."

She offers half a smile and licks her lips. "You're in my bed."

"Because you weren't in mine."

She stares at me as though waiting for me to say something. "If you like this bed, then it's yours for whenever you stay over." I roll onto my back to give her some space.

She lifts the covers and frowns. "You're almost naked."

"Because I was sleeping."

She grins. "You sleep naked?"

"Always, but I kept my underwear on for you."

Penny is smiling. I follow her gaze to my hips and the bulge in the blanket. It's morning, and I'm beside Penny. No apology.

"If I were to accept your contract, and I worked late on weekends, the offer of this room stands?"

I nod.

"If I hire you, then the house is yours to style in whatever way you choose. I'll draw up a contract."

Her eyes flick over mine. "What if you pay me as we go? You might not like some of my ideas and..." she bites her lip, and I home in on those lips, wanting a taste, "... we could have a disagreement."

Her concern is not only about business but also whether we fight or become involved, so I answer with, "My business decisions are compartmentalized from friendship."

Her eyes lock with mine as though she's waiting for me to say something else.

"What's your favorite color?"

I pull back. "Why?"

"I want to understand your tastes."

"Green or blue, but that doesn't mean I want the walls painted in those colors."

She agrees. "Favorite animal?"

I take a moment to think about it. "Dolphins."

A smile creeps over her lips. "Is it because dolphins are one of the smartest animals on the planet?"

"I didn't know that. There is something therapeutic about watching dolphins in the water."

Penny leans onto one elbow. "Have you been to SeaWorld in San Diego?"

I place a hand on her hip. "Not really a fan of supporting captured animals."

"I get it, but they also rescue and rehabilitate wild animals that are sick."

"True."

"The dolphin show was my favorite as a kid. You couldn't help being in awe of their intelligence and be hypnotized watching them glide through the water with ease." She places a hand over mine resting on her hip. "I could take you some time."

I smile. "You're making a lot of plans for someone who doesn't like to have days off."

"Well, as your new employee, I understand the

importance of recreational days for pleasure. I'm helping you."

"Should I fire my massage therapist, personal trainer, and dietician now?"

"Yes!" She taps my chest. "I can save you money just by adding a little fun to your life."

I believe her. "I'm not firing anyone, but I could add a fun-therapist to my calendar every fourth Sunday."

"Once a month. How boring." She flops back onto the pillow with an exasperated expression on her face.

"Have you forgotten you're here working every weekend? No fun days for you either, cupcake."

She places a hand on my cheek and leaves it there. Penny's stares unnerve me as though she's hoping for more than I can give. "We could plan our own fun during lunch breaks."

"I'd love to have lunch with you... but..."

"What do you mean?"

"I'm in New York once a month for a week. I have planned trips to London every three months. Plus international trips to Singapore and Australia."

Penny nods slowly, seeming to absorb what I'm telling her. My cell vibrates on the table beside me. For once, I want to be left alone for a few minutes. I reach over in case it's Bill, only it's my mother so I silence it.

A message pops up on the screen.

Mom.

> We need to chat about my fundraiser.
> Please make time for me. Btw your father
> had lunch with Daphne in Italy.

I close my cell.

Dammit! Daphne is the last person I want to be thinking about right now.

"Is everything okay?"

"My mother wants to chat about one of her charity balls."

A woman's voice calls out from down stairs.

Penny's eyes round, fixed on the closed bedroom door as she springs upright in the bed. "Is she here now?"

I place a hand over her stomach to stop her from propelling off the sheets. "It's okay. It's my chef."

"You have a personal chef, and she is a woman?"

I chuckle at the hint of jealousy she is showing. "Sally is in her sixties and is happily married with adult children."

"Oh." Her cheeks blush, and I can't help but kiss her. It's light and quick. Penny grabs the back of my neck and holds my lips to hers a moment longer.

"Is there anything you would like her to cook?" I ask against her lips.

She pulls away and stares at the door. "Maybe I should go."

Placing my arms under Penny, I roll her so she is lying along the length of me. "Or you could stay. If you're going to be here on weekends, then I should introduce you to Sally."

She places her hands under her chin and meets my gaze.

I can't read her. Yet I sense the longing and fear.

"Shouldn't we keep this as a business relationship?" she asks.

"If that's what you want? You're not on the clock now, though, Penny."

She pecks my nose with a kiss. "No, I'm not." Her expression changes, and suddenly her mouth is on mine, and her tongue is inside my mouth.

It's the only sign I need.

With my arms around her back, I kiss Penny hard while my body wants more. I try to ignore the desire to rip her dress from her back. Only I can't stand it with her this close, and all that material stops me from touching her skin.

"I need to get this dress off you."

"Please do," she whispers.

I work fast to get her dress, bra, and panties off, then flip her on her back, and before my mouth finds her pussy, her hands are in my hair.

"Wait." She edges up in the bed. "I want you on your back."

I don't ask questions and move into the requested position.

"No. Lay across the bed with your head toward the ocean."

"Easy." I flip over and reach out to touch her.

"Place your hands behind your head. No touching."

I groan but do what I'm told. "Wait." I pull out a drawer, and thankfully, there is a condom. I roll it on and reposition myself.

She places a hand on my chest and straddles my body. She glides her pussy over my dick, and I moan and thrust, needing to touch her. "I got this," she tells me. She grabs my dick, strokes it, and then eases onto it.

Hands behind my head, I watch how Penny slides slowly to take me in. Her eyes are closed, she's moaning softly, and I'm enjoying the view. Her eyes flash open. She leans forward onto her hands and stares out the window. "Orgasms with the best view in the world are my new favorite thing."

It could also become mine.

Curling up, I take her breast in my mouth and suck her nipple until she moans loudly, and I switch to her other breast. Penny pants, she's so close. Fuck this! I release my arms, grab hold of her ass, and pump her hard and fast until she is crying out my name. She comes. Her arms weaken, and her body slumps, but the girl I remember is capable of coming again.

"C'mon, Pen." I thrust deep and fast as I pull her face down to mine and kiss her with all I have. Our tongues lash about, the animal in me wanting to devour every part of her.

"Franklin," she whimpers against my mouth.

I pull out and flip her onto her stomach, shove a pillow under her hips, spread her legs, and ease back into her. I'm close.

Penny's head lifts. "My God." Then her back arches, and her pussy is mine for the taking. I hammer into her, my elbows by her head. She breathes hard and fast, and then, with a low moan, her body slumps into the bed.

"Beautiful."

Suddenly, she pushes up onto her elbows, her ass high in the air.

I love her ass.

I thrust deeper and harder until I come hard then fall onto the bed beside her and lie still for a moment. "You're amazing."

"Thank you," she whispers, eyes hooded. "I needed that."

I chuckle. "Don't thank me. We all need to fuck, Penny."

"It's the second-best orgasm I've had in my life."

"The second."

"Don't worry. You're in first and second place."

"I need to up my game to overtake first place again."

She moves her hips from side to side. "Are you taking reservations for next Sunday? Same place. Same time."

Fuck, I want to say yes.

14

PENELOPE

SALLY SERVES me pancakes after blending Franklin's protein smoothie.

I'm wearing Franklin's sweater and boxers.

It's obvious the clothes are his and highlight my unplanned stayover.

In the short time I've sat on the stool at the counter, I have noticed Sally's salt and pepper hair pulled back in a bun, her slim body under her navy top and trousers, and her pale skin. Sally has barely given me a glance, yet I'm stressing about what she thinks of me.

How many other overnight women does Sally cook for?

Does she feel sorry for me?

Franklin kisses my cheek. "What?"

"Nothing. Just thinking about everything I have to do."

He rubs my thigh. "Stop worrying about work."

"Says the workaholic." I eye his cell on the counter.

He kisses my cheek again. "I'm not thinking about it

while I'm with you." His dark eyes with thick lashes suck me in, and I can't look away. He smiles, and it's like the sun has brightened everything around Franklin. I see him and the world in this beautiful light. Only I'm Mercury and orbiting around him faster than I should.

Sally glances up from the sink and smiles at Franklin. Then her eyes dart to mine, and there's a hint of acceptance. "Is there anything else I can do for you, Mr. Hendricks?"

He hesitates. "Why don't you head on home? I can clean up here. Take the rest of the morning off."

Sally's face drops. Then she pulls a face, and I can't help but giggle as I'm sure she's thinking Franklin won't know how to do the dishes.

"I can clean up, Sally." I give her a knowing smile.

Sally nods once. "Okay. You're both very kind. My grandchildren are visiting today, and I would like to spend some time with them." She wipes her hands on the dish towel.

"Thank you. It was lovely to meet you, Sally."

"I'll see you next weekend, Ms. Penny."

"I, um..." I stutter.

"Yes, you will. I won't be here, but I have asked Penny to stay while she works on the house."

"There will be some changes, and for a while, no *kitchen*," I emphasize.

Sally's eyes widen. "Okay. I'll see you then." The side entrance door clicks shut after she leaves.

"Sally has a code to the back gate and a key to this door. I can send you her number so if you need her to visit more frequently, you can call her."

"I can?"

"I'm going to need your contact details to send her number." He glances up from his cell, his expression serious.

I give him my number, wanting to say *you could have asked for it in Oregon*. Now he has a business reason to need it, and the thought that this is *all business* makes my stomach tighten. Am I getting myself in too deep?

"Why me?" I whisper. "When you could've asked the most influential decorators in California?"

He sets down his cell on the counter and pivots on the stool so he is facing me. He places both palms on my bare thighs. Heat flows from his skin into me at a cellular level, and it hits that spot between my legs. The man only has to look at me, and I turn to mush.

"I'm not going to lie... I like you. Really like you, and that means I trust you."

A ball of doubt grows in my chest. "You don't know me," I rasp out. "You might know my body, but that's not all of me. I might be crap at what I do and completely mess up your house. Did you think of that?"

His eyes dart over my face, but there is no humor in his expression. "Know that I don't make rash decisions. The calculated risks *with* the probability of a desired outcome are considered. If I fuck up, I have strategies to overcome any problem." He lowers his face, and when he looks up, there is a gleam of mischievousness in his eyes. "I need to emphasize the word *desire*. Personal desire is something I'm very considerate about." He leans closer so his mouth is only inches from mine. "I also like giving people a chance. Is it a crime to stare at my beautiful decorator all day and imagine what I could do with that ass?" His hands squeeze my thighs.

My thighs open for him.

"Not a crime," I murmur. "So it'll be decorator and client... with benefits. And I'm also an interior designer. You have a two for one deal." I reach up and cup his cheek. "I prefer to think of you as a friend than my client."

Large hands slide under my rear. He lifts me, and I squeal, grabbing hold of his shoulders to balance. I land on the counter, and Franklin slides the dishes and food into the sink. Crockery clashes with a bang, and I'm sure some of it broke.

"Consider breakfast cleared away."

I laugh, my head falling back, and I imagine Sally's reaction if she knew how Franklin cleared the breakfast dishes.

Franklin's eyes darken with sexual craving.

Leaning back on my elbows, I stare at his handsome face as my bent knees fall to the sides.

Franklin slides *his* boxers over my thighs, and then I'm pulled closer, my back now on the cool tile and my legs wrapped over his shoulders. He kisses my pussy, licks, and tastes me.

"I'm ready for dessert," he says, almost in a growl.

I giggle. "You don't eat dessert after breakfast."

Then I'm silenced, my hands slamming against the cold tile as Franklin's mouth and fingers leave me breathless.

EVERY DAY FOR THE NEXT WEEK FEELS LIKE A MONTH. I MISS seeing Franklin's beautiful face and have to be satisfied with listening to his sexy voice over the cell phone when I leave voice messages about how I'm remodeling the house in a way I think will suit him.

I'm living off the excitement of being with someone new.

The sex is like an adrenaline hit, and I don't want it to end.

In the back of my mind, a voice warns me I'm mixing business with sexual benefits, and it could end badly. The way I feel when I'm with Franklin makes me reckless because I feel like a different person.

My cell is beside my laptop on my desk. I sigh as I stare at the screen, waiting for it to light up with Franklin's name.

"You've had that same expression on your face all week." Hugh edges his rear onto the corner of my desk. "I swear you're a different person lately."

With bent elbows on the table, I lean my chin in my palms and stare at him. I can't hide my smile. "I'm happy, okay?"

"You should be. We have secured two contracts this week on twenty-million-dollar properties in the OC."

A text comes through on my cell, so I immediately pick it up to read.

Franklin.

> Please feel free to stay at the house all weekend. Use the time to decide what the house needs and what needs to change. Living somewhere helps with decision-making. See you when I get back from San Fran on Tuesday?

He's away, and yet he wants to see me on Tuesday.

A weekday.

> BTW I'll send you the codes to park your car in the garage. There's a different code to the door.

He's sending me all his codes.

Shit! He had a Lamborghini parked there the other day. What if I hit it?

"Penelope."

I look up. Hugh only ever calls me Penelope if he's concerned or mad at me.

"What's going on?"

"Um... Franklin just sent me the codes to his Malibu house."

He slides off my desk and leans over with two arms on the table. "Shut the front door."

I laugh. "He wants me to do some work for him," I say in a quieter voice. "It will be on weekends so as not to clash with my work here."

"Like a friend helping a friend?" he asks cautiously.

"Right." Hugh is staring at me, and I know what he's thinking.

"A business decision?"

"Yes."

Hugh stands. "What are you doing tonight?"

I let out a sigh. "I don't want to stay there on my own. So I'll go in the morning and check it out again."

"He won't be there?"

I shake my head. "Franklin's in San Fran."

"And that's why he gave you the codes?"

"Yup."

Hugh undoes the top button of his yellow shirt and pulls off his emerald tie. He always dresses in color, and most of the time, I look bland standing beside him. "I think we should order pizza and come to yours tonight. We need to have a private discussion."

"Hugh, I really am fine."

TWO HOURS LATER, WE ARE SITTING AT THE SMALL KITCHEN table in my tiny apartment. Lily and her boyfriend are out on a date night, so I have the apartment to myself so my friends and I can hang out together. Pizza boxes are spread over the dining table and counter. Hugh, Sienna, and Zara are here.

"Shall we watch a romance movie with a good meet-cute?" Sienna asks. "I'm in the mood—"

"No," Zara and Hugh chime together.

"Sorry," Zara says. She spins her glass on the table. "We haven't chatted for ages, and I want to hear about Franklin."

"There's not much more to tell you. I don't know what you want me to say?"

"I just want you to be careful," Zara says.

"I know you guys care and think you're looking out for me." I acknowledge each of my friends before continuing, "Only I'm old and wise enough to know when I'm in over my head. Franklin and I like spending time together. He has offered *me* the contract to remodel his home as he said he likes giving people a chance."

"It's great, Penelope. Only he could afford the best stylist in California. Yet he chose you, and I don't think it was about giving a new, upcoming designer a chance because we know he's got the cash to hire high-end designers."

"And you can't get your head around why he chose me when I'm relatively new at Style Line Designs," I say in frustration.

Hugh frowns. "Not at all. You're a natural, which is why I recommended you to my boss." He glances at Sienna and then Zara. "We care about you, babe. We don't want you to—"

"I know." I grab the bottle and fill my glass before passing it to Zara. "If I sense it turning bad, I'll get my reinforcements to come and save me. Besides, the renovation should only take a month or two, then I'll probably never see him again." My heart aches at the thought. "Please don't ruin the moment when I haven't been this happy in years."

Zara reaches out and takes my hand. "I'm confused why he wants you to sleep at his home when he's not there. It's not like you're together-together. It's freaking weird."

I chuckle. "It freaked me out a little. But hey, why don't you all come and stay there with me tomorrow night? Then I could run my ideas for each room past you all."

Hugh's eyebrows rise into his forehead. "You want us to sleep over at Franklin Hendricks' vacation house?" Hugh's voice cracks. "Um... yes. I'm not crazy enough to turn down an offer like that, especially if it helps my friend sleep at night."

Sienna frowns at Hugh. "It's weird, Hugh. We're sleeping at one of the most influential men in America's home, and he doesn't know it. It's like being sixteen and gate-crashing a party. It makes me uncomfortable."

With a piece of pizza in one hand, I wave at my friends with the other in an it-will-be-fine way. "Then I'll ask him if it's okay?"

Zara is staring at me as though I've grown six heads.

I'm waiting for her to say something. She doesn't, so I have to ask the question, "If he says it's fine, will you stay?"

"Sure."

Lily and her boyfriend arrive home, slamming the door behind them.

"Hi." She waves at everyone before they head into her bedroom, giggling and stumbling as if they've had too much to drink.

Hugh stares at her bedroom door. "The entertainment is about to start."

Zara stands. "I'm still scarred from the last time."

"Is it that bad?" Sienna asks.

She is the only one of us not to have witnessed the sex screams and moans of my roommate.

"It is." Hugh stands and tucks his chair under the table.

"Ah." Loud gasp. "Ah." Loud gasp. "Ah."

Sienna places a hand over her mouth.

"That's nothing," Zara says, with the biggest smirk on her face. "Wait until—"

"Yeeesss. Yeeesss. *Yeeesss*. Yes. Yes. *Yes*."

Zara snorts a laugh. "There it is."

"I'm used to it." I shrug. "I'll put my AirPods in, and eventually, they tire. It never lasts all night."

Sienna giggles. "We better go. Nice seeing you, Pen."

Hugh wraps an arm around her shoulder. "If you sounded like that, our apartment neighbors would be banging on the door."

Sienna giggles. "Harder. Harder. Give it to me. Give it to me."

"I'm tapping out." Zara hugs me before heading toward the door.

"Wait for us," Hugh calls to her, then he turns to me. "Enjoy your night," he mocks me. "We'll chat tomorrow."

As I stand in the kitchen, the sounds of sex fill my apartment.

I head to my room and shut the door.

It's time I found my own place.

15

FRANKLIN

It's the last morning meeting before I head to the airport.

I remained in San Francisco for another three days and had to cancel my date night with Penny. The contract is drawn up, and I'll send it to her when I land in New York. Trades and stock have consumed my time, so we've barely spoken in the last couple of days.

I agreed for her friends to stay over. If that's what she needs to be comfortable in the house, then so be it. She said her friend, Hugh, brainstormed ideas with her.

Employing Penny was about giving her a break and using her ideas. I don't want her to be influenced by friends or colleagues who think they have more experience than her. She needs to take a risk and believe in herself. With a splash of confidence, Penny could do great things.

I have set up a meeting for you to meet my brother, Jobe. Run your ideas by him, and he'll provide a contact list of suppliers and trades. He also has a great architect who will be ready to go as you need him. Let me know if you need anything else.

The following morning, I burst into the HCM NY boardroom.

"Gentlemen, what do you have for me?" The meeting is in progress. I remain standing and don't take a seat at the head of the long table. I walk slowly around the room as my portfolio managers and analysts pitch their best money-making ideas.

Caleb, my COO in New York, opens the meeting at nine o'clock for the West Coast to attend online. Finding a suitable time for all country zones is troublesome. I glance at my screen to analyze the numbers.

"Morning, LA, afternoon, London, and for those of you still awake in Singapore, welcome. We're now twenty-eight percent up for the year to date. We're here for short and long, sells, covers, all alpha welcome."

Keeping out of the eye of the camera, I take each step as slowly as I would if I were balancing on a tightrope. It gives me a chance to assess my team's body language. "Lana, where are we with that IT company?"

She glances at me and then at her screen. "It's promising."

"Are you confident?"

She fidgets in her chair before folding her arms. "I'm certain."

I eye her a moment before looking at George, a portfolio manager. Our compliance officers are watching staff like an eagle eyeing its prey. Only it's a trade and a due diligence process. At Hendricks Capital Management, we pride ourselves on good ethics and honest trading, unlike some crooks who slip under the radar with borderline illegal trades.

My grandfather and father set up outstanding, long-term investment strategies to get this company where we are today. I'm steering HCM to bigger investments, taking larger risks with solid backing.

If Lana has any insider information, she knows it's a risk. Her risk. Not mine. The authorities use software to find patterns in data and trading. We have been investigated twice, and it's brought unwanted attention to every hedge fund. A dozen companies are out there that would like to bring HCM down, and it dates back to years of doing business with my father.

"George, how is that technology company handling the supply issues in China?" I grab the back of a leather chair, and all my attention for the next thirty seconds is on George.

"The short is promising. It's been a positive event. A more marginal growth than people would have you believe."

I give him a nod and turn to Caleb. He's the meeting moderator today, though the portfolio managers usually lead it.

For the next twenty minutes, we have people around the globe sharing their research on how we can profit from buys. My LA analysts have logged in from their homes before work to check the market and confirm if stock is up.

"What insights and ideas can we offer?" Caleb asks.

I take a seat in the back corner of the room and listen. I don't intervene even for a lemon. Researching a lemon might lead to a great idea. This is the time for my employees to be heard.

When the meeting concludes, I head into my office for a private discussion with Caleb.

As I sink into my leather seat, I can't help but glance at

my cell on the desk—no new message from Penny, not that I'm expecting one. She is my designer, that's all. But God, I can't help thinking about her long hair and how good it feels in my fist, her perfectly fuckable mouth, and her rounded ass.

"Whose idea has you on edge?" Caleb scratches at the salt and pepper whiskers along his jawline.

"What?" I snap out of the fog, clouding my brain. "No, the meeting was positive."

"I agree. So why the face?"

Fuck. For someone who is usually void of emotion, I'm acting like a freaking teenage boy with too much testosterone. I can't date and focus on business. The two things don't go hand in hand.

"I suggest we divest from PetroDepend."

I stare at Caleb. "Why? We have good returns, and the numbers are great."

"I see those figures, yet I have a gut feeling something is up. I'm going to investigate it further."

"Good. Let me know what you find."

We go back and forth for another thirty minutes.

I check the time on my watch—another two hours before I board my flight. Caleb and I talk shop for a few minutes, largely about the Sharks buy and when we will officially confirm the purchase. I check the time again. "I need to go. See you next month."

While driving to the jet, I'm thinking about Penny and her meeting with Jobe. He better fucking listen and not drill her.

I'm more nervous about that meeting than any of the work meetings I have set up for the week. It's exactly why I have to pull myself together.

16

PENELOPE

DURING MY LUNCH BREAK, I walk out of the office to a black
Bentley waiting to drive me to Hendricks Realty.

Royce gets out of the driver's seat and comes around to
greet me. "Hello, Penny." He opens the back door.

"Hi, Royce. How are you?"

"Fine, thank you."

He closes my door and strides around to the driver's
side. He slides in and focuses on the traffic to veer out into
the Downtown LA chaos.

"Is Franklin home tonight?"

"Yes. His flight arrives at six-thirty."

"Right." I can't wait to see him and show him my ideas if
I get through this meeting unscathed.

We park out in front of Hendricks Realty, and before
Royce closes my door, Jobe, Franklin's brother, is standing
on the street to greet me. He looks exactly like the pictures

on social media. No Photoshop is required for these handsome men.

"The famous Penny Gilbert." His smile is as infectious as Franklin's, only it produces less stress lines around his eyes and brows. Closer up, I see he has a smooth forehead with no expression lines.

My first impression?

Jobe is *all* about appearances.

Is it weird he knows my full name? Who am I kidding? This family has probably searched the crap out of my profile. My heart beats faster with every step toward the huge automatic sliding doors.

Jobe has the same dark hair, brown eyes and facial features as Franklin. He holds a card to a sensor box, and the doors slide open. Jobe places a hand on my lower back as we enter the building, the doors closing behind us. The foyer has one receptionist, and a hallway and staircase are behind her. The space is decorated in sage green and ivory, with decorative brass items placed around the foyer and on a coffee table.

"We'll talk in the private meeting room." He leads me down the hall to the only door on the right. There is a huge table that seats twenty-four people. In the corner are two couches with a coffee table and a rug between them. The niche has a cozy, intimate feel and is less formal than the meeting table.

Jobe pours himself a whiskey from a table by the wall. "Can I get you anything?"

I don't want alcohol, but I'm not judging why he needs to drink at midday. "Just a water, please."

He peers over his shoulder. "Nothing else?"

"No thanks." If my nerves don't settle down, I may need a shot of something, though.

After handing me a glass of water, he sits on the couch

and points for me to join him. "Franklin tells me you have ideas on how to remodel the haunted house."

I choke on the water as I swallow. "It's haunted?"

He smirks. "Maybe not haunted, but someone died there. Drank too much, then fell over the balcony during high tide in a storm."

"So, not *in* the house?"

"No." Jobe is smirking, and I'm unsure whether to believe him.

"It's a beautiful home with potential. I'm excited to make her shine."

He peruses me for a moment and crosses his legs so his navy trousers creep up, revealing Christian Louboutin leather Derby shoes. I recognize the designer brand after window shopping with Hugh.

"And you think you're the best person to do this?"

"I do. I have spent some time there and think I could turn it into a home Franklin can relax in."

He scratches the slight stubble along his jaw. "You know that isn't Franklin's home. He barely stays there and prefers to spend most of his time at his penthouse or at his Colorado place."

I pretend this is not news to me. "I love a challenge, and I think Franklin will appreciate the transformation I have in mind."

Jobe's eyes feel like nails scraping over my skin, assessing every part of me. He begins the conversation about his company and mentions some of the beachfront homes he has sold or manages. He continues to describe high-end homes, and yet he hasn't asked me what my ideas are for the house. "Do you have builders and other trades you prefer to work with?"

"I do, but they're tied to my work projects." I uncross and cross my legs. Franklin mentioned an informal meeting.

The way Jobe is judging me, it's like I'm trying to take off with his money.

He pulls out his cell and hands it to me. "Give me your details, and I'll email a list of trades that will be available for you. Just tell them you're working with Franklin. If there are any problems, call me, and I'll sort it out."

I tap in my contact details and hand it back to him. "Thank you. I appreciate the list, especially if it's people you trust."

He stands, tapping away, before popping his cell into his suit pocket.

It's my cue the meeting is over.

He holds out a hand. "It was lovely to meet you, Penny. I assume we'll be seeing each other again soon." He shakes, gently squeezing my hand. "I can see why Franklin fell hard for you."

My cheeks heat. Pulling my hand from his, I don't know where to look. "Franklin and I are friends."

Franklin has *not* fallen for me. He'd be messaging and calling me every day if he had, and he'd send more than business-like texts. His words would hint at something romantic if that was the case.

He chuckles. "Let's call it that, yet it's been almost a decade since he was this reckless."

"Reckless? I haven't seen that side of him."

"Maybe it's the Franklin before Penny you didn't meet."

I want to say I did meet him, and he acted spontaneously, not recklessly, when he asked me to set up the beach scene for him to propose to Daphne.

My stomach drops.

Daphne.

I'm no Daphne.

A wave of nausea hits me at the thought of his family blaming me for any reckless behavior.

Jobe walks me out, and I scurry into the back of the Bentley before Royce can open the door.

Jobe holds up a hand but doesn't move it. He offers me a stiff goodbye before he turns, the automatic sliding doors opening at his step.

"Is everything okay, Penny?"

I meet Royce's eyes in the mirror. "Yes. I need to get back to work for a meeting."

And possibly puke.

Royce steers the Bentley into traffic faster than he did on our journey here. I close my eyes as we drive farther away from Jobe and his judgment.

I'm insulted at the idea that I have influenced Franklin to be reckless. No one has that kind of control over Franklin. He's one of the most influential men in the country.

On opening my emails, I find the one from Jobe with an attached list of contacts for the renovation. *God, I'm delusional.* Last night, I had a vision this could be a step toward my own business.

Instead, it's going to be a make-or-break situation.

If I mess up, I'll be the one who breaks.

My reputation will be ruined, while Franklin can simply hire someone else to fix my mistakes.

This is not about us spending time together while I have fun renovating his property. I'm going to be watched by all the remodeling and decorating influencers around the world as I create a home for one of the most powerful men in America.

This is not as easy as breathing new life into something old.

This is not about saving beautiful things and money.

Can I really create something that is not in line with my values? Because the idea of starting my own business is to showcase my creativity and environmentally friendly ideas.

Is it too late to reject Franklin's offer?

THE STAFF MEETING ENDS.

Hugh rounds the table before I close my laptop. He waits until most of the people have left the room before speaking, "So, how did it go?"

Packing my laptop under my arm, I wait for the remaining staff to exit the room. "Good," I reply without giving him eye contact.

I walk from the meeting room and down the hall while Hugh maintains a pace beside me. "You were quicker than I thought."

I hold my laptop over my chest as though it can shield me from the emotion of thinking about Jobe's words. "Yes. It was brief. He basically wanted to meet me before emailing the list of contacts their family uses for building requirements."

"Ugh. But what was he like? Jobe Hendricks only sells real estate to the rich and fabulous."

"Yeah, I got that feeling too. His shoes were probably my entire month's pay."

Hugh audibly gasps and places a hand over his chest. "Don't tell me..."

I laugh. "Yep. The ones you've eyed when we've been shopping."

"Christian Louboutin," he says with a wail.

"They'd look better on you." I bump his hip, and he lands a hand over my shoulder.

"That's why I love you, my little Penelope." He follows me into my office. I eye Hugh in his pink and green button-up shirt and with a yellow sweater looped over his shoulders. Forest green pants finish his attire.

The red fitted dress with flared sleeves, red heels, and red lipstick give me a classical and stylish appearance. Against Hugh, I might as well be wearing gray. After making my way around my desk, I slide onto the chair.

Hugh sits on the corner of my desk.

I lean forward with my elbows on the dark wood. "Do you think it's too late to say no to Franklin?"

"Why would you do that?"

I close my eyes momentarily before meeting his gaze. "So I don't fail and look like a fool."

"You're not going to fail. Do you know how jealous I am that you get to do this?"

I force a smile.

"I am here for you. If you want to bounce any ideas off me, I'll be honest with you. I mean, you have *Malibu* at your feet," he emphasizes. "Jody has assigned me to a preschool project." He rolls his eyes.

I smother a smirk. The last project Hugh managed was a little too colorful and flamboyant for the owners, so Jody, our boss, has him toning down his creative flair for a while.

"I'm sure the preschool center will love the bold colors you work with. It will stimulate the kids' little brains."

"Penny, I'm the one who needs stimulation." His brow furrows. "I'm dying to help you." He holds out his hands as though he is balancing weights. "Preschool versus billionaire's Malibu house."

I laugh. "I get it." Hugh always manages to make me feel worthy. "But if Franklin hates it, then I'm blaming you."

Hugh rubs his hands together as though he already has a kazillion ideas. "Oh darling, he is going to love it."

THE FOLLOWING NIGHT, I'M DRESSED AND WAITING FOR Franklin to pick me up for dinner. He didn't tell me anything except to be ready by six-thirty as he has a restaurant reservation. It sounds like a date—*no, it's just a business dinner.* I mean, plenty of people have working meals. It's common, even.

I'm reapplying gloss to my red lips when my cell rings with an incoming call.

My heart misses a beat when I see Franklin's name on the screen. My thoughts race into how the night will pan out, and I'm already wishing the dinner could be over so I can curl up in his arms, only the two of us in a room. I mean, I'm nervous about tonight, where he is taking me, and if I'll stick out like a sore thumb in a fancy restaurant. My etiquette is fine. Only I can't help slipping inside myself when surrounded by high-class wealth, which Franklin is used to associating with.

I hold my breath before answering and stop the thoughts from steamrolling toward *why me?* He could have anyone, so why is he wasting his time with someone like me?

I know the answer.

It's always the same.

Because he knows it's just sex while we're working together.

I swipe the screen before it rings out. "Hey."

"Hello, Penny," Franklin says in his smooth voice that has my ovaries sparking to life. "Royce has parked out front."

"Just give me a minute." I end the call and stare at my reflection a few seconds longer. "Enjoy it while it lasts," I murmur. "You have nothing to lose."

Except your heart.

I clench my eyes shut.

Stop being an idiot. You are worthy. Be with him and enjoy the night.

Running my hands over the navy material of my long, flared skirt, I can't do anything else to improve my appearance except adjust the plunging neckline of my white top so you can see a little cleavage but not too much. When I reach the ground level, Franklin is standing outside the car, leaning on the door, arms crossed. He is edible in a black suit, white shirt, and a bow tie. His eyes meet mine before the glass doors to my building open. He pushes off the car with a smile that warms my heart. Holding the rail, I take each step carefully in my higher-than-usual heels, and when I'm on the pavement, Franklin is beside me, wrapping me in those biceps and lifting my chin so all I see is him.

"I've missed you," he says softly before his lips are on mine, and for once, I stop thinking and allow myself to enjoy whatever this man has to give.

Royce coughs from behind, and Franklin pulls his lips away, grinning, his forehead resting on mine.

"We have a schedule, sir," Royce says.

Franklin reaches down for another kiss, only this time it's quick. "Shall we?" He takes my hand, leading me to the car.

"Where are we going?"

"It's a surprise."

In the back seat of his car, I curl into his side, strong arms wrap around me, and I'm quite happy to stay like this and skip dinner.

He runs his fingers along my arm, soothing any nerves. He leans in close to my ear, the whisper of his breath causing goose bumps to rise on my warmed skin. "You are beautiful."

I smile and squeeze his thigh. "Thank you. I don't need to tell you how handsome you look because you're always..." I hitch in a breath as his eyes meet mine. His eyes darken, and I sense the lust flowing between us.

"Always, what?" he asks in a husky voice.

"Always... desirable," I whisper. *Oh God, the way he stares at me, I dare not turn away.*

He leans in and whispers, "Open your legs for me, Penny."

I do so while he scoops up the material of my skirt and slides a hand between my thighs. The movement is slow, deliberate, and heading in one direction. He forces the elastic so his entire hand fits under the material. One, two, three fingers slip inside, and my body is his in seconds.

I'm vaguely aware of Royce.

Pleasure flows through my body.

I keep an eye on the rearview mirror, hoping Royce doesn't glance back.

He doesn't, not once.

I don't care if this is a regular occurrence for Royce to be chauffeuring while Franklin makes out with women in the back seat. Tonight, the woman here is me, and lust sparks in my every cell, overriding logic, only to leave me fulfilled with an orgasm. Franklin's fingers are magic, and I feel the need to explode, climb and climb, my legs spreading wider, my panting faster.

A groan fills the car, bringing me back to the now.

The sound came from me.

I sound sexually deprived, like I'm receiving my first orgasm. Franklin covers my lips with his, inhaling my groans as I come hard and loud. When he removes his mouth, I'm starved for oxygen and breathe fast and deep like a marathon runner.

"I love that sound," he murmurs.

"What sound?" I manage. My eyes are closed, and I'm not ready to come down from the high just yet.

"The sound of *Penny* coming for me," he growls out the words.

I move my hand and find his thick, erect cock. My fingers move over the bulging material of his trousers, rubbing the length of him. I find his zipper and his other hand covers mine, halting any movement.

"Penny," he rasps out. "I'm on the edge. Let's avoid a mark on my trousers."

Before I offer to go down on him, he pulls his hand from my panties and stares at it. With every passing streetlight, I see the glimmer of my orgasm on his fingers. He takes one finger and places it in his mouth. Eyes closed, he sucks the length of each finger, and it turns me on in a way I've never felt before.

"You're my new favorite taste," he whispers.

"We're here, sir." Royce's gaze remains forward. He exits the car, walks to the front, and stands by the pavement to wait for us.

"In a few seconds, Royce will open the door," he says while adjusting my skirt. I take over, fixing it while staring out the darkened windows, trying to orient myself to our whereabouts. While enjoying the ride, I took zero notice of where we were headed. "He'll walk you inside and then drive around the back before I get out of the car."

I turn back to Franklin and study his face, but nothing in his expression hints as to why he doesn't want to be seen with me.

"It's better this way."

"I'm a secret," I whisper, leaving out the word *dirty*.

"No. Only to the public who have no business knowing my private life. My family prefers to keep our personal lives hidden as best we can."

I understand somewhat what he's inferring. Only my stomach is already filled with dread.

The door opens. I slide across the seat and step out onto the sidewalk. A flash of the camera while others are raised, only to lower when the photographers realize I'm of no importance.

Royce loops his arm in mine and walks me inside. He speaks with a woman behind a counter, then turns to me. "Mr. Hendricks will see you inside," he says quietly then leaves me with the woman. She makes a call while I stand awkwardly and alone.

Bloom.

I know of the restaurant and have heard about the food. Never made a reservation as someone like me would need to book months in advance, and that's if I didn't get hung up on when I inquired. Bloom is known for Hollywood-star clientele, so how did Franklin get us a last-minute reservation? I clench my purse, playing with the strap.

"Ms. Gilbert," a man says. I turn to the waiter, who's wearing a suit. "I'm Aidan, and I'll be serving you tonight. Please follow me."

I follow Aidan as we weave around multiple tables to the back corner of the room. He pulls out a chair, and I sit, careful not to catch the white tablecloth and have the contents of the table fall into my lap. Then I hear a loud, familiar, deep, obnoxious laugh, and my entire body stiffens.

The sound penetrates my heart, and I want to stand and dash out the back door.

Where is Franklin?

I don't want to be here alone.

17

FRANKLIN

ROYCE DRIVES to a side alley near a secret back door to the restaurant. I'm about to text Penny when Bill's name appears on my screen.

"Bill."

"I just spoke to Theo. You need to call him."

"Now?"

"It's about the resort in Bali."

"What about it?"

"Call Theo."

"For fuck's sake." I stare at the blue door. It's a contrast against the red-brick building, and it's calling to me like a secret getaway so I can forget all this bullshit for a few hours.

"Thanks for the heads-up. Say hi to Bridgette for me."

"I will. We're heading out to dinner now."

Burdening Bill with trivial things about my life is something I've never done. He gives me ninety percent of his time, and it's not his fault when deals sour. He deserves a private social life, and if anyone should forfeit their time, it's me.

I call Theo.

"Franklin."

"I'm about to have dinner with the most beautiful girl in the world, so this better be good."

"Anyone I know?"

"No."

There's a moment of silence.

"The last thing I want is to deliver bad news on a Friday night. I didn't realize you were out."

I haven't taken my eyes off the blue door. "You have thirty seconds."

"Someone got wind of your idea. The price has escalated by another ten million."

"Ten million!" *Fuck.* "We both know my offer of fifteen was generous, especially when it's worth five in the current condition. Twenty-five mill is fucking ridiculous when I need to spend another thirty mill before reopening."

"Someone is messing with you."

"You fucking think." I work my temple with my thumb and finger—there's a hint of a headache coming on. For a few minutes, we discuss strategy.

"What's your next step?"

I shake my head. "Nothing. We're done here. I'm not playing this game. Call me on Monday and let me know how any other deals go down."

I check the time. I've wasted ten minutes on calls. I jump out of the car and knock on the door. In a matter of seconds, my mood is black. What I should be doing is heading to the office to make some calls, sort this shit out, and figure out who is trying to ruin my deal. Only someone is inside waiting for me, and I want to be with her more than I want to fix this crap. Being around Penny is like having a set of imaginary hands working my shoulders and neck, and I always come away from time with her feeling unusually relaxed.

I need her in my life.

The thought has me taking a step back.

What the hell am I thinking?

I can't be involved with anyone.

The blue door opens to Aidan awaiting me. "Mr. Hendricks, Ms. Gilbert is waiting for you."

"Thank you."

He leads me along a narrow hallway with dim lighting. Rubbing my temples one last time, I expel the conversation from my mind as the door opens to the restaurant. Penny is in the corner. Head dipped. She's reading the menu. Only she's not moving at all. When I come closer, I notice a dent between her eyebrows. *Is she worrying about the price?*

She stares at me, her expression unchanged. I lean down and kiss her cheek before taking my seat. "Is everything okay?"

She picks up a glass of water and downs it. Frowning, she says, "You tell me?"

"I apologize. I had to take a call."

She shrugs her shoulders. "I could have stayed in the car with you rather than sitting here feeling like I've been stood up on a date."

I lean forward. "I thought you could have enjoyed a glass of wine while you waited. No one gets stood up here when it takes at least a month to acquire a table."

She raises one eyebrow. "When did you book? Was it for someone else?"

Aidan places the white napkin over Penny's hips. I lean back for him to do the same to me.

"Sir, would you like the usual tonight?" he asks.

I look to Penny. "Are you drinking white or red?"

She picks up the menu, glances over the wine, then places the menu aside. "I'll have whatever you drink."

I nod to Aidan. "We'll have a bottle of chardonnay along with a glass of Blanton's on ice."

She peers down at her hands in her lap.

"What is it?"

She shrugs again, and it annoys me.

"Just say it, Penny."

When her eyes meet mine, the dent between her brows is back. "Fine. I wanted to pay for our meal tonight."

"Why?"

"Because it's what..." she shakes her head, "... you know, what friends do. Even business partners share the cost of dining out."

I can't help but smile at her gesture. The seriousness in her eyes is amusing. "You know," I don't finish the sentence because her eyes narrow like she's about to shoot poisonous arrows at me from one look.

I thrum my fingers on the table, contemplating how to explain tonight without sounding like a douche. "I didn't have to reserve tonight because I—"

"You know the owner?" Her eyes are wide.

"You could say that."

Aidan appears with my glass of whiskey and a bottle of chardonnay. He pours some in a glass for Penny to taste. She nods as I'd hoped she would since it's the best chardonnay in the restaurant.

I give a little wave of a hand for him to leave us.

"I could ask the owner for a discount if that helps." I wink at Penny.

Her shoulders rise and fall. "A ninety percent discount would help."

"Something else is bothering you."

Her head tilts to the side. "Could your friend add three hundred percent to a certain table?"

Why would she ask that? Scanning the room, I spy no one of significance. "What table?"

She shrugs again. I'm starting to see a pattern of shrugging to avoid the uncomfortable within her.

"What. Table?"

"It's okay. At least I distracted you from your call." She smiles, and this time, it almost reaches her eyes. "How was your week?"

Small talk.

"My week is better now I'm with you." I tap my glass with one finger while she fiddles with the cutlery.

Who the fuck is here?

Tonight was supposed to be about relaxing and enjoying fine food and wine. Spoiling Penny. She is not going to enjoy the food with her stomach in knots.

"You know what? Let's get out of here."

Her eyes widen.

"I can have food sent to my penthouse or to wherever. We can head to the beach house. We could go to yours?"

She shakes her head. "Not mine." She shakes her head again. "You'd hate it."

I sit back and fold my arms. "Why? Because right now, I don't care where we go as long as I'm alone with you."

She giggles. "Yeah, that. Not only is my entire apartment the size of your bedroom, but I share it with someone." She makes a face. "Two someone's at night."

"Someone?" *Someone better be a fucking female.* "I'm to assume it's more than one bedroom."

"Yes, but—"

"What do you mean two at night?" My fingers turn red around my glass. Why is Penny backtracking?

She giggles. "You'd be entertained."

141

I raise a brow. "Would I?"

"My roommate and her partner are..." she rolls her eyes, "... loud."

Placing my glass on the table, I lean closer to Penny so no one overhears our conversation. "This is a problem for you?"

She shrugs again.

And I have my answer.

"I'm used to it, but I don't expect anyone else not to get a good night's sleep."

I wait a moment before asking more questions. I take a mouthful of whiskey and another. "Why do you stay?"

Penny sips her wine and casually places it on the table. "Cheaper rent for a good location. We stay out of one another's lives, and I prefer it that way."

"If you found a better place for the same rent, would you take it?"

She eyes me curiously. "You are aware there is a housing deficit?"

"You forget my brother works in real estate."

She nods slowly. "Right."

"If it's fine with you, then I can ask him to keep an eye out for any vacancies?"

Penny tilts her head as a slow smile creeps across her lips. "Thank you. I appreciate it."

My shoulders relax. "Are you happy to stay and eat, or do you still want to leave?"

The waiter appears at the table. "Excuse me, sir, are you ready to order?"

I place the menu aside. "It is up to the beautiful lady to decide."

"I don't suppose you have takeout?" Penny says playfully.

Aidan frowns. He is confused, considering I own the restaurant and am aware there is not a takeout option.

At first, he stammers, and I eyeball him. "If you prefer to take the food with you, I can speak with the chef," he says.

"Penny?"

She looks embarrassed for me. "We'll just order now and eat in."

I tilt my head at Aidan. "The lady would like to stay. What do you recommend?"

Aidan reads out the chef's special meals, asking her what she prefers and if there is anything she would like to add to her meal.

With Penny more relaxed, we finish our meals and the bottle of wine.

The conversation flows onto the renovation. "You didn't answer my email," I say. "I was waiting for a response, so I assumed you were happy with the contract terms."

"I didn't get it. Did you accept my excessive hourly rate?" She grins at me as though her proposal is excessive, and when we last spoke, she said we could negotiate the terms. "When did you send it?"

"When I landed in New York." I pluck my cell from my pocket and scroll through the sent mail. "For fuck's sake." I shake my head. "It stayed in draft mode." Now, she doesn't know how much she means to me since I multiplied her terms fivefold.

She giggles. God, I love the sound of her happiness. "Sent," I say and smile at her, hoping when she reads the terms, she'll know how appreciated she is. "You're not to read this until we're home. No more business tonight."

She places her chin on her palm while her elbow rests on the table. She stares at me with a warmth that makes me want to cocoon her from the rest of the world.

"What is it?" I ask.

She grins and shakes her head. "I was thinking about my ex. I'm so glad he dumped me. Otherwise, I would never have met you." She glances up at me through long lashes, almost coy. "I'm really glad you found me on the beach." Her eyes widen. "Not under the circumstances, and I'm s-sorry," her voice falters. Grabbing her crystal glass, she drains the last of the wine.

"Hey." I reach across and squeeze her delicate hand. "I'm glad you were there too." What I don't fucking understand is why she is thinking of her dickwad ex when she is with me. Thoughts of Daphne rarely come to mind when I'm with Penny because I'm completely consumed by her. *Only her.*

Her head tilts. "Let's get out of here."

"Done." I signal for Aidan. "I'll call Royce to bring the car around."

"Do you want me to walk out first?" Her eyes are wide. "Or can I take the back exit with you?" Her big eyes plead with me. I have no idea why she's uneasy, and my gut is telling me not to leave her, although my head is screaming that it's premature for her to be known as my new girlfriend. Not together. Whatever this is, we will be seen as being on a date, and that's all the media needs to scrutinize her past, like she is running for governor.

"Royce." I keep my eyes on Penny. "Bring the car around to the back."

Her shoulders rise and fall, and her eyes never leave mine. Her lips part with a hint of a smile. Before either one of us speaks, acknowledging we will be seen together, Aidan presents the bill. After I pay, like any other diner would, we stand. Before we leave, I must speak with Aidan to inform him the tip is all his, but he has moved to the front foyer.

"Thank you for a beautiful meal." She rises on her toes to kiss my cheek.

With my hand on her lower back, we walk toward the front of the restaurant. I step past the customers congregating in the foyer to speak to Aidan and quietly thank him for his discretion.

"Penny. I'm surprised to see you in this restaurant," a deep voice comes from behind me.

I spin to see a middle-aged man in a suit standing over Penny. Everyone heard his blatant opinionated statement. My stomach clenches at the sight of her distressed face. Her eyes are wide, like a deer in headlights about to be struck by a fucking truck. Then her brow furrows, and she stutters. *Fucking stutters.* She clears her throat and lifts her chin. "Mr. Wagner. It's been some time. How are you?"

I step toward Mr. Douchebag Wagner and stand behind him and another two men wearing black tuxedos. Hairs prick on the back of my neck. These three stand over her like bullies. My girl doesn't cower, and I give her a moment.

"Did you hear about Bernard's engagement? I've never seen my son happier. I know you wanted him to be happy."

The fuck?

"That is great news. *I* am also happy." Her eyes dart to mine. "In fact, *I* can't remember being happier in my life."

Mr. Wagner takes a step closer, and I don't give two fucks what he is about to say. I doubt he is happy for Penny, so I slip in beside her, wrap an arm around her waist, and pull her to my side. I want to tuck her behind me and protect her from the bastards. "Hello, gentlemen." I memorize each of their faces. The one on the end looks familiar. "I'm Franklin Hendricks." The familiar guy's face turns pale. *Is he a client?* "I'm the owner of Bloom. I hope you enjoyed your meal tonight."

Penny stiffens beside me.

Mr. Wagner stares at me, his eyes narrowed. "Are you dating her?"

Penny's chin drops.

I'm guessing she thinks I'm going to say no, and she'll look like a fool.

"You stand in my restaurant and have the audacity to question my personal life after I've asked if you've enjoyed your meal? If the food hasn't left you feeling satisfied, then please let it be the last time you dine here, as reservations have a long waitlist." I step closer so I'm in his face. "In answering your question, yes. Penny and I are together. Now leave before I have you thrown out."

Aidan comes to stand beside us.

The other two men thank us for a wonderful meal, and I raise a hand to dismiss them while speaking quietly to Aidan, "Please ensure Mr. Wagner *never* eats in my restaurant again."

18

PENELOPE

FRANKLIN TAKES my hand and leads me to the back of the restaurant and through a blue door. We are only ten feet from the car when cameras flash and blind me. Shouting comes from the corner as more paparazzi scramble toward us.

Eyes down, I shield my face with my hands.

Royce is ready, the car door open, and I'm the first to slide across the seat.

"Go," Franklin commands as soon as Royce's door slams.

Royce guns the engine until we merge with traffic. A few minutes pass before he glances into the rearview mirror. His eyes are on Franklin, staring out of his window, his finger and thumb digging into his chin, deep in thought.

Neither one of us speaks.

Royce's gaze fixates on me, perhaps checking if I'm okay.

The paparazzi didn't rattle me. I'm silenced by Franklin's admission about owning the restaurant.

Why didn't he mention it to me rather than act like we were regular diners?

Now I'm wondering what else he is keeping from me.

I don't know this man.

He doesn't act like he is better than me, and when I'm with him, I think of nothing except us—we're in our own small bubble. Only I can't help feeling like I'm not enough, and worse than that is the knowledge that what we have is temporary.

The insecurity is eating me up because I'm falling hard for Franklin.

My hands tremble in my lap.

Bernard's father was about to belittle me in front of everyone before Franklin stepped in.

"To your penthouse, sir?"

"No, Malibu." It's all Franklin murmurs without taking his focus from the window.

"Do you mind dropping me home first, Royce?" My voice cracks on the last word.

I need to be alone.

No matter how much I feel for him, Franklin will probably need to pay someone to stop the pictures of us from reaching the internet. He doesn't need to have his image tied to someone like me.

Franklin straightens, and I feel his gaze on me. His hand covers mine in my lap. "Why?" he whispers. He gently squeezes my hand and slides closer to me. It's reassuring that he cares, but I can't be with him tonight.

We have sexual chemistry.

Tonight, my heart needs more.

What Franklin and I have is more than I ever felt with Bernard. Our conversations are easy, and I've never been more comfortable with any guy than I am with Franklin.

Glancing down to his hands, I savor the warmth of them

on mine. He gives me a sensation of protection. I have to let him go because the longer we are together having casual, regular sex, the harder it will be when he no longer needs me.

"I want to be alone tonight." I avert my gaze to the window because it hurts to look at him.

"Take Penny home," he instructs Royce.

His eyes remain on me. Every part of me feels him. Back straight, chin up, I remain strong. We both need time, and what I'm feeling inside cannot be fixed by sex.

I need to be loved.

Protected from people like the Wagners and not just on a dinner date.

I need someone who wants to be with me for me, to feel safe, and not have an expiration date where my heart will be broken when my body is no longer needed.

And Franklin has said he is not seeking a relationship.

I wanted the sex even after Hugh warned me about Franklin. Now, I want what he can't give me.

I quickly glance at Franklin, staring at the city lights.

What is he thinking?

Will this be goodbye?

The silence surrounds us.

We finally turn onto my street. Royce double parks, ignoring the car horns behind us.

"I'll walk Penny inside. Park the car somewhere."

"No need," I murmur. Only Franklin frowns, and I know he won't listen to what I say. I slide out of the seat, and he is right behind me. The wind whips my hair around my face as I brush it out of my eyes.

I place a hand on his chest. "I don't need a chaperone."

Franklin takes my hand in his, wrapping it between both his palms. His eyes are apologetic. I swallow hard, ready for whatever he is about to tell me. "I'm sorry about tonight. I promise you that man will never set foot in my restaurant again."

"That's heroic, although unnecessary, and not wise for your business."

"Penny. When you're with me, *you* are my business." His eyes flick over my face. "Mine to protect. Now, shall we head inside out of this breeze?"

I lead him into the small foyer and the glass doors close behind us. My head is spinning, his words touching my heart. I turn to him, ready to kiss him goodbye.

"Are we heading up to your place?"

I step back. "You want to see where I live?"

"If it's okay, I would like to see you safely home." He takes my hand as I lead him to the elevator. I have dreamed about making out with Franklin in an elevator, but tonight, we stand apart, yet we're still holding hands.

He stands behind me as I unlock the door and is right there when I walk inside. "Lily must be out partying."

He glances around the small living area. "How long have you lived here?"

"A few years. My roommate furnished it, and nothing is mine except what's in my room. When I get my own place, I'll fill it with the things I love." I smile at him, imagining how I'll decorate my place with a neutral palette and all sorts of things I can restore.

"What's stopping you?"

I choke out a laugh. "Finances. This place has a great location for work. It's fine for now, albeit temporary."

"Do you have a date when you'll move out? A location in mind?"

"No. I've been so busy at work. It's really just a place to sleep."

"And where do you sleep?"

My breath hitches. *Shit. Did I pick up my dirty clothes from the floor?*

There are two doors leading from the kitchen-living room. One is Lily's bedroom, and the other is mine.

I open the door, and he peers in. "May I?"

"Sure."

Franklin walks to the end of the bed and stares at the covers. "So this is where Penny spends her nights." He grins. "At least there is room for two."

My heart threatens to burst. "You want to spend the night here. In my apartment?"

He takes a step closer. "If it means being with you, then yes."

There is a slam of the entry door.

Laughter.

Franklin's eyes dart to my bedroom door.

"It's my roommate. Prepare yourself."

"For what?"

Lily's door slams. There's more laughter, and Franklin stares at me.

"Lily only comes home to..." I shrug. "You'll see."

"See?"

"Hear," I say with a giggle.

It always starts with a steady, repetitive knock on the wall. Gentle almost. Then their sex gears up a notch, and it's a loud bang, over and over and over.

Franklin's eyes widen. "They waste no time."

I grin at him.

"How long does it last?"

"For an hour or more."

His expression sags. Anything he wanted to discuss is lost to the wall banging. He watches the rhythmic jerks of a landscape print on my wall as he pulls off his jacket and places it on the chair. Then he unbuttons his shirt and loosens his trouser belt.

"What are you doing?"

"Do you want to give them a run for their money?"

I smother a laugh. "Hell, yes." I get to work on removing my top and skirt as quickly as Franklin. He pauses to watch me strip, then pushes his trousers over his thighs, and that beautiful erection bounces free.

The heartache of before is lost in the moment of fun, mindless sex. Everything is forgotten as I jump onto the bed, while the thud, thud, thud sounds against my bedroom wall.

Franklin slips on a condom, "Are you ready?" He winks at me.

"Always."

Franklin slides two fingers in. He hisses, leans down, and kisses me. "Lily is going to hear us."

"Fine."

He climbs on top of me. He begins sliding in and out, allowing me to stretch with him. He slowly builds, his face serious. Then he finds his rhythm, picking up the pace and sinking deeper inside.

I pant loudly.

"Don't hold back, Pen."

I shake my head and close my eyes.

Franklin's momentum switches, and my headboard thumps against the wall with such force a giggle erupts from me. I hold Franklin's ass while he pummels into me over and over.

"Are we winning?" he whispers between breaths. I laugh, and my pussy clenches around him.

"Stop it. You'll make me come quicker."

I laugh more at his seriousness.

"Penny!" He growls out the word.

I exaggerate my moans, but the sound comes out wrong.

It's a forced moan, and then my voice cracks with the pleasure whipping through me. I sound like a dying animal.

Franklin covers my mouth with his hand. "For fuck's sake, let the walls do the talking." I love seeing this playful side of him. He rolls his hips as he thrusts harder and faster, and I let out the groans of all groans when I come right before him.

"Good girl," he croaks as he comes hard, shudders, and then flops over me.

My door swings open, with Lily and Toby rushing into my room. "Penny, are you okay?"

I scream and fling myself off the side of the bed onto the floor, trying to grab the sheet to cover myself as I go. In a split second, the sheet is entangled around Franklin, and he falls with me.

We land on the carpet.

I'm relieved to be covered by the sheet, which is somehow wrapped around Franklin's head. Only everything from his stomach down, including his glistening semi-hard dick, is on display. He struggles with the sheet until I whisper, "Don't move."

Lily and Toby's eyes bulge like cartoon characters.

Lily's face turns beet red. "Shit. Sorry. I thought you were having a fit or something."

I smile innocently. "I'm okay. We're okay."

"We can see that," Toby says, holding back his laughter.

They leave us, the door clicking shut.

Franklin wrestles with the sheet, and his face appears when the sheet falls away. He takes a deep breath as though I'm suffocating him.

"Is it safe?"

I burst out laughing with the image of him stuck in my head. "We're good. They didn't see much."

He holds up one arm, fist clenched. "Winners."

I can't help it.

I'm laughing uncontrollably.

My Frankie.

I stop laughing and gaze into his eyes, with happiness filling my heart.

Then, without thinking, I blurt out, "I love you."

Sitting at my favorite café in Santa Monica Beach, I stare at the froth on top of my coffee decorated with a cute heart. I take a sip and recap last night to Zara and Hugh. Hugh snorts as he laughs when I tell them how Franklin had all his bits exposed while his head was wrapped in a sheet.

"I wish I'd been there," Zara says, gasping for breath. "Not that I want to see Franklin's bits, but oh... to have been a fly on the wall."

I laugh along with my friends until I say, "And then I told him I loved him."

"What?" Zara laughs again, but her face changes in understanding about what I just said. "Did he say it back?"

I shake my head.

Hugh folds his arms and stares at me the same way when he gets all protective.

I shrug. "I know. The damn words slipped out."

"Like a rebound remark?" Hugh asks.

"Maybe. To say I don't have feelings for him would be a lie. I do, and it's more than lust."

"You mean great sex," Zara adds. She is aware of how much I love having sex with Franklin.

"The sex is great. Is it love? I don't know. I feel happier with Franklin than I ever did with Bernard, and I thought I loved him. This might be the closest version of love I get since I'm aware there is no future with Franklin. He has made it clear he has no time for a relationship as his work comes first."

"Yet he proposed to Daphne." Hugh raises one brow.

I let out a sigh. "He thought it was what *she* wanted. At the time, he didn't want to lose her, but he came to realize they were not right for each other."

My friends stare at me as though I have two heads. "It's fine. I don't need protection from Franklin or my stupid brain since I know what it is. It felt right to say it in a moment of happiness. Unfortunately, there's no dial to take it back."

Zara looks sympathetic. "Did he look like he was going to say it?"

I stall for a moment. "He frowned at me, a mixture of surprise and... I don't know. But he kissed me, and I quickly changed the subject."

Zara places her elbows on the table and leans closer. "When are you seeing him next?"

"This afternoon. He's visiting his family this morning."

"I'm curious what you said to distract him from those three words?" Hugh won't let it go. I know it's because he wants to protect me from getting hurt.

"We jumped up and sorted the bed. I made light conversation as though I didn't say it. Then he messaged his driver and told him to go home as he wanted to stay with me until morning."

"See?" Zara pipes in. "That's a good sign. He could've just left."

"True. Then we had a conversation about why he always needs a driver when he has half a dozen expensive cars."

"Only half a dozen." Hugh rolls his eyes. "I can be

jealous of him. Though I won't hate him... no one else has stuck it to Bernard's dad like Franklin did last night."

"He was rather heroic," Zara purrs.

Heroic.

Warmth blossoms in my chest.

"I didn't allow it to sink in as I was caught by surprise at him announcing he owned Bloom to Mr. Wagner." I turn to Hugh. "Heard of any other businesses he might own?"

"One second." Hugh signals for the bill. "Sorry, ladies, I have to run. I'm running late to meet Sienna. More wedding planning," he almost sings.

He stands and focuses on me. "Besides HCM, Dricks, and Bloom?" Hugh shakes his head. "Although your man is quite private and dislikes being in the media."

I didn't tell my friends the lengths Franklin went to for us to arrive at Bloom at different times.

"Though I have heard whispers of multiple properties, some in other countries. As for businesses, he keeps that a secret. Until now, I didn't know he owned Bloom." He blows us a kiss. "*Ciao, bellas.*"

"I now realize what HCM stands for?"

Zara stares at me bewildered because we all know what it is.

"Hendricks Cliterature Management." I bite my tongue. "Franklin Hendricks, that is."

Zara and I burst out laughing.

"Wait. Did he agree to your contract terms?"

"I haven't had time to read it." I set my cell on the terrazzo café table to open the emails and wait for it to load. There is an unopened email in my inbox from Franklin Hendricks at HCM.

I skim over the new contract he had drawn up.

All the air leaves my lungs.

I cover my mouth with my hand, still staring at the total

amount owing to Penelope Gilbert on completion of the renovation.

"What is it?" Zara slides my cell toward her. "Holy fucking hell. Is this a joke?"

I shake my head. "How should I know? We did *not* agree to this. I estimated ninety-thousand and thought I overcharged him. I expected him to challenge the price."

Zara's expression is deadpan. She picks up my phone so it's closer to her face. "In other words, you thought he may have suggested $50K? Could the extra zero be a mistake?"

"Possibly," I murmur. "I'm sure it's an oversight."

If it's not an error, then I will ask Franklin to draft a new contract.

I *will* set the terms, and the five-hundred-thousand-dollar remuneration will be rejected. Because apart from being excessive, I feel like it's a payment of other sorts.

And now I feel sick thinking about it.

19

FRANKLIN

A THICK VINE twists around the overhead wood structure, purple flowers hanging like lanterns above us. The inviting blue pool with a waterfall cascading from the back wall tricks my mind into a state of calm.

Much of my teenage years were spent by this pool. During college, semester breaks were spent at home. I studied for hours out here until my younger siblings' guests would arrive and destroy the peace.

My mother requested her family to meet at nine to discuss her plans for the gala ball. No excuse will be tolerated when it comes to doing our part at her favorite fundraising event. No one else has arrived yet, and it's a relief because all I can think about is Penny. Last night, she seemed just as surprised as I was by those three words. *Could we be more?*

Lola pours spring water from a jug and fills my glass. "Have you eaten breakfast, Mr. Hendricks?"

"I have, thank you, Lola." She moves to fill the other glasses at the unoccupied table. My father steps out of the house and sits across from me. "How was your trip?" I ask him.

He smiles. "Never a complaint when business takes you to Italy."

I take a sip of water and place the glass within reach. "Mom mentioned you had dinner with Daphne."

"I did." His eyes hold mine. "She's split from Stephano."

"I didn't think they were a good match."

"Daphne also mentioned she is not over you."

A while ago, I would have rejoiced at the news. I offer no emotion. No response. I feel nothing. No regret.

"You are, however, over her?"

"I am. I wanted a second chance for so long. Now," I shrug, and his eyes widen. I'm even picking up Penny's habits. "That chapter has closed. I can see myself heading in another direction."

"Orange juice, Mr. Hendricks?" Lola offers to pour Dad his juice.

He waves her on. "No, thank you. Lola, please ask my family to hurry up." Lola disappears inside, and my father sets his focus on me. "She's coming to your mother's gala to support her."

"As long as she isn't seated beside me."

"But you are friends? Maybe I was hasty in my judgment about her being wrong for you."

"No, your instinct was dead right."

He eyes me carefully. "I'm proud of you moving on."

"That's because he has found the perfect distraction." Jobe pats my shoulder and then takes a seat beside me. "After our meeting the other day, I understand the attraction."

Dad's brow furrows. "What meeting?"

I respond before Jobe says anything stupid, "I've hired someone to remodel the Malibu home. We get on quite well. Her ideas are unique. I offered her a contract so I can sell it in six months."

"Only you didn't make it clear you hired her to bring profit. She told me about creating the perfect home for you and remodeling it to *your* needs."

"Penny isn't privy to my intentions after the renovation. I'm hiring her to make it appealing to a certain buyer."

Jobe assesses me. "Yet she seemed to be privy to your private life last night." He raises his brow, challenging me.

"What am I missing?" my father asks.

A sly grin creeps into Jobe's expression. "Have you checked the tabloids this morning?"

I yank my cell from my suit pocket.

My father does the same with his.

I type in my name, and a stream of photographs of Penny and me leaving the restaurant fills my feed. There is one taken through the front glass of the restaurant of the men I addressed last night in the foyer. Penny is there, her back to the camera.

"Who is this?" Dad asks.

"Penny, the interior designer and decorator."

"Are you with her?"

"No."

Jobe coughs out, "Bullshit."

My father glares at him. "What do you know of it?"

"Franklin sent her to me to set up a liaison with our contractors." Jobe swivels so he can see me. "Why are you denying it? Penny is great for you."

My father's gaze has been fixed on me the entire time. I sense the questions burning behind his eyes. He knows Penny is new and not known by our family ties. He can guess all he wants, as I'm not in the mood to hear his opinion about an average girl with no significant family who is only with me to snare our family's billions.

Daphne earned his respect.

She also led me to Penny.

"Who is Penny?" Mom takes a seat beside my father. She picks up her glass of water and takes a few mouthfuls. "Franklin?"

"Franklin's new girlfriend." Jobe presses his hands behind his head and leans back with a smug grin on his face.

She chokes on the last mouthful. She looks at Jobe, then to me. "Is this true?"

"We spend time together because she is working for me."

Mom tilts her head, and her freshly styled hair falls into place. "Are you bringing Penny to the gala?"

"No." I could kill Jobe for bringing Penny into this. Once our relationship is out, she'll be followed and photographed when she least expects it.

Daphne loved the attention.

Penny is the polar opposite of her.

"Bring her," Mom says with a gentle yet firm tone. "A date attracts positive feedback for the family. It makes you appear—"

"Less of a Casanova," Byron says as he sits beside Mom and she gives him the side-eye.

"Likeable and less serious," Mom adds.

Byron chuckles. "Right."

"Just get out of bed?" I snap at him. He looks ridiculous in purple-striped sweatpants and a matching sweater.

"This is the latest trend, not that you have any interest in athletic wear."

He is right about that.

Charlotte waves and takes a seat on the opposite side of Byron. My two youngest siblings have always been close.

"Have I missed anything?"

"No," I snap again. "You all interrupted the conversation about Dad's trip and any potential investors."

Charlotte leans forward to see our father. "I thought you said you're retiring?"

Is she serious? "He's been saying that for years but always manages to keep a finger on the pulse when it comes to him researching current market conditions and analyzing investment trends worldwide."

Dad takes my mother's hand. He appears resigned, and it confuses me. "Your mother and I had a discussion, only I haven't broken the news to you." His gaze flits to me. "It depends if you're ready to take the wheel."

"I've had the wheel for years."

"Complete control," he adds.

Everyone is silent.

Hendricks Capital Management will be my responsibility. I have been groomed for this position my entire life. It will own all my time—all of me—and right now, I'm not sure if I'm ready.

What am I thinking?

I am ready.

"This is a matter for discussion at a later date." Mom gives Charlotte a firm look. "Today, I want to chat with you about ideas for extra sponsorship."

When the day comes for me to step into my father's shoes, there will be zero time for a relationship.

It has to be temporary.

Eventually, I'll have to let Penny go, and I'm queasy at the thought.

My father's cell dings. He reads the text message.

"Sorry, Sophia, but we need to see this." He stands and asks for us to follow him.

We gather in the living room and hover around the television. My father says a command, and it turns on. The sports broadcaster announces the first-ever Hendricks-owned sports team.

"Son..." my father slaps my back, "... we are now the owners of the LA Sharks. Get ready to work some pretty big weekends for the next few months as we gear up for the season. I hope you like attending basketball games." His hearty laugh vibrates around the room.

Byron is smiling from ear to ear.

Jobe rubs at his jaw.

Charlotte stands to hug Dad, then me.

Mom kisses Dad on his cheek. "This is new for you, Carson. I like it very much." She turns to Charlotte, and I wonder what these two have discussed. Is my mother paving the way for a career for her?

My cell buzzes.

Penny.

> Finished coffee with my friends. Do you
> want me to meet you in Malibu?

"Excuse me," I say and step out of the room to call her.

"Hey, did you get my message?" The sound of her voice stirs happiness deep inside me.

"I did. I'll have Royce pick you up, and we'll head there together."

"I can drive myself, Franklin."

"There is no room in the garage for your car."

"I can park at the Malibu Barefoot Bar and walk to your house."

Why does she argue every point?

"No. Head to yours, and Royce can meet you. Just say a time."

"Okay. An hour."

"See you soon."

"I received your email."

Finally, I have a reason to smile. "Are you happy with the terms?"

"I can't sign it. There's a mistake... like an extra zero added. I thought at first you were playing with me before realizing it was an oversight."

"It's not an oversight, Penny. I had my lawyer draw it up, and it's what your time and creative skill is worth to give up your weekends to work on the house."

She is quiet for a long period.

"I'm sorry, but I can't accept your offer. We'll discuss the terms later."

"There's scope for us to agree to other monetary arrangements."

"I'll talk to you soon. Bye, Franklin."

I head back into the room, rather surprised by Penny's rejection of the contract. She is the only person I know who undersells her worth. "Tell me whatever you need me to do, and I'll do it. I'm sorry to cut this meeting short. I need to be somewhere."

"With Penny?" Charlotte jokes and gives me the widest smile.

"Yes, with Penny," I say seriously, hoping they don't read anything into it. I don't want Dad doubting that I'm ready to lead the business in a new direction.

Mom links her arm through mine, tilting her head back as she assesses me. "*I want* you to bring her to the gala."

"Fine." I dismiss her while I tap on Royce's name. "I'm heading out front now."

Nonchalance has worked for me before. Only I get a glimpse of Mom's reaction, and her expression tells me I shouldn't be fine. Everyone has an expectation of my personal love life.

"Are you staying to celebrate?" My father pours Blanton's into several glasses.

"Sorry. Work calls."

Mom walks with me to the front door. Her silence is worse than the questions on her lips. She reaches up and kisses my cheek. "The world is right again." Dainty fingers brush over my shoulder, removing invisible lint. "I'll be in touch."

I smile at my mother's positivity. "Tell Dad I am happy and will celebrate some other time. I just have—"

"Too much on your mind to relax right now." She places a hand on my cheek. "Be kind to yourself, Franklin. Give this young lady a chance."

I can't look at my mother because her eyes are filled with hope.

For once, I'm not assessing the future with a short or long-term strategy being the answer to all my troubles.

One day at a time.

AFTER ARRIVING AT THE MALIBU HOUSE, I TELL ROYCE TO head home and I'll see him on Monday. I punch in the code to open the door and take Penny's hand. She stalls and peers over her shoulder.

I slide stray strands of hair from her mouth. Her pouty lips entice me to kiss her and carry her to the bedroom. Ignoring those thoughts, I lead her into the kitchen. "Take a seat while I fix us a drink."

165

"Do you want to hear my plans?"

"Absolutely."

She shoots me her beautiful smile, and I feel it in my chest and all the way to my cock. "Your kitchen has enough room for a double counter." She pauses and waits for my reaction.

"Go on."

"And we could add walls here for a butler's kitchen. I love the idea of the first counter having appliances and a sink, and it being wide enough for people to sit at and chat to whoever is preparing the meal."

What? "I never sit to simply chat to our staff."

"Maybe you should." She gives me her you-should-try-it-sometime look. "Not all families have chefs and cooks. Many like to do it themselves, and sitting around the counter unites the family. I think it will give your kitchen a whole different feel for you."

"So why the second island? Personally, I like a butler's kitchen to hide the mess."

"You could have that too, especially if you hire a chef for the night."

I cock a brow. "The night? My mother has never cooked in her kitchen."

"As far as you know. I'm sure there are nights she cooks to help with the stress. It's quite therapeutic. You should try it."

"I'll take your word for it." I place a glass of wine in front of her and pour myself a whiskey. "Sally prepares my meals. If I turn on the oven, does that count?"

"No." She stands with her wine in her hand as she paces forward and makes a circular action with her free hand. "The second counter has storage and more stools around it in case you have a party."

"Why wouldn't we be civilized and sit at the dining table? Or outside on the balcony."

She shoots me a mischievous grin. "Sometimes people don't want to be civilized. You can stand and move around the charcuterie board." She stares as though envisioning the food. "Then the dining table is here where the glass doors will extend, allowing people on the bottom level to view the ocean no matter where they're standing."

"I like the sound of that."

"I want to use the old kitchen wood somewhere. I hate waste... we could use it on the wall."

"I can't picture it. If something is old, then just get rid of it."

"But it's wasteful."

"We can talk about it later. Tell me more of your ideas."

"I thought you could combine it with a stone wall."

"Stone walls are a nice feature around fireplaces."

"And that's exactly what we'll be doing here." She points to the center of the room. "A modular couch here."

"Flooring?"

"Hardwood. And more windows."

"Right. It sounds good, but I want to build something impressive. Something no one else has, so when someone —" I stop myself not wanting to tell Penny I'm only hiring her to sell the property. While it's just the two of us here together, it's nice to pretend she is remodeling the house for me—*us*. "So that guests are impressed by the grandeur and uniqueness of the house."

She drinks her wine and spins to me. "Downstairs is about using the space to bring the outdoors in. We want to see the ocean. Upstairs..." she takes another sip, "... is also about the ocean with a massive balcony. Only your bedroom will have a retractable ceiling so you can stare up at the stars. There is the option of a window or air view."

"Now you're talking."

"The bathroom will have glass doors so you feel like you're showering on the beach."

"Everyone will see me fucking you in the shower."

Her eyes widen. She comes to me and places her crystal wine glass on the counter. "With the number of windows I have in mind, everyone will see you fucking me on every counter, every piece of furniture, and..." she points to the ocean, "... out on the balcony."

"I love all of your suggestions." I take her hand, pull her to my side, and kiss those plump lips. "Best interior designer and decorator I've ever hired." I lift her onto the counter and spread her legs with my thigh. "We'll start by christening the old."

PENNY IS ASLEEP BESIDE ME. THERE'S AN IMAGE OF HER ASS I can't get out of my head. On all fours, she wiggles her ass right before I push inside her. The best ass I've ever seen, and I want to make it mine.

I want as much Penny as I can get.

I slip out of the sheets and grab my cell, closing the balcony door behind me. There are a few walkers on Malibu Beach. I turn my back, giving them a view of my rear rather than my dick. I'm staring through the glass at Penny. Watching her sleep calms me. She calms me. I don't know how to deal with the emotions I'm feeling.

I call Jobe.

"Franklin, what do I owe the honor?"

"How was yesterday?"

"After you left and didn't celebrate with Dad? The conversation became all about you. Your fault. One drink, man. That's all you needed to commit to so you could silence Dad's questions about why you suddenly left after the news or, more to the point, to see who? He saw right through your lies."

"He wouldn't have asked those questions if you didn't mention Penny."

"I guess you have to ask yourself why you're keeping her a secret?"

I press a finger to my temple. "It's for her sake."

"You think you can protect Penny from the Hendricks' madness?" He chuckles. "Have you asked her if she wants to be in the shadows?"

"Not something I'm willing to discuss when the future is unclear. We're happy, and this is just a bit of fun."

"Keep telling yourself that. Let's not rock the perfect world of Franklin Hendricks."

My blood heats, and tension rips through my neck and shoulders. "I gotta go. Just wanted to check in on yesterday and see if Mom had other requests."

I end the call and spin, leaning my arms on the railing. I stare out to the ocean and inhale deeply before bowing my head.

Shit.

I call Jobe again. "You're right."

"You didn't call to talk about yesterday?"

"No." I clench my eyes shut. "I'm scared." The words come out in a whisper. "How do I balance work and her? Because I don't think I can. My gut is in knots until I'm with her. Then the pain disappears."

"What now?"

"I need to protect her. Can you get a condo for her?"

"What's wrong with the one she has?"

"It's a small space she rents with a couple of wall bangers."

169

He laughs. I groan, remembering how we fell out of bed. Fucking ridiculous setup. A smile creeps across my face. It was a little funny, but I'm not mentioning that to Jobe.

"Send me a list of locations, and I'll find something. Price range?"

"Whatever it costs for her to have something nice and private with a view and balcony."

"The comfort needs to be at a level to accommodate you when you stay over?"

I don't respond.

"Why don't you just let her stay at your penthouse?"

"We're not at that stage."

"Bullshit. I'll get her a condo but stop being a dick and accept that she is good for you."

"Rich coming from you. When was the last time you had a relationship?"

"I don't see the need to have one girl. I like two at a time in my bed. I'm not old and boring like you."

"I was twenty-four when I was with Daphne. It's not old." But he's right. I only wanted relationships as they gave me the certainty of continuity. While my work life is all calculated risks, I can't live my private life in the same way. Only now, I'm so fucking time-poor, there isn't space for anyone.

"Do you miss her?"

"No. Not like I did. I loved our conversations about the economy and finance, but we're still friends. It's different with Penny."

"Penny is real. She is a breath of fresh air and not governed by the dollar. I bet your wealth scares her. Be careful, bro. I'd be asking her about the condo first before bankrolling it for her."

"We haven't negotiated her contract, and it might be a form of payment that suits her."

"I'm not sure, Franklin."

The door squeaks behind me.

Penny is naked, her knotted hair falling over her shoulders.

My cock twitches.

"I gotta go."

20

PENELOPE

On Wednesday, an email comes through from my boss about the next project Hugh and I will be working on together. I should be excited, except all I can think about is Franklin's house. We spent most of Sunday discussing ideas, choosing tiles and wall paint, and researching state-of-the-art bathroom cabinetry and accessories. I've never worked on a project with endless cash flow, and I need to research more about some fancy shit that can make his home stand out. Excitement streamed through me as we discussed all my ideas, yet every time I offered to recycle or repurpose furniture, he shut me down, saying *out with the old.*

It left me a little stunned.

That's not how I live or how I'm used to living.

We need to be mindful of the environment, and his disregard for repurposing good wood is a shock.

Hugh comes into my office and sits on the side of my

desk. "What ideas do you have for the Manhattan Beach project?"

I push up from my chair. "Do you want to discuss it over coffee?"

He agrees, so we take the elevator to the ground level and cross the street to the café. I take a seat while Hugh orders our lattes.

I open my cell and send Franklin a text.

> When can I contact the tradesmen to start on your home?

Hugh returns and sits beside me. "Ready to brainstorm?"

"I'm already looking into environmental-friendly ideas for Franklin's house. We could carry through the same ideas into this project."

"I want to ask what ideas only I'm nervous about mixing a work contract with a personal one."

"I'm not doing anything that could bring Style Line Designs into disrepute."

Our coffees are delivered, and Hugh waits until the server leaves before speaking. Most of our office comes here for lunch, and we never know if the staff is friendly with our boss.

"I know. Only if she hears you have taken on a private role instead of telling a client to go through the company, she may cause problems for you."

I take a sip of coffee and wonder why he is worried about this now. He's known about the project for weeks, but now he's seen the budget.

Why would she be upset when it's weekend work?

"We don't work weekends for Courtney."

"Have you ever asked yourself why it's only weekends, Pen?" Hugh's expression is almost sad.

173

"What are you implying?" I take a sip of coffee to calm me as I know exactly where this is going.

"How did Franklin find your work? Did you show him your portfolio?"

"Okay, stop there. I know you're looking out for me but don't question my creditability. You only have the right to do that if the contract is complete and not up to scratch."

Hugh nods. "My apologies. Just be careful, okay? Men like him are used to buying things they want, even women."

"Thanks, but Franklin's not like that."

He takes a sip from his mug and then wipes the froth from his lips. "I *am* curious about your ideas for the Manhattan Beach project."

I smile at him because I'm eager to chat about it. As much as his offhanded comment annoys me, he would do anything to protect me. "What do you think about using biodegradable and natural materials?"

His eyebrows arch high into his forehead. "Tell me more."

"An outdoor living area using recycled materials and a green roof that can help with insulation. We could source artwork from local artists or use recycled or sustainable materials, keeping it unique and classy."

"I understand what you want to do because these are your values, but we must be careful when clients want lux living."

"We can also do that with the environment."

He takes another sip. "Right. We might need to negotiate some things because Courtney will never go for it. Let's focus on the job at hand."

"Fine. But I'm researching environment-friendly products for Franklin, so it's no effort to do the same for this project."

"That's Franklin. These are our clients." Hugh

unbuttons the sleeves of his neon orange shirt and rolls them up. "It surprises me Franklin has agreed to this. I imagined him wanting everything to be dripping with gold."

"He doesn't know exactly what I have in mind. He trusts me to bring my touch to his home."

Hugh eyes me carefully. "Be careful, Pen."

When I return to work, Hugh and I form a plan and a list of companies we could use for the project. We agree on a paint color from the pictures of the home sent to us and schedule a viewing on our way home after work.

Before we leave, I receive a message from Franklin.

> You can start now. Any trouble, call Jobe.
> BTW, are you free tonight? I want to show you something. Don't ask what. It's a surprise.

I giggle as the first thing I was going to ask is what he wants to show me.

> Sure. Send me the address. I'll meet you there.

I pack up my desk, ready to head out with Hugh.

> Royce will pick you up at your place at 6:30.

ROYCE DRIVES US TO THE HEART OF LA ON WILSHIRE Boulevard and parks in an apartment complex. Franklin refuses to tell me anything, so I go along with him. Is this one of his investment properties? Am I getting another remodeling job?

"Take a look around before you comment," Franklin says as we exit the car.

He punches in a code, we step into an elevator, he punches in another code, and then swipes a card. He takes my hand, his eyes set on the numbers flashing at each level. It stops at twenty-three.

"Jobe is here to help with any questions."

Franklin is wearing his usual suit. He dresses smartly all the time, but today, something about him is different. He appears fresher—hair perfect, clean-shaven, and he smells as though he just stepped from the shower. Am I missing something? I'm still in my work attire, and my white blouse is crumpled after a long day in the office.

The doors open, and we step out to glass doors. Jobe is on the other side. This condominium must take up the entire floor. Franklin holds a card to a security reader, and the doors open.

"I'm getting this changed for extra security," he says.

"I can see why when the person can see you through the glass doors."

"The elevator will not stop at this level unless you have the code. But I wanted extra security beyond the doors."

"I see."

Jobe strides toward us, looking equally as smart as Franklin. "Good to see you again, Penny." Jobe takes my hand and shakes it. "I'll let you two look around, and I'll be here if you have any questions."

"Thanks," Franklin says, and I don't miss the shakiness of his voice.

We head into the primary bedroom. There's a beautiful bed styled with natural colors. It has floor-to-ceiling windows with a great view of downtown LA.

"For part of the year, you can see the sun set through

these windows." He points toward the street, and to where the sun is setting, only now it is blocked by skyscrapers.

"It has a nice feel." I keep walking around. A modern en suite bathroom is all black and white. There are also two other bedrooms. The walls are an off-white color, and it feels clean and refreshing. The kitchen is a good size, with a living area leading out to a balcony. Franklin follows me outside to a modern setting with large planters, trees, and a herb garden. Has someone else decorated it for him, and he wants my opinion?

Jobe enters the room. "Something urgent requires my attention in the office. Email me any concerns. I'm interested in hearing your thoughts, Penny." He smiles at me and waves before leaving. I'm equally flattered and dumbfounded.

Jobe values my advice?

"You haven't said much." Franklin stands beside me as we gaze out over sprawling LA as lights flicker on and day turns to dusk.

"What do you want my opinion on? I like it and think it's a good investment, although I don't need to tell you that."

"No." He steps behind me and wraps both arms around my chest. His chin presses against the top of my head. We both stare out to the slither of skyline between the buildings, and I'm oblivious to the horns and sirens below. "I bought it for you."

21

FRANKLIN

PENNY JUMPS out of my arms. "You what?"

"It's yours, Pen. Jobe has kept an eye on the market, and this place ticks all the boxes." Her fists dig into her hips, and by her frown, it hasn't had the effect I hoped for. "It's close to your work, although a better location than your old apartment, with great security and space for you to do as you please."

Penny jabs a finger toward me. "I don't understand why you think I need all this from you. I don't need rescuing. For years, I had to prove to my parents how capable and independent I am, and now you're treating me like a kept woman."

"No," I say firmly. "I'm keeping you safe."

"Argh." She throws her arms in the air. "First, it's the ridiculous contract, and now this."

My cell buzzes in my pocket.

Penny stares at me.

It rings out and immediately buzzes again.

It's not going to stop until I answer it.

The expression on Penny's face screams, *don't you dare*.

I check the screen.

It's Paul, and he only calls out of business hours if the world of HCM is about to be hit with a monetary hurricane. "I'm sorry, I have to take this." Penny holds my gaze, her eyes narrowed. "Paul, it's not a good time."

"It's never a good time to tell you that one of your biggest investments has turned sour, and you could end up in court."

"What?" I growl.

"Organize your jet now. I'll travel with you to New York and give you the rundown on the plane."

Paul knows to be careful what he communicates in emails, so we need to discuss this face-to-face.

"Penny. I'm so sorry, but I have to go." Thoughts of a fallout of a court case cloud my mind. "It's the worst timing, but we can discuss this lat—"

"Are you serious? You need to go *now* when *we* need to discuss what has happened here tonight?"

"Unfortunately, the matter I need to attend to is very serious."

"And what is happening between us isn't?"

I can't do this with her now. "Pen, I'm sorry. We will talk about it. It just has to wait—"

"Because your work has to come first. I get it." She storms toward the elevator glass doors. Penny stares straight ahead and doesn't give me another look.

We stand apart and in silence in the elevator. During the time it takes to drive to her apartment, I am on my cell organizing the jet to be ready to leave in two hours.

When we pull up out front, I get out of the car and walk her to the door. "The timing is bad, and I apologize, but please understand how much you mean to me." We kiss. It's brief as Penny pulls away. "Good night, Franklin." She turns and walks through the doors.

Is she walking away from me?

⊂○

Midflight to New York, I write several emails to Penny.

In the end, I don't send any of them.

I want to gift the condominium to her because I can. It is already in her name. She simply needs to sign the papers with my lawyer, Jobe and me present. Whatever she intends to do with it is up to her. She can rent it out or live in it. Or do nothing. I simply wanted somewhere for her to stay without anyone intruding on her privacy.

It's done, and I can't think about it when I need to focus on why I'm on our private jet to New York. Paul received an anonymous tip that an old college acquaintance is filing an environmental lawsuit against PetroDepend for illegally disposing of hazardous waste into the ocean, causing significant damage to the marine ecosystem. My investors are about to lose a shit ton of money.

It places me in an awkward situation as any contact with this person might be misconstrued as an attempt to influence the lawsuit or gain insider information.

My grandfather and father built Hendricks Capital Management on integrity. I expect PetroDepend management will attempt to silence me. Any unusual movement of stock from their portfolio could attract the attention of financial regulators, increasing the risk if I decide to sell.

I'm not a whistleblower. Yet there's the risk of backlash

from clients and the investment community. We have worked with PetroDepend for five years. Nothing like this has happened before. So, where were the safety indicators? Who fucked up?

I check my folders after sending a brief email to George and Caleb, so they won't be surprised when I rock into the New York office tomorrow.

There are countless emails regarding the takeover of the Sharks basketball team. Worst fucking timing. My father can deal with all of it.

Jesus. There's an email from my mother I missed. She needs details on sponsorship and wants me to host the live auction for her gala.

I nominate Jobe.

If everything goes to shit in New York, the gala will be the least of my worries because I won't be attending. I'll still be on the other side of the country.

"Can I fix you a drink, Mr. Hendricks?" Heidi has been part of the crew on our jets for the past five years and can read my mood.

"Double. On the rocks. Thanks, Heidi."

The lawsuit can fuck our company as well as investors, and I'm going to have to tighten my spending so as not to appear shady with our clients. Maybe the condominium for Penny was premature.

THE FOLLOWING MORNING, HEADS TURN AS I WALK THROUGH the New York office.

"Morning, Franklin," echoes through the long room.

I close the glass door behind me. George, Caleb, and Lana are the only staff privy to the briefing.

"What's your plan?" George asks before my laptop fires up.

"There isn't one until I learn more about the lawsuit. I'm heading out to PetroDepend today and hopefully get answers if they don't lie to my fucking face. Then there is the public-interest complication. One of the clients Caleb secured years ago is a pension fund that represents many small-time investors who rely on our expertise to secure their retirement savings. Their potential loss is on my conscience. Their retirement funds could fucking evaporate. That weighs heavier than the losses to our company."

"What can we do?" Lana asks.

"Stay calm and speak to no one."

My cell rings, and while I said no interruptions, it's Jobe, so I answer anyway. "What's up?"

"Penny has a list of what work she wants to happen this week. I want to confirm again she has a green light to do everything?"

The Malibu renovation is the least of my concerns. "Yes. You don't need to call me about this. Just make it happen. Whatever she needs, get it done, and if she manages it in a smaller time frame, even better."

"How long are you staying in New York?"

"As long as I need to be here. Why?"

"Because I need the jet. There's a house in Italy I want to check out."

"It's all yours. I can't see myself leaving here in the next month."

"What about Mom's fundraiser?"

"I'll be there."

No point in letting anyone down yet.

THE NEW YORK PENTHOUSE ON BROADWAY IS A LUXURIOUS space with the best technology—criteria I won't negotiate. Tonight, it feels empty. Lifeless. I imagine Penny here with me, waiting for me to come home from the office, spending our nights together—an unattainable dream.

I step out on the balcony and gaze over the endless skyscrapers and blinding lights. I'm surrounded by eight million people, yet I've never felt more alone.

I call her.

It rings and rings.

I listen to her voice asking me to leave a message.

I almost say *I love you*, but it's the wrong time to say it and in the wrong way.

I tap out a short message.

> I'm lonely here without you.

Delete.

> I miss you.

Delete.

Jesus, it's been a matter of hours.

> Hi Penny. Please think about the condo. It's yours to move into or rent out. We can discuss it more when you are ready.

I never send emojis, but maybe I should add a heart. Fuck knows what I should do. I'd rather send an email, or a voice message might have been a better option, only I couldn't trust myself not to say something irrational. I hit send and go to bed. I need a good night's rest to gather my thoughts and focus on the bigger problem.

The following morning, I head to the gym at four o'clock after barely sleeping. All night, I fixated on the lawsuit and everything that could go wrong. I checked my messages every hour for something from Penny.

I can't control how she feels.

I scroll through my emails and then toss my cell on the table.

How the fuck am I going to fix this?

22

PENELOPE

ON FRIDAY AFTERNOON, I pack up my desk hurriedly to get out of the office and have a glass of wine somewhere. I haven't spoken to Franklin since he blindsided me with the condominium, except for the text asking him to give me space.

Hugh waltzes into the office with a huge grin, clearly as happy about it being Friday as I am. "Are you ready?"

"Absolutely. I'm ready for a drink before heading to Franklin's Malibu house."

"He's away, right?" Hugh carries my computer bag while I stuff a few things into my handbag.

"He is. For a month, his brother said."

"And he didn't tell you this himself?"

"Nope. He had to rush off for business but didn't say for how long. He texted, but I'm not ready to talk to him after Wednesday night."

"Wait." Hugh is silent momentarily. "What happened Wednesday night?"

I shake my head, still trying to make sense of what happened. "He surprised me by buying a condo a few blocks from here..." I point out the window, "... and said it's mine."

"The condo? You can stay in it. Or rent it from him?"

"No. It's mine and in my name. I just have to sign the papers."

"Woah." Hugh's eyes widen. He leans one hand on the desk. "Is that his way of saying he loves you back?"

"No," I snap. "It's like you said... this is his way of telling me my place is not good enough and buying me something he thinks is better for me. I didn't make him stay over. Everything about Malibu is business now. I'll get it finished ASAP. He can't buy my love." I let out a frustrated groan. I thought he was different. "Why can't men just admit their feelings? He either likes me or he doesn't. I don't need gifts or..." I lift my hands then drop my arms to my side, "... or saving."

"So, I'm not following exactly. Do you think it's your payment for the remodel? It could be a tax thing for him."

He did mention working something out for both of our taxes. "Who knows because the man doesn't talk to me unless—" I stop talking and look at Hugh, my eyes burning. I fight it so the tears don't well. "I think you were right," I whisper. "It's a sex thing because it's fucking great, and is it bad that I don't want it to end?"

Hugh smirks, and a single laugh bursts from me, yet it's not humorous. "So you both need each other for sex. Nothing wrong with that."

"Only I'm not the one trying to buy him or manipulate what we have."

Hugh takes in what I'm saying. "What did his message say?"

"In a nutshell, he apologized and told me to think about the condo."

"And have you?"

"No. Nothing in that message convinced me to think any more about it. No emotion. Just a statement as though I'm a business colleague with benefits." I stop and stare at Hugh with it all making sense. "Malibu *is* a business project. Hopefully, I can get most of it finished before he returns."

"Sienna is away until Sunday. Do you want me to help you tomorrow?"

I smile at my friend. "Please. I need to shop at local artisan stores and start collecting the furnishings. There are two bedrooms upstairs we can sleep in and a bathroom. The rest of the house is being gutted. And since yesterday, Franklin's bedroom doesn't have a roof."

"Why don't we skip work drinks, grab a bottle, and head there tonight? We can go over everything, and when the workmen arrive in the morning, we can go shopping."

I hug Hugh and grab my keys. Franklin told me to use Royce, but he deserves a break while Franklin's away. I send him a message telling him I don't require him to drive me this weekend, and I'll see him maybe when Franklin returns.

Before I'm on the Santa Monica Freeway, my cell buzzes with a call from Franklin. The car screen lights up. "Don't answer it," I say to Hugh, and I switch to my Spotify playlist. A message flashes across the screen, and I flick it away.

"Do you want me to read it to you?" Hugh has my cell in his hand.

"No, it can wait."

I turn the music up, and Hugh and I belt out the lyrics to Abba. They were my parents' favorite band, and Hugh appreciates my love of the seventies and eighties music.

While singing my heart out, I wonder what music

Franklin loves. It doesn't matter. Franklin was a bad decision, just like Bernard. I should have never given my heart to a man I barely know other than what we have between the sheets.

BEFORE THE LIGHTS SWITCH ON, DUST HITS MY NOSTRILS. I lock the door to the garage and step into what used to be the kitchen.

"What a mess," Hugh mutters as we step over planks of wood and small pieces of concrete from the wall. "What's your plan for here?"

"I'll tell you after we eat." We head out to the balcony with our takeout burgers, fries, and a bottle of wine. "I'm not sure where the glasses are, so we'll just have to drink from the bottle."

"Reminds me of when we were in college." He grins. "Only our taste in wine has improved one hundred percent."

I laugh. "Yes, but are we classier?"

We are both famished, so we remain silent, eating our food and taking swigs from the bottle. The moon is high in the sky, sending a shimmer across the dark ocean. The air is crisp and filled with salt. I can't wait for another couple of months when it will be warm enough to be on the beach, basking in the sunlight.

"My focus will be on the view," I say between mouthfuls. "Floor-to-ceiling windows to bring in natural light and warmth and double glazed to regulate temperature. It can help him save on energy bills."

"Franklin doesn't strike me as someone who is concerned about energy bills."

"Sustainability doesn't have to affect luxury," I say with

half a mouth full of food. "Everyone needs to be mindful of their impact on the environment. Capturing the natural breeze from the ocean is part of my layout to produce cross-ventilation and reduce the need for air-conditioning."

"I like this way of thinking, especially with mindfulness of the environment. It's something we can market with *our* project."

I nod. "And I have already done the research."

My cell lights up with a message from Franklin. I'll read it after I wash my hands. Can he see us on the security cameras?

We finish our burgers with the ocean waves breaking near the balcony. I love how the ocean tide flows under the house, and I imagine being in the Maldives, surrounded by the cerulean sea.

"Okay, I'm ready for this tour," Hugh says, scrunching his burger paper with emphasis.

I lock the balcony doors behind us, then weave through the debris to the staircase. "New sweeping staircases with curves are my favorite, but I want to add a clear glass railing and paint the stairs off-white to blend in with the walls. It will aid airflow and give it a weightless appearance, as though the stairs are floating. What do you think?"

Hugh pauses and peers over the railing to what used to be the living room below. "I like it. I want to hear all your ideas."

WHEN I WAKE, I READ OVER THE MESSAGES FROM FRANKLIN last night. Ugh. Again, they are business-related. One contractor is no longer available, and he gave me a number for another.

I miss him.

But I'm too damn angry to call him.

I need a few more days to air my thoughts to Hugh and get on with business. If I'm only here for casual sex, it has to stop because my heart wants more.

I didn't know the man was so damn addictive. I'm going to need counseling to give him up.

For now, I have got to maintain a business attitude, so I text him our plans.

> I'm at the Malibu house working today. Hugh and I will go shopping for accessories in neutral palettes to give your home a coastal feel. If there are certain colors you hate, now is the time to speak up. I'm thinking sustainable decking for the upstairs balcony. I'm also using VOC paint in white and light gray color schemes. If you're not familiar with VOC, it is volatile organic compounds to maintain better air quality inside. Healthier for you and better for the environment. It's why I'm sourcing reclaimed wood for the flooring and beams. I know you said you don't really see the need, but it's important. You said I could do what I wanted with this project. I'm so excited and thankful you have given me a chance to remodel and decorate your home.

> Enjoy your time away, and please try to relax when you get a second.

> I'll send you progress notes and take photos every day that I'm here.

I hit send and take a deep breath.

My cell buzzes with an incoming call—an unknown number.

I assume it's Franklin and hesitate before answering, but it could be one of the tradesmen coming to the house today.

"Hello, Penelope speaking."

"Penelope," a female voice says, and despite only saying one word, there is a clear hint of upper class in her tone. "My name is Sophia Hendricks. My son, Jobe, gave me your number. Have I caught you at a bad time?"

"Hi. Um... no. I..." *Shit. What do I say?* I'm actually here at your eldest son's house in Malibu, even though he is on the other side of the country. Have I done something wrong? "Now is fine. How can I help you?"

Hugh walks into the room wearing his boxers. I hold up a finger to my lips, eyes wide for emphasis.

"Did Franklin mention my gala ball to you?"

I have no idea what she is talking about. "Sorry, he didn't."

Hugh bounces onto the bed beside me, his head on the other pillow. He mouths, *Who is it?*

Franklin's mother, I mouth back.

Hugh's eyes round like saucers.

"That doesn't surprise me." I hear a sigh in her voice. "I hold a gala ball to fundraise for a charity that is close to my heart every year. My family is involved, and Franklin or Jobe usually do the live auction together. I hear Franklin and you are spending time together, and I would like to invite you to sit at our family table."

I can't speak.

"It sounds daunting, but we are not a scary family. You don't have to give me your answer now. There will be a chair for you, so speak to Franklin. I think you'll have a fun night."

"O-okay. I'll see if I'm free."

"Please meet me for lunch in a few weeks to talk it over. I'd love to tell you more about it in person."

"Thank you, Sophia."

"Have a good day, Penelope."

"You, too, Sophia. Thank you for the call and invitation."

Holding the cell to my chest, I stare at Hugh. "Holy fuck. Sophia Hendricks just invited me to her gala fundraiser. Franklin doesn't even know."

He slaps my shoulder. "Get up. You have just added ballgown shopping to our list of things to do today."

23

FRANKLIN

Working seventeen-hour days and sleeping three hours a night for a straight twenty days messes with a man's mind, especially when I'm distracted by a brunette who is in my house, thousands of miles away.

I wake to more emails, updates, photographs, and invoices from contractors.

The house is unrecognizable, as is my heart. On weekends, I open the security app, hoping Penny is in my home before closing my eyes at night. The weekend I saw a guy in my house, I almost called demanding questions in a state of being majorly pissed off.

I am losing my mind.

Hugh is her friend, and he's engaged to someone else.

Overtired, I flipped out.

Penny is not mine.

She won't even talk to me apart from updates on the house. Who knew buying someone a new place would make them run this fast? I overlooked what it represented, but I'm not trying to buy her.

> Your ideas for the house are impressive. I'm excited to see it in person when I return.

There's a knock on my office door.

"Come in."

Ruby enters and places a coffee on my desk.

I need a damn whiskey, not caffeine.

"Thanks, Ruby."

"Just a reminder... Mr. Hicks will be here in an hour."

"Thank you." The douchebag from PetroDepend won't budge, but my lawyer will be here in ten minutes, ready to take this idiot down.

> Do you have a return date?

I stare at the text from Penny. I want nothing more than to engage with her and take my mind off all the fuckery going on here. Then I realize the time. It's just after seven, making it four in the morning in LA.

> No. I'll be back for Mother's Day weekend.
> Why are you awake?

I'm not happy about Penny being awake, especially if she's stressed.

I don't mention my return will be the same weekend as my mother's gala. I have three missed calls from my mother. After today, I'll have answers and can talk about her fundraiser because if I don't do something about this lawsuit, she'll be fundraising for our company instead of the charity.

> Most of my planning begins before work. I
> want to reassure you that your home will be
> luxurious and eco-conscious. I'm using
> reclaimed wood and incorporating state-of-
> the-art energy-efficient systems, such as
> solar panels, a rainwater harvesting system,
> and a gray-water recycling system. These
> will not only make the house stand out but
> also significantly reduce its environmental
> impact.

I toss my cell onto the desk.

Fuck.

HCM has always operated on ethics. Now, this lawsuit will be splashed all over the press. Why didn't I listen to Caleb when he suggested divesting from PetroDepend?

The environmental impact will be huge news.

Penny will hate me.

I spring from my chair. "Penny, you're a genius," I murmur.

Penny is portraying how important it is to be eco-conscious with my renovation. I walk to the window and stare at the gray skies blending with the architecture.

Penny, unknowingly, is the best thing in my life.

And I can't even tell her.

I can only commend her work.

> Reducing the environmental impact is
> important to me. Thank you for being
> mindful of the remodeling.

> Yet you fly around the world in a private jet.

She got me there.

Only when necessary. I'm using a commercial flight to return home as Jobe has the jet in Italy.

Is that why he's not returning my calls?

The fuck.

What do you need? I can help you.

Jobe said not to contact you as you have 'a lot going on.'

He what?

Penny. YOU can contact me anytime.

All I want is to hear her voice.

Okay. I'll wait until lunchtime since it's a workday. I'll try the contractor on my break, and if he doesn't answer, I'll have you call him.

Deal.

If this guy knows what's best for him, he'll pick up Penny's call.

I send Jobe a text.

Answer Penny's calls. I'm not asking.

Knock. Knock.

"Come in."

Paul walks in and closes the door behind him. "Are you

ready to knock this idiot off his perch?" He drops his legal files on my desk. "Are we doing it here?"

"Yes. I don't want the staff to even lipread what is happening in the boardroom." The boardroom has all glass walls, and it's easy to see and hear what's happening in there.

"Let's talk strategy for the session with Hicks. One of your options is transparency with clients. You might consider having a carefully framed, indirect conversation with your clients about potential risks in the energy sector due to environmental concerns. You cannot disclose the specifics, but you could encourage them to diversify their investments to minimize risk."

I take a seat at my desk. "Understood."

There are three chairs on the other side of the room. Paul sits on the end chair on my right.

"You might cooperate with the regulators. If you decide to whistleblow..." he tilts his head, "... and work with financial regulators, you can provide them with the necessary information about PetroDepend's impending lawsuit without compromising your clients' interests."

"What else?"

"Reassess PetroDepend's standing in your portfolio and reconsider whether it aligns with your clients' ethical standards. You might then gradually divest from PetroDepend as part of a long-term strategy unrelated to the lawsuit."

I rake my fingers along my jaw to ease the tension. I should have kept that damn mouthpiece my mother had made for me in college to stop grinding my teeth. "Caleb had suggested that months ago before any of this came to light."

"Now, if Hicks surprises us and comes with his tail between his thighs, you could use your influence as a significant investor to push for change within PetroDepend, perhaps by demanding more transparency or stronger commitment to ethical practices. This might not prevent the immediate impact of the lawsuit but could present a way forward for PetroDepend to regain investor confidence."

"Be a nice guy all around."

Paul ignores my comment. "The chance that will happen is like five percent. Do you have the data open?"

I move my untouched coffee aside and bring up all the information on the screen Lana sent through.

"Can I have this?" Paul indicates to my coffee.

"It's cold. I'll have Ruby make you a fresh one."

"I'll need that too. Haven't eaten yet. I'll need all the caffeine I can get."

By five o'clock, the office clears. George and Lana come into the room where I'm sitting with Caleb, and he tells them to go home.

"You should go home too and get some rest for once. There's not much you can do until you hear from Paul with the right action to take against Hicks," Caleb adds. He's right. Paul is flying back to LA as we speak since his office is there. I pay him well to be where I need him, and after speaking with Hicks, we won't know more until tomorrow at the earliest.

My cell buzzes. It's Penny. It must be around two in the afternoon. "Sorry, I need to take this," I tell Caleb.

He waves.

"Catch you tomorrow."

The door clicks behind him.

"Afternoon, Penny."

"Hello, Franklin."

Her voice is warm and soothing. I stretch out my neck, the tension slightly easing. "How are you?"

I hear the sigh through the speaker. "Okay, I guess. Frustrated."

I will take anyone down. She only has to say the word.

"How can I help?"

"Your brother called me back. The contractor had a family emergency. He sent me the contact details of the other workers on his team. So, work should recommence tomorrow."

"Good. I'm loving all the progress images you've sent. You should do a reel or whatever interior decorators and designers do on Instagram."

"Could I? Would you mind? I mean, it would be great marketing for me if I ever..." She hesitates. "I think you're going to be surprised when you return. Everyone has been working long hours. You're going to love your *new* Malibu home."

Home.

"I'm looking forward to it, Pen. And yes, share those pictures. It's your vision coming to life."

She sighs a happy sigh over the phone. "I know you're busy, but will I see you when you come home?"

"You will." *I miss you.* "Take care of yourself, Penny."

She is silent for a moment.

What is she thinking?

"Bye, Franklin."

My heart fucking hurts, and I hate it.

In a dash, I pack my laptop into my bag. When I'm inside my penthouse, I send another message to Jobe. It's around midnight in Rome.

I spoke to Penny. Thanks for sorting it out.

Jobe is calling me.

I answer, "You're up late."

"Time zones kill me."

I chuckle. Music plays in the background. "Are you at a bar?"

"No. Damn piano music is supposed to relax me."

I laugh again. "Did you take a bottle of Michter's with you?"

"No. I thought I'd get into the wine while I'm here, but their reds don't go down the same."

"I hear you. We could also debate whiskey."

"I'd take any right now."

"I'm opening a fresh bottle of Blanton's." I pour the gold liquid into a small glass. Add ice. Swirl it. "Hear that?"

"A deep cut, brother. Does it piss you off that I've spoken to Penny more than you have in the past week?"

"Don't go there."

"You're already showing signs of addiction."

"You're way off the mark."

"We'll see. Have you seen your therapist lately?"

"Jobe." I grunt.

"At least get your yoga instructor back to the office. Stop firing everyone who tries to help you."

I pour another drink. "I'm fine."

"Don't blow it with Penny."

I whip my neck back and down the contents in one go. "Bye, Jobe."

24

PENELOPE

Three weeks later...

At midday on Saturday, I'm standing in the foyer of the Rose Garden Tea Room at The Huntington Library, Art Museum, and Botanical Gardens, waiting for Sophia Hendricks to arrive. I had to google the tea rooms. Then, I searched for images of Sophia. As I'd expected, every photograph emanated sophistication. When a lady wearing a navy dress walks in, I recognize her immediately.

"Penelope." Her voice is genteel. She holds out her delicate hand. Shellac nail tips match her dress. Diamonds sparkle under the recessed lights with two ringed fingers to the knuckles. "It's lovely to meet you." Her blue eyes are bright and sparkly, a contrast in color to Franklin's dark brown ones. "Shall we head inside?"

I follow Sophia as she gives her name, and the staff leads

us to an outside table with more privacy than in the main room. We overlook a stunning fountain, and the gardens surrounding us are surreal.

"Are you happy for us to have the Huntington Tea option?"

"Of course." I fidget in my seat. I glance down at the cutlery and pretty plates.

The server appears, and Sophia orders for us. She looks directly at me. "Is it too early for champagne?"

I shake my head.

Am I about to get drunk with Franklin's mother?

"You can bring them now," she tells him. Sophia glances at me and smiles. "It will help break the ice, so to speak."

I giggle nervously. I need something other than tea.

"Firstly, thank you for meeting me here. I wanted us to chat without the men so you won't be nervous at the gala."

"I'll still be nervous," I confess.

She reaches over and touches my hand that's fiddling with the butter knife. "Don't be. We don't bite. You'll see how my boys misbehave as much as others. And meet Charlotte. She'll be home from college for the weekend. She is younger than you, but I'm sure you'll get on fine."

I smile, though I'm not convinced.

"Does Franklin know you have invited me to the gala?"

"No." She winks. "I want it to be a surprise. This work he has in New York..." She blinks slowly. "He works himself to the bone. He's more like his father than our other children." Her gaze meets mine, and I sense I'm missing something.

The server places our champagne flutes in front of us, and I take mine, guzzling a couple of mouthfuls. "Can I please have some water?" I ask the server, then smile at Sophia. "I'm so thirsty."

"You are working hard, especially in your spare time, to

make the Malibu house extraordinary. Jobe is raving about you."

"He is?" *What about Franklin?*

"We both came up with an idea. Next weekend you could take the jet to see Franklin in New York. Surprise him. Make him take some time away from his work."

I'm stunned into silence.

"Do you like New York?"

"I've only been twice. I thought Jobe had the jet in Italy?"

"He arrived home today," she says as though she has all the answers.

"Oh, it's too expensive with the jet and the price of fuel." I sound dumb, but I don't see the need when he could be home the following weekend. Surprising Franklin might not be the smartest idea if he doesn't want to see me.

"Please. It's for Franklin. He'll appreciate it."

Sophia hasn't read the business-like texts he's sent. He could have another woman there to relieve any other tension. Hands in my lap, I collect the end of the white tablecloth and twist it in my fingers.

"The Malibu house will be fine. Leave instructions with Jobe. Go see Franklin."

"If I do, I'll book my own flight." I withhold the urge to mention the gas emissions from jets.

We are interrupted when the server places a tiered plate of biscuits and cupcakes on the table before us. The sides include salmon, cream cheese and dill, and caviar. He places another plate of lobster salad and shaves black truffle over the top.

"Thank you." I give Sophia a gratuitous smile.

"No, Penelope. Thank you."

I DECLINE SOPHIA'S INVITATION TO TAKE THE JET TO SEE Franklin, choosing to tie up the loose ends on the renovation instead.

Besides, I don't want to turn up only to be a burden when he is busy with work. The lower floor is complete, as is his bedroom and ensuite. The retractable ceiling and skylights are finished, and I have amazed myself at the brilliant idea of lying in his bed and staring up at the stars.

Today, Hugh and I are collecting the last of the artwork sculptures and floor rugs from local artisans. Zara is waiting at the house for the delivery of the balcony chairs. The spare bedrooms are receiving the final paint, then the last two bedrooms can be decorated.

I can see the light at the end of the tunnel, and I'm excited to surprise Franklin with the finished product, even if I don't know where things stand between us. I'm excited, yet sadness has settled on me. When he was here, I had an excuse to see him. With no reason to visit his home, I'm afraid I won't see him.

And that hurts bad.

Why do my emotions have to complicate everything?

Why couldn't I fall for a partner and not a part-time lover?

"Next project..." Hugh says, interrupting my daydream, "... is my wedding." He wiggles his shoulders a little. "Four months, baby."

"That has come around fast."

"Yeah, Sienna is set on an early autumn wedding with the colored foliage. Will you need a plus one?"

"Maybe." I side-bump him with my hip, then open my cell to see if there are any messages from Franklin. "Maybe not."

Two weeks later...

As I clasp my sapphire drop necklace, handed down from my grandmother, I stare into the mirror. My dress is long, black, and snug. The black-tie event stipulated the guests wear black, making shopping for a gown considerably easier.

All morning, I sat in a chair for my hair to be styled perfectly before having makeup professionally applied. It's the same beauty salon I visited last year before attending the Interior Decorator Awards with Hugh, so fancy is not a new thing. It doesn't mean I'm comfortable in my skin, even though the mirror reflects beauty I don't recognize.

My cell buzzes with a message from Zara.

I'm parked out front.

Coming.

After grabbing an overnight bag, I head down to the foyer where Zara is waiting.

"You look stunning, Pen."

I twirl. "Thank you."

Zara takes my bag and sets it in the trunk of her car. "Call me when you want to be picked up."

"I can catch an Uber," I tell her while sliding into the front seat, barely bending at the waist. "I think this dress is a bit much."

"It's not. Don't drink too much champagne. You'll feel bloated and uncomfortable. Besides, I don't want you with a hangover in my car when we drive home tomorrow."

I laugh. "I won't. Tomorrow is about our moms."

The only place to stop for me to exit the car is farther along Wilshire Boulevard. Limousines line the street as guests walk a red carpet into the hotel. "I'm so freaking nervous." I wipe my hands on my dress.

"Don't do that." Zara grabs my hands. "Think of tonight as a tick off your bucket list."

"Attending my fuck-buddy's mother's charity gala was never on my bucket list."

She giggles. "What's the worst that can happen?"

I give her a sideways glance. "Let's see... I could fall going up the stairs. I could trip in these shoes and spill my drink on some influential men. I could embarrass myself in front of Franklin's family. I won't know what to say when they ask me intelligent questions about the economy or for some random comment about the world."

"Okay, okay. You're not meeting English royalty. Just do the oldest trick in the book."

"What's that?"

"Imagine everyone at the table is naked."

I grab my purse and lift my dress before stepping out of the car. "No help at all."

"Okay, then focus on the best thing that can happen." She grins at me.

My breath hitches.

Franklin loving me. Taking a step back from his work to spend a little time with me. Ugh. Never going to happen.

"Really? No, we need to meet somewhere in the middle. Otherwise, I might not make it back for Mother's Day."

"Right. Not the best and not the worst. Sit with someone who makes you laugh and who you're not attracted to."

I shake my head at my friend. "I'll message you." I swing the car door shut and walk toward the swanky hotel.

25

PENELOPE

ALL IN BLACK, I line up with a group of middle-aged ladies and men. Despite being almost incognito, among them, I feel like a fraud. They have come to bid their thousands and raise money for a brain injury charity. I arrived with a gifted ticket, and somehow, I'm at the Hendricks' family table. I want to puke. I step to the front of the line, where the burly, suited security guard asks for my name.

"Penelope Gilbert."

"Enjoy your night, ma'am."

I take one, two, then three steps inside. Before I have time to assess where to go, I'm herded toward the foyer, where trays of champagne and hors d'oeuvres are offered to the crowd.

As expected, I don't recognize anyone.

Swiping a champagne glass from a tray as a server strides past, I head to the far corner, out of sight, but before I make it, a hand slides through my arm.

"Penelope."

Sophia.

Her hair is swept into a French twist. She glitters from her ears to her neck and her black sequined gown. Her makeup is classy, and she is absolutely beautiful.

"I asked Tim to notify me the moment you arrived." She smiles, red lipstick smooth on her lips. "Come. I have matters to attend, but I'll introduce you to Charlotte."

Sophia constantly says "Hello" to guests as we weave toward huge open double doors. My hand is tucked in hers, and I take sips of my drink, careful not to spill it on me or anyone else. I'm led to a table front and center in the room. Standing around the table are two guys. One has longish, curly blond hair. He looks nothing like Franklin. He stands between a guy with dark hair and a girl with fair hair wearing a standard long black gown. They turn, and all three sets of blue eyes lock with mine.

"Darlings, this is Penelope. She will be sitting with us. Introduce yourselves and assist her with anything she needs." She turns to me and rests a soft hand on my forearm. "Penelope, I have to take care of a few things. There's fresh champagne on the table."

I hold her arm a fraction longer and whisper close to her ear, "Is Franklin coming?"

Her gaze flits over mine. "I hope so."

Sophia leaves, and I turn to her other adult children.

"So this is the famous Penelope Gilbert," the dark-haired man says as he pours champagne into a flute and hands it to me.

"Thanks." I raise my glass. "I already have a drink, and I'm not famous."

He chuckles as though I'm not in on his joke. "You'll need another," he quips. "By the way, my mother and brothers are saying you are the most interesting person at our dinner table."

My face flushes. Praise be to thick makeup and concealer.

He holds out a hand. "I'm Byron. Third in line to the Hendricks' throne." He shakes my hand. He smiles, and it reaches his alluring blue eyes.

"He's a bloody dickhead, that's who he is." The blond-haired guy steps forward. He sounds... odd.

"Are you from the East Coast?"

His smile is broad and cheeky. "The southern coast of Australia... Adelaide. Heard of it?"

"Um... no." Is it a trick question? "So, you're Australian?"

"This Aussie is part of the family." Byron ruffles his hair.

The Aussie holds out a hand. "Brandon Johns. Not a Hendricks."

I shake his hand and hope I'm sitting next to him. Brandon looks like fun.

"We call him BJ," says the female I assume to be Charlotte.

I choke on my drink.

"Yeah, I like her." She leans in and takes my hand. "I'm Lottie. The fourth in line." She rolls her eyes. "The smartest of these idiots, except for Franklin. No one is smarter than Franklin." I smile at Charlotte, not knowing whether to call her Lottie or not.

"I'm Penny." I raise my glass.

"Penny, if you haven't already noticed, my mother likes to use our birth names." Charlotte takes my hand and leads me to a seat on the side of the table, where we can see the stage and the doors to the foyer. "We're sitting here."

A bell chimes and the crowd spills into the ballroom.

Sitting next to Charlotte, I take a moment to appreciate the decorations. Fairy lights cover the ceiling, and crystal chandeliers project a kaleidoscope of light around the room. The main chandelier hangs centrally over the dance floor. Front and center to the main stage are a screen and table, along with a microphone and some auction items. The walls are donned in artwork, which is part of the auction.

The table centerpiece is a three-foot glass vase with a white-flower bouquet almost the width of the round table. Throughout the assortment of flowers, lights twinkle—a spectacular sight around the room.

"My mom knows how to throw a gala ball." Charlotte must have been watching me as I took in the room.

"It is impressive."

Brandon takes the seat to my left, then Byron sits on the other side of him with their backs to the stage. If Franklin were to come, I wonder where he would sit. Opposite me?

Jobe wanders in with a female on his arm. His gaze meets mine. His lips curl into a grin. "Penny, I assume you have met everyone?"

"I have, thank you."

He sits beside Byron. He introduces his companion to me. "Elsa, I would like you to meet Penny. She is advising my brother on remodeling his Malibu Beach house. She is a great decorator, and her innovative ideas for renovating are impressive."

Elsa stands and shakes my hand. "Good to meet you, Penny. I would love to chat with you later about an upcoming project. I only come with Jobe to all the formal events to improve his image." She winks at me.

Jobe coughs and pretends to choke on his champagne.

Elsa shakes her head. "I'm actually his executive assistant, and he would be lost without me. I asked for a raise to do all this PR stuff."

Byron chuckles. "Good to see you again, Elsa."

"Hey, I'm in the top ten eligible bachelors. You should feel privileged." Jobe jabs a playful elbow at his date.

"The only reason you made that list is because Franklin is no longer on it," Charlotte quips.

A tall gentleman with graying hair strides to the table. On his arm is the most important person in the room.

Sophia.

The Hendricks smile at everyone they pass.

He walks with his head high, shoulders back, self-importance oozing from him.

They're a *real* power couple.

Mr. Hendricks pulls out the chair for Sophia, and they sit so they are facing the stage, the chairs on either side of them vacant.

A female laughs, and it is familiar. It's not until she pulls out the chair beside Elsa and next to Mr. Hendricks that I realize who she is. The hem of her black puffy dress finishes midthigh, revealing the longest, slim, and shapely legs. She's wearing a sleeveless silk dress, her long blonde hair flowing over her shoulders, tanned from the European sunshine.

Daphne is a walking supermodel.

She waves at everyone. "Hello. I've missed you all and especially Sophia's gala events."

Sophia smiles at her. "I'm privileged you could make it, Daph."

Daph.

An affectionate abbreviated name.

What the hell am I doing here?

"After Carson invited me, I cleared my calendar for you."

Sophia nods at her. "Your kind donations are appreciated."

I feel like the biggest imposter at the table. I'm staring at the space between Sophia and Charlotte. Did Sophia want her son next to her? I pick up my drink and take a gulp. Is he even coming?

Mr. Hendricks' eyes land on me. A dent forms between his bushy brows until he lifts his head with a subtle nod.

"Ms. Gilbert, I presume." This man's booming voice is intimidating.

"Yes. I'm sorry I didn't want to interrupt to introduce myself. Penny Gilbert."

"I look forward to speaking with you after the formalities."

If I'm here, because if there is any chance of leaving, then I'm sneaking out.

I smile and do my best not to look nervous.

"If you could excuse me." Jobe stands and takes the stage beside the emcee. Sophia beams at her son, oblivious to the awkwardness at the table.

"Get in line, Dad," Charlotte jokes. "We all want to chat with Penny."

I smile, hoping it's a compliment, only to meet the glare of Daphne. Scooping my champagne glass from the table, I take a few more mouthfuls, wanting the desired effect to kick in soon.

"Penny. Right. Didn't I see you at Noah's wedding?"

My cheeks heat.

Yes, it was the weekend I fucked your ex's brains out. Had the best orgasms of my life.

"Yes, you must have. Good to see you again, Daphne. Italy agrees with you," I say pleasantly.

"It does, only I miss home and am making plans to return." Her smile is less than pleasant, and her eyes seem to calculate my response.

Why does she seem so interested in me? Does she know I'm remodeling Franklin's house?

Jobe addresses the room, and I'm saved from an embarrassing response.

We sit quietly while he introduces the emcee and calls his mother to the stage. Sophia glides across the hardwood floor and hugs her son before giving her address to the room. Without peering at Daphne, I feel her eyes crawling over my skin as if she's assessing my worthiness of being here. But Franklin is not here, and for all she knows, I could be Charlotte's plus one. So, in the next break, I get chummy with Charlotte.

"Has your college break commenced?" I ask in a soft voice.

"I return Sunday night for exams, then I'm on break... although I'm nervous for senior year."

"Nervous? I loved my senior year." I smile at Charlotte as though we are bonding over our college experiences.

"My father expects me to prove myself," she says quietly. "It's been fun and games until now, but this year will be different. I'll be studying all the time. I'm smart, but I'm no Franklin. Anything less than a high distinction is unacceptable." She pulls a face. "Unlike these two goons." She tilts her head in the direction of Byron and Brandon. "Both are riding their athleticism and hoping for the NBA draft."

I gape at her. "They're that good?"

"They think they are."

Her expression makes me giggle. "Didn't your father buy a team?"

Her hand taps mine. "I know what you're thinking. The LA Sharks won't pick up these dicks unless they prove themselves more valuable than other draftees."

Charlotte knows her basketball, or at least she knows how her dad operates.

"Have you ever been to a game?" she asks.

I shake my head. "I don't even know the rules."

She grins. "I'm sure Franklin will get you courtside tickets to the first home game opener. You'll soon pick it up." She laughs low, and I laugh with her as though we are in on an inside joke. The joke is me being clueless about the Hendricks family, and I sense Charlotte likes that I haven't done my homework.

I take another mouthful of champagne. My body begins to tingle.

Hallelujah.

Jobe takes to the microphone and sings his mother's praises for all her hard work organizing the gala. At the end of his speech, the crowd applauds and cheers as Sophia makes her way to stand beside him. She thanks him and everyone in the room for all their donations and talks about a friend of her family who has been affected by a brain injury.

At the end of her speech, the room falls quiet.

More applause.

"Jobe tells me you're remodeling Franklin's beach house," Daphne says from across the table. Her timing is off after Sophia's speech.

I nod and say quietly, "I am."

"Are you just starting out?"

Sophia is talking quietly to Jobe. "Kind of." I take another sip of my champagne. "It's my first as an independent, but I work for another company."

She stares at me a little longer before smiling. Only it's more of a smirk.

Thankfully, Sophia interrupts us and announces the rules of the auction.

She asks everyone to dig deep into their pockets tonight. She stops talking and smiles. Instinctively, heads turn toward the main doors to where she is staring.

I stop breathing.

Franklin has arrived and is standing at the back of the room, his presence like smoke, wafting over the crowd and demanding attention.

As handsome as the Adonis himself, still as a statue, he ignores the crowd only to nod at his mother. I take a few seconds of pleasure in admiring his handsome face and the way he stands—strong and full of importance.

My insides spark to life. Heat is smoldering between my thighs. I turn away before I embarrass myself, only his siblings have noticed how I'm ogling him. The only thing worse is the way Daphne is smiling at Franklin, pining almost.

Shit, she wants him back.

Jesus, what a fun night this is going to be.

Would anyone notice if I slid under the table? My time with Franklin is best when we're alone and can be ourselves. Well, not just ourselves. We always end up naked, except we are not exactly on friendly terms at the moment. Does he want me here? We have barely spoken to each other. Did he invite Daphne, and I'm here to prove a point not to mess with them?

My mind is filled with crazy assumptions.

"Please take a seat, son." Sophia offers an understanding smile, and Franklin holds up a hand in apology as he makes his way to his family's table. His gaze rakes over the guests, and he nods at Byron and Elsa. His face alters ever so slightly when he finds Daphne. Then he places a hand on his father's shoulder. His father turns and shakes his hand before he stands behind the chair beside Charlotte. He smiles at Charlotte, and then his eyes lock with mine. Everything onward happens in slow motion.

The slight widening of his eyes.

The shock causing his lips to part.

The intensity of his gaze is like an electric shock to every cell in my body.

I feel alive just by his proximity, with a need to touch him. Only he might as well be in New York as I cannot. He places a hand on Charlotte's shoulder before he quietly says something to her. Pulling my gaze from his, I take another sip of my drink, the one mouthful remaining in my flute.

Can someone please pass me the bottle? I don't need a glass.

I freeze when his breath is close to my ear. He gives me a quick peck on my cheek. I'm the only recipient of those lips at the table. My shoulders stupidly ease until his voice is in my ear. "You can stop drinking now. I want you to feel everything I do to you tonight."

I swallow hard. And just like that, the frustration dividing us evaporates. All I can think is *yes, please.*

Charlotte leans forward to get our attention. "I heard that, you dumbass," she whispers and frowns at Franklin. "Sit down. Mom is waiting."

26

FRANKLIN

IN A SEA OF BLACK, I didn't notice her.

My dick did.

Immediately.

How?

Sitting beside my father, I keep stealing glimpses of her while paying attention to the auction as she pretends to listen intently to something I know must be boring to her. This is not her scene, so why is she here?

The night is now bearable. I have socialites to speak with. My father will expect it, yet all I want is to be with her.

I glance up at Daphne watching me closely.

Last week, she emailed me to confirm she was donating to my mother's cause. I thanked her for her support, as I know my mother appreciates it. I also indicated her attendance was not required since she now resided in Italy. I didn't give another thought to why she emailed me instead of my mother until now.

Did she know Penny was also invited?

Why did she want to come?

She knows there's no future for us.

The entrée is served, and the table breaks into trivial chatter.

"Can we swap seats?" I ask Charlotte.

"Not a chance." She sticks a fork into a prawn without looking at me. "When Mom is on the stage, Dad will want to speak with you."

"Dad has all of tomorrow to question me since I'm spending the day with Mom," I snap under my breath.

Charlotte glares at me. "Soon," she whispers. "Stop making it so obvious."

"What?"

She rolls her eyes, turns to Penny, and starts a conversation.

Is she cockblocking me?

Jobe announces the current bids on the main auction pieces and that the bidding will close after dessert. It no longer has my focus, and I'm happy to give my mother a fat check at the end.

Dad leans in closer to me. "Penelope is a lovely young lady."

"Yeah, Dad, she is." I drop the cutlery, no longer hungry. "When did you meet her?"

"When I sat at the table," he says in a deep voice. I'm not accusing him of anything.

"Who invited her?"

He frowns at me. I shake my head.

"It must have been your mother."

My family is killing me.

I rub the spot above my left eyebrow to ease a sudden pain. "When did Mom meet Penny?"

My father gives me his side-eye look as though he is

paying attention to the auction. "Your mother keeps her cards close to her chest."

What play is my mother planning? She knew Daphne was coming.

Jobe announces a five-minute break.

"Penny," Daphne says from across the table.

I glare at Daphne.

"Perhaps you should come and work with me for a while in Italy. The Italian designers influence many great decorators. I think you'll love it, even for just a few months of experience."

Out the side of my eye, I see Penny glance at me with wide eyes and then back to Daphne. I don't shift my gaze from Daphne. What is she up to?

"I, um... I'll think about it. Thank you. I have several projects I'm committed to at work."

Daphne's gaze flicks to me, then back at Penny. "Did he nit-pick your ideas?" She rolls her eyes like they're co-conspirators.

"He hasn't seen it yet." The nervousness in her voice has everyone smiling.

"Oh." Echoes around the table.

I lean forward so Penny has to look at me. "As long as you did what you promised, I'm sure I'll love it."

Her green eyes widen. *Good.*

"Excuse me." I head to the restrooms, unbuttoning the button under my bow tie. Now that Penny is no longer a secret, I can no longer protect her from the opinionated bullshit, mindless questions, backstabbing and fucking games.

Daphne.

I punch the door, and it swings open.

"Woah," a guy says on the other side.

"I'll get maintenance to check it out." I stride past him.

When I return to the foyer, my father is conversing with two other men, all holding a glass of bourbon.

"Franklin." He signals for me to join them.

"What is happening with the retirement funds?" he says it low so no one overhears.

"I have it under control." Penny walks past with Charlotte toward the restrooms. "Excuse me, gentlemen."

I catch up and match their stride. "Penny, may I speak to you for a moment?"

"Not now," Charlotte says. "We won't be long."

Leaning against the wall, I wait for both girls.

Jesus, what do they do in there?

They finally exit, and I can't take my eyes off Penny—her long black dress and her hair swept off her shoulders, revealing her long neck. My dick twitches, knowing I'll claim that neck tonight. She smiles and laughs with my sister. With a closed fist, I rub the material over my chest.

She gets on well with my family.

I push off the wall and stop when Byron and Brandon join them in a circle. They laugh, enjoying Brandon's joke.

The man has a death wish.

I join the circle.

Byron slaps my shoulder. "How long are you back?"

"Just the weekend." I sneak a glance at Penny.

Penny smiles at me, and the tension in my neck eases a little. She's not mad.

"Are you excited about your home?" Her eyes sparkle with excitement.

"Home?" Byron repeats.

Charlotte frowns at me.

I'm a dickwad for not setting her straight.

I will.

Soon.

"The house you—"

I cut Byron off. "I am. From the images I received, your work is remarkable. I can't wait to see it."

"When?" Her face is deadpan.

"I'd like you to be with me when I check it out."

"Monday?"

"I'm flying back to New York on Monday. I could change up a few meetings to Tuesday."

"At least he didn't say tonight," Charlotte moans. "I'll leave you two alone. She loops her arm through Brandon's and Byron's and guides them back to the ballroom.

Finally, I'm alone with Penny.

"Those two get on well," Penny remarks.

I turn and observe Charlotte and Brandon. "Those two? They're just friends."

"If you say so."

I'm momentarily dumbfounded. How didn't I see it? "Byron will kill him. That's a guy's best friend code he is crossing."

"Right. That's why no one has noticed but me."

"Jesus." I rub the spot above my brow. "Neither can afford that sort of distraction if they are serious about getting drafted. Imagine the fights."

"Lottie is smart enough not to let her feelings get in the way of business."

I stare at Penny. "You got all that with the few hours you have been with my family?"

"There are some things women just know. As for you..." her shoulders rise and fall, "... I can't read you, Franklin. I have whiplash trying to work you out."

"I call it as it is, Pen. Ask me anything, and I'll give you an honest answer."

She smiles, lowers her eyes to her hands, and fiddles with her purse.

"Pen." I reach out and take her hand in mine. "Can we go somewhere to chat?"

"Chat?" Her quiet laugh is mocking. "When do we just chat? I can't do this anymore with you. It hurts," she rasps.

"Do what?"

"You come, you go. You don't give me a second thought until—" She shakes her head. "Then you act like you missed me."

"I do," I interrupt. "A lot."

"You say that now because you need me physically." She waves a hand. "Daphne's here, and she's willing."

"Penny," I growl. She strides past me, and I go to stop her when a hand lands on my shoulder.

"Franklin." Jobe is on my other side. "Mom is waiting for you to do your part."

I turn and watch Penny disappear into the ballroom.

I take the stage alongside Jobe and persuade the crowd to up their bids for the auction. When I find Penny in the crowd, she is clapping and smiling at me in approval.

Who is giving who whiplash?

After the formalities, I round the table, stop at Penny, lean down, and whisper, "Royce will be waiting for you outside. If you don't want to be seen with me, I'll exit ten minutes after you leave."

When I straighten, everyone at the table is watching us.

"What a great idea," Penny exclaims. "I'll speak to your mom about a remodeling donation for the future."

I take my seat.

"You're a dick," Charlotte says under her breath.

I ignore her.

After dessert is finished, my mother and father, Jobe, and I address the room.

My father has the final word, expressing our gratitude to everyone for the kindness in supporting his wife in a fundraiser she is passionate about, as is he. He talks about neurological diseases and how more research is required so people don't have to suffer in silence.

When he finishes, the crowd claps enthusiastically. As do I. My mother's fundraising galas all began after my friend, Damien suffered a brain injury in our college years.

There is purpose behind the glamour.

Penny slips out the main doors.

No one else notices.

I do.

As soon as I'm back in my seat, I take my cell in my lap and text Royce.

> Is Penny with you?

He texts back immediately.

> No, sir. She refused to get into the car and instead got into a car with another female.

Whatever noise erupts from my throat gets my father's attention.

"Is everything all right, son?"

"No."

THE FOLLOWING MORNING, I'M THE FIRST TO BREAKFAST.

I couldn't be more frustrated than I was last night when Penny refused to take my calls, and with the added stress of the court case, I barely slept.

The folding doors to the pool are open, and Lola is setting the outside table.

I step outside. "Morning, Lola. Are we dining here?"

"Morning, Franklin. We are, at your mother's wishes."

I place the gift to my mother, wrapped in a gold ribbon, on the table. "What has my mother requested for breakfast?"

"Her favorite fruits and yogurts followed by eggs and mushrooms."

"No bacon?"

"No, Franklin, she is minimizing her meat in meals." She tries to hide her smile.

"It is Mother's Day."

My father appears and pats my shoulder. "Franklin, did you sleep well?"

"I did," I lie. "I didn't consume my body weight in alcohol like my brothers. Though it might have helped me."

"Your sister tried to keep them in line. She lectured Brandon and Byron on their professional appearances if they were serious about getting drafted." His expression is one of amusement. "Made it clear that being drafted isn't just about talent but about appearances and discipline as well."

I smirk at my father. "Lottie could surprise us and be CEO material."

Dad rubs a finger and thumb over his chin, grooming an invisible beard. "Sophia has high hopes for Charlotte. She might just come through and prove her brothers wrong."

"She has more assertiveness in her at this age than all of us."

"Not you, son."

"I think she does. I had no one to compare to with Jobe being five years younger than me."

"In fairness, Byron is five years younger than him." Is Dad showing leniency to my brothers?

"And Charlotte is only fifteen months younger than Byron," Mom says as she steps outside. "Franklin is right.

Charlotte's potential stems from being a strong woman... something I taught her."

"You?" Dad acts offended.

"Yes, me. You were barely around, Carson, and while I was playing referee to the older boys, I juggled two young toddlers. Charlotte quickly learned to defend herself from her older brothers." She takes a seat beside my father. "The credit is mine."

I can't help admiring my mother. "Happy Mother's Day, Mom." I stand and kiss her cheek before handing her the gift.

Lola appears with the bunch of peonies I also organized, all neatly arranged in a vase. "For you."

"Franklin, you always manage to put a smile on my face even though I say I need for nothing but to have my children with me. Oh, my darling," Mom says after she's unwrapped the box. "My favorite Roja perfume. Ah, what's this?" She pulls out a candle. "Oh, Franklin." She studies the Jo Malone London label. "Peony." She removes the lid and inhales the scent. "You always seem to know what I like." Her expression is filled with gratitude.

"I'm glad you approve."

Mom smiles at me. "Thank you."

Dad wraps an arm around Mom's shoulder. "You deserve the world, my love."

She leans a head on his shoulder. "I'm too tired to argue."

"Talking about last night..." Dad looks at me, "... did Penelope have an enjoyable evening?"

"She appeared to, although it was not the plan I had for her meeting you all."

"My apologies. I met her for lunch and invited her. Jobe had told us how much she means to you. And if we were to wait for you for an introduction—" Mom stops and stares at me.

"You're lucky it's Mother's Day."

"Morning," Charlotte almost sings as she comes to the table. She hands Mom a small box and kisses her cheek before sitting beside me. "Something small since I'm on a student's budget."

I choke on my pineapple juice. "Don't act as though you're poor."

"Actually, Franklin, I'm taking limited money from Mom and Dad and trying to blend with the other students."

I shake my head. "After almost three years, you've decided to rough it?"

"No, it's a *trial*."

Mom laughs.

"You..." she pokes me in the shoulder, "... usually fight for what you want."

"Are we talking about college here?"

"Nope. About you being grateful."

I stare at my mother for a clue if she knows what Charlotte is on about.

"For what?"

"For having an awesome sister."

I take another sip of my juice, my frustration levels still climbing. "I think the boasting should be left to Mom since it's her day."

Charlotte leans close as though she has a secret. "Penny told me where she is spending Mother's Day."

What?

She laughs at my shocked expression.

She lifts her chin. "I know where her parents live."

27

PENELOPE

Zara parks the car outside my family home. I stare at the crème-colored cottage with a small porch, and a host of memories flood my mind.

"Remember the first time we went to a party, and you got drunk on Melissa's dad's bourbon?"

I laugh. "It was a dare I soon regretted."

"Your saving grace was you slept at mine."

"Oohh yeah." My parents are Christians, and I would have been grounded until I turned twenty if they'd found out. "They loved me but never understood teenagers. They thought time stood still and my teen years replicated theirs."

"Not telling them what we got up to was your way of being kind."

I giggle with Zara, then become sentimental. "You've been with me through some hard times."

She takes my hand and squeezes it. "I'll always be here for you."

I smile at her. "Thank you. And I'll be there for you."

"You better go in, and I better get to my family's breakfast. Although..." she checks her cell, "... I'm already late."

"See you around eight."

She honks the horn before driving away.

Pansies, snapdragons, and daisies line the garden path. Near the posts grows a hot pink bougainvillea. My father clips it to keep it under control. This year it has spread, encroaching onto the other plants. I learned early not to play near it and ended up in tears once after tripping on the porch steps and falling victim to its spikes. I take the first step and expect the screen door to fling open. The creaky sound is etched in my mind, along with the bang, when it slams since Dad has never replaced the old hinges.

I hold the screen door open and, no surprise, the front door opens. When are they going to lock their doors during the day?

"Here's our Poppy." Dad appears and hugs me. "Why, look at you dressed all fancy in those boots and that smart coat." He takes my coat and hangs it on the hook on the wall. He leads me along the small hallway. "We just got back from church... it's why the front door is open." He winks at me.

"I'm glad you listen to me." I stop in the sitting room, and Mom waddles over to me. "Happy Mother's Day, Mom."

Holding out her arms, she comes to me with the biggest smile. "Thank you, honey."

"You're limping worse than last time," I say as I hug her.

"Don't you worry about me... it's just my silly hip. Let me see you." Mom stands back and assesses me. "My, you look well." She hugs me again.

"I am well, but I hate the thought of you in pain." I pull out the gift from my handbag. "I have something for you."

Mom unwraps the pink bow on the box and lifts a gold necklace with three entwined hearts dangling from it. "Penelope, it's beautiful." Mom smiles, and it reaches her green eyes. The same eyes I inherited. "Look, Ray."

Mom holds it up, and I clip it around her neck. "It's the three of us."

Her eyes water. "It's all I ever wanted." She hugs me, and Dad comes and joins in the group hug.

"Tears already?" Dad lovingly pats both our backs. "We'll have to change that. You two go and sit, and I'll get us some coffee to go with the pancakes your mom cooked."

The table has a cloth over one end where they eat, and the other end has the contents of Mom's craft box scattered across it. After years of being an interior decorator and designer, it's hard not to notice the mess, but this is how my parents have lived all their lives and rarely get visitors.

"What's this?" I hold up an old wire candle jar with fishing line attached.

Mom smiles proudly. "I'm making a wind chime out of your grandmother's old spoons." She takes it from me, the candle holder upside down, the wires dangling, then holds a spoon to it. "Like this."

"I see."

"I've gone through some things, decided I don't use half of it, and want to do something useful."

"What else do you have here?" I move scissors and ribbons away from me. "Why are all my old T-shirts here? I thought I threw them away?"

"You put them in a sack, and I kept it. We now have a use for them."

I hold one up. It's a pink tie-dyed top I had when I was fifteen. "What use?"

She shuffles through until she finds something. "Tote bags." She holds it up, and I can see it's a tote, but why?

"Like this." She cuts out the neck and both sleeves. Then she cuts a fringe about an inch apart along the T-shirt's hem. She ties the end of each fringe piece of each side together in a knot. "See? A perfectly good tote bag for shopping and no sewing required." She passes three to me. "Take these, love, for when you go to the markets to buy your fruit and vegetables."

"Mom, it's fine. You keep them."

"Honey, I have plenty."

"Are you ladies ready?" Dad carries over a plate of pancakes. He places the maple syrup and whipped cream on the table.

"Always for the best pancakes in all of California."

"Stop it." Mom grins. "I'll just get some berries." She makes a noise as she stands and grabs her hip.

"Mom. Let me."

"I'm okay. It's just this silly hip. The pain will go away."

"You're sixty-five, Mom. The pain might not go away. You may need a hip replacement."

"Now, we won't get all gloomy. I'll be fine."

Dad sighs, then smiles as if trying to mask his concern.

"Your health insurance will cover it," I remind them.

Neither respond.

"You didn't let your insurance go, did you?"

"We are on a lower level," Dad admits. "Money was tight. We were healthy. You were doing fine."

"Oh, Mom." I inhale a deep, cleansing breath. "Let me pay for your insurance."

"Penelope, you can't afford it. You don't even own your own home," Mom says with her arms wide as though they are wealthy since they own this little cottage.

"I've just finished some work where I'll be paid well. I can pay for the next year's insurance."

Dad places a hand on my shoulder. "That's lovely, Poppy.

But your mother and I agreed years ago we'd never take from you. We knew what it was like to give everything to our parents for the family's benefit. We don't want that for you."

"Dad, listen—"

"Not today, please." Mom forces a smile. "Eat your pancakes, and let's enjoy our time together."

AFTER LUNCH, I STACK THE DISHES IN THE SINK. "I'M DOING the dishes." I wave my parents away.

Dad stands and heads to the cupboard. "I'll get the Scrabble board ready."

"Can we sit outside in the afternoon sun for a bit?" Mom asks. "I'd like to rest a while."

"Of course, whatever you want. I'll serve the pumpkin pie and bring it out to you." My parents like to rest in the afternoon. Only Mom appears more tired today than usual. Is it the pain getting her down? I lay a hand on her shoulder. "Are you okay?"

"I am, dear. I'm not sleeping well with this hip." Mom hobbles, grabbing furniture to lean on as she goes.

"You go out with her, Dad." While waiting for the pie to warm, I wash dishes and stack the plates. Through the door screen, I watch Mom close her eyes. She did most of the food preparation yesterday, and I wish she left it for today so I could have helped her.

Her face lights up when a dog appears and races around the table.

"Huh." I push open the screen door.

"Noo," Mom shouts.

Oomph. The dog bounds up, and I stumble back. "Down, boy." I pet his head. "Whose dog is this?"

Mom laughs when it licks my face. "Meet Riddick, the friendly Retriever."

"No, his real name is Goldie the Golden Retriever," Dad says.

Mom laughs again. "His balance is ridiculous. Something gets knocked over and broken with every visit. So, I named him Riddick."

"Every time?" I'm struggling to keep my balance with the dog on his hind legs and his front paws on my arms. He's walking, and I'm moving with him. "He's very strong."

Dad comes to my rescue, and the dog leaves me to sit beside Mom. "Our neighbors are away, so we're feeding him. He's created a gate between our fences."

"What do you mean created a gate?" The dog trots over to me, and I hold out my hand in warning. "Down, boy."

"Don't make him sound like a bad dog. Come here," she says, patting her thigh. Mom has pepped up with a new lease of energy.

This dog has won Mom over. It surprises me as I was never allowed a dog growing up. We only had cats.

"Lacey, I'm not going to chastise him, but if he breaks something, I'm not pretending he didn't do it." Dad points to the wooden fence. "He broke the fence and kept pushing until part gave way."

Mom rubs the dog's face and chest and scratches behind his ears, making cute noises as though she knows how to speak dog.

"And that's why I haven't fixed it..." Dad continues, "... because your mother loves it when he visits us."

I raise a finger to the dog. "Goldie-Riddick better behave and not eat the pie when I bring it out." I head inside, gather everything I need, return with the pie, and place it on the wrought iron table. The dog surprises me and sits away from us under the shade of a tree while we eat.

"See? I told you he'd be fine," Mom says in a cocky tone.

"Why don't you get a dog?" I ask.

"Because our boy would get jealous," she says between mouthfuls.

"He's not your dog, Mom."

"He's here enough to be, and besides, he's not our worry when our neighbors return at night, so it's a win. We keep each other company." She calls the dog over and feeds him some of her pie. It surprises me how he takes it so gently from her fingers.

"At least he's calm now."

After we finish eating, we go inside to play Scrabble, Mom's favorite game. Goldie walks inside with us. What? He lies near the table and sleeps for the next hour while we play the board game.

There's a knock at the door, and the dog's head lifts. He *ruffs* a little bark.

"That'll scare 'em away." Dad grins. "Are you expecting anyone?"

Mom shakes her head.

Pushing up from my chair, I tell Dad, "I'll get it. You take your turn."

Just before I open the door, Dad says, "Sit, Goldie."

I blink, unbelieving.

"I hoped I had the right house." Franklin's deep voice hypnotizes me. "I was in the area and thought you might need a ride back to LA. I have a few things to do so..." he jabs a thumb over his shoulder, "... I can come back."

"You were in the area?" I shake my head to clear my thoughts. I'm distracted by him wearing faded denim jeans and a tan shirt. I've never seen him in anything but trousers. With a looped finger, he holds his designer coat over his shoulder. "I, um... am driving back with Zara. How did you know where I lived?"

"*Gold-ie*," Dad shouts.

I'm knocked sideways into the door as the dog bounds past me and onto Franklin's chest. Goldie must be ninety pounds, and she's airborne with momentum. Franklin groans with the impact. His coat goes flying as he flaps his arms for balance.

"Nooo," I yell, reaching for him as he stumbles back, trips on the stairs, and attempts to grab the railing, only he topples over it and—

"Jesus! Mother of God," he screams in pain. He rolls off the bougainvillea and into the bed of daisies.

Goldie is all over him, licking his face, and Franklin splutters as her tongue licks his mouth.

"What the fuck is happening?" He shoos away the dog and checks his hands.

"Goldie, come here," Dad says from behind us.

I crouch beside Franklin. His head has a long cut running down the side of his face, and both his palms are cut. His shirt has numerous rips, and I'm sure he is bleeding on his back. It was a heavy landing.

"Oh, shit." I lay a gentle hand on his shoulder as he studies his hands. "What hurts the most?"

He peers up at me and tentatively touches his face. "My ego."

"Let me help you up."

He shakes his head. "I'll take it slow. I hurt everywhere."

"Can I do anything for you, son?"

I turn to Dad standing and watching us. He picks up Franklin's coat, brushes it off, and eyes us seriously. "I'm sorry about the dog."

Franklin bows his head. "I've made quite the first impression."

"C'mon, let's get you inside and cleaned up. I know what it's like to come out second best to that damn plant. The problem is the thorns can be poisonous, so we need to clean your cuts now."

"Terrific." Franklin unrolls carefully. He grimaces before he is fully upright.

"You might need to see a doctor if they swell. You could get an infection and even end up with dermatitis."

"What was I thinking?" he murmurs.

I lead Franklin inside and formally introduce him to my parents in a rush. I need to attend to him quickly.

Dad pats his shoulder. "Nice to meet you, Franklin. The handshake can wait."

Franklin assesses the scratches on his hands before meeting my father's caring gaze. "Thank you, sir. Please call me, Frank."

Frank?

My beautiful man wants to be less formal around my parents and the gesture pulls at my heartstrings.

Dad shoves the Scrabble game back into its torn box and clears a space at the table.

"You need to remove your shirt." I leave him to prepare a bowl of soapy water and grab a towel and the first-aid kit. When I return, my parents are seated at the table, but no one is talking.

Franklin has his face in his hands.

I place a hand on Franklin's shoulder. "Do you need some pain meds?"

He removes his hands from his face. "Please."

Dad springs to his feet. "I'll get some. Do you need anything else, Poppy?" Dad calls over his shoulder.

"No thanks."

"Poppy?" Franklin raises an eyebrow.

"My father has always called me Poppy. Don't try to distract me," I warn him. "Before I start, I'll need to squeeze each cut so it bleeds to rid some of the poison." His gaze meets mine when I touch his cheek. His eyes water and clench when I squeeze. "It's like a bad pimple," I say, trying to ease the tension.

"I rarely had a pimple growing up," he says, deadpan.

I tap his shoulder. "Done. Lean forward while I check your back."

Dad returns and places the medication on the table. "This should help," he murmurs.

"Thank you, Mr. Gilbert."

I trace my fingers over his perfectly tanned skin. Not so long ago, I admired him in other ways. His shoulders flinch. "Sorry." I squeeze again. "There's a thorn in that cut. I'll need the tweezers to get it. You're lucky there is only one thorn."

"Lucky," he repeats, seeming unamused.

My fingertips trail over the rest of his back. "That's it. I'll bathe your cuts, and it will hopefully soothe the sting." He nods without glancing up, his elbows on his knees. After washing his back, I dab at his cheeks. His gaze flicks to mine, and for the first time, I see a vulnerable man.

"I'm going to apply some cream, and it should help with the pain." I hold up the tube of antibiotic cream.

"It will help," Mom finally speaks. "I keep stock of it for when Ray prunes the tree."

"Prune it? I'd kill it," he mumbles.

Dad chuckles under his breath. "There's been times I've thought about it, son."

Franklin manages a smile. It's small, but it's there.

The ice breaks, and the tension in the room eases.

Mom hobbles to the cupboard and grabs another box. She places it on the table. Judging by Franklin's expression, he's noticed her limp. She slides the medication across the table with a glass of water. "You should get checked out tomorrow."

"Thank you, Mrs. Gilbert. I apologize for the interruption. I hope you're enjoying your special day. I have some flowers in the car."

"You do?" I ask. He always surprises me. "For my mom?"

"I didn't want to be presumptuous and assume I would be invited in. Could you please get them?"

He hands me the remote to his car. I dash out, not wanting to leave Franklin alone for long when he's feeling awkward.

The bouquet is tied with a pink ribbon. The flowers are all the colors of the rainbow and include gerberas, peonies, and carnations. How can I stay angry at him when he does things like this?

Inside, I hand the bouquet to Mom. "How beautiful."

"Frank." She shakes her head at him like she does at me when I've bought her something, and she's told me not to waste my money on her. "They're beautiful. Thank you."

I sit beside him and take his hand. "Thank you. Mom tells me not to get her anything and save my money as she has everything she needs."

His gaze flits around the room, and when our eyes meet, there is a tiny dent between his brows. In that moment, understanding crosses between us. "Your parents are wise in telling you to save your money," he says.

Gratitude fills me with him coming here to be with my family.

With a smile, Mom hobbles away to get water for the flowers.

"Here, son." Dad passes Franklin some medication. "This is a bit stronger." Dad looks at me as though he is letting me in on a secret. "Your mother doesn't know I take these when I've been cut, as I need something stronger than what's in our cabinet."

"Dad!" I say under my breath. "You can't hand out pills without knowing Franklin's medical history."

Franklin reads the back of the packet, then throws one down his throat. "It's fine. I've taken these before."

"Jesus." I shake my head.

"Can I get you a whiskey?"

Franklin nods at my father. "I'd appreciate a drink, sir."

28

PENELOPE

FOUR DRINKS LATER, Franklin is incapable of driving.

I text Zara.

> I'm driving Franklin back to LA as he's incapable of driving after drinking with my dad and a host of other things I'll explain later. Long story. Hope you had a great day with your mom. We'll catch up during the week.

My cell buzzes. It's Zara. "I better take this." I leave the room and explain what has gone down with Franklin after he appeared at my door.

Zara bursts out laughing. "Is he sitting in your kitchen getting drunk with your dad?"

"Uh-huh."

"I can just picture it."

I sigh loudly. "That's not even the worst bit. He drove his

Lamborghini here. I've never driven something so expensive before. Hell, I'll probably crash it."

"A freaking Lamborghini. Don't crash it. Take a picture."

My hand rests on my throat, and my heart is racing. "Under other circumstances... maybe, but my anxiety is about to spill over. I'm waiting for the questions from my parents. The only conversation is about whiskey. Apparently, my father knows more about distilling and fermentation than I realized."

Zara giggles again. "It's a good thing, Pen."

"Maybe."

"So, you and Franklin are good again because I thought we were mad at him for ghosting you?"

"It's hard to stay annoyed at him when he is here and trying so hard."

"I know. I just wish he'd make up his mind so you know where you stand."

"Yeah. Hey, I better go. Franklin or my parents might need saving."

Dropping my cell in my bra, I walk into the kitchen. Everyone is sitting around one end of the table, laughing and in deep conversation.

Into what freaking parallel universe have I traveled?

Dad holds up his glass—mainly ice remains. "Frank is sending me a bottle of Blanton's. Says I'll like it better than my old friend Jack."

His words stun me momentarily. Does my father know how much a bottle is? I didn't think he'd want to drink something so expensive.

"And tickets to the basketball." Mom rolls her eyes. "Did you know your father has been watching it these past couple of years?"

"No, I didn't." My parents never liked sports as it could bring out the worst side in people. They never liked aggression. It dawns on me how the conversation must have started.

"Courtside seats for your parents." Franklin cheers with his glass.

Oh boy.

"Not for me, but thank you for the offer," Mom says pleasantly.

I sit beside my mother and take her hand in mine. "Would you like me to do anything for you?"

She squeezes my hand, her eyes searching mine as though she is trying to understand me. "Visit me more."

I place my other hand over Mom's. "I will." I tune back into what Dad and Franklin are talking about.

"So how did you meet Poppy?"

I expect Franklin to say at a wedding, but he goes into detail about how he was on the beach thinking about how to propose. "Then I saw her. Penny was as beautiful as the sunlight glistening over the ocean right before it sets. She caught my eye, and I couldn't look away. I watched her for a while as she created a romantic setting, making sure the finishing touches were perfect and memorable for another couple. I thought if she cares this much about making other people happy, does she care equally for her own happiness? The moment touched me, so I asked her to set up the same scenario for me. What could go wrong?"

Mom and Dad's expressions are of shock. He doesn't give them long to ponder an answer.

"The following night, everything was set for a romantic proposal. Only my ex-girlfriend is... a perfectionist." I giggle but don't interrupt him. "She said no." His eyes round as though he is implying, *can you believe it*? "I was heartbroken. I don't take rejection well. I missed cues projecting what my heart was telling me. The girl of my dreams was not the one I'd proposed to... she was the one who created an intimate space for couples to confess their love. My ex wanted me to shout my feelings to the world. It wasn't about just the two of us. In hindsight, fate led me to Penny."

The girl of his dreams.

I am speechless.

"A relationship should always be about the people in it, first and foremost." Dad squeezes Mom's hand. "I'm glad Poppy has you, Frank. It's good to know a man is looking out for her."

I want to tell them both to stop being so melodramatic, only Franklin is possessed, and his mouth has taken on a mind of its own.

"Okay, that's our cue to leave." I stand. "You're delirious and talking nonsense. Enough of the whiskey chatter."

Franklin's excitement has me laughing.

"Are you sure you want to see the house tonight?" I ask.

"Yeeesss," he says, exaggerating the word. "I waited until I was with you, and I'm flying out tomorrow."

"Can't you stay longer, pleassse? You just got back."

He groans and rubs at his temple. "I want to, only shit's going down on the East Coast. Trust me, I'd rather be here with you."

I glance at him, then set my gaze back on the road, easing my foot off the accelerator.

"FYI, this car has never been driven by a grannie."

"A grannie? Seriously? You're not capable of making any sound decisions, so excuse me if I ignore you because I don't understand this drunken code you're speaking." I veer off the road and wait for the garage door to slide open. Automatic lights flicker on to highlight the other two prestigious cars parked side by side. I ease into a space and kill the engine. "Are you ready?"

Franklin is out of the car and tapping the security pad for the door before I've even grabbed my handbag.

"You've answered my question," I murmur. This man makes me smile more than I want to admit. "Wait for me," I shout at him.

Franklin opens the door, steps aside, and sweeps one arm into the air like a gentleman waiting for a lady to walk first. "Should I close my eyes?"

"No, you idiot." I laugh, feeling nervous and excited about his reaction.

The lights automatically flick on, and pride swells in my chest at how I've created a special coastal sanctuary for his home. There are white walls, an expansive kitchen, hardwood floors, and an uninterrupted ocean view.

Franklin's face lights up. "It's amazing, Penny. And the remodeling is perfect."

"Thank you. I want to explain some things to you about how I sourced each piece and the special touches of the house, but I'll wait until daylight hours and when you're not so... drunk."

"I'm not drunk. Only love drunk." He pulls me into his chest, takes my face in his hands, and kisses me. It's tender, loving, and not what I expected.

"If this is my payment, sign me up for your next project." I kiss him again.

"Consider it done," he murmurs against my lips. "Want to show me upstairs?"

"Saving the best for last." I walk Franklin up the floating stairs like they're leading us to heaven. I reveal each bedroom, bathroom, and study before guiding him to his bedroom—the grand finale. He responds to each with praise. He'll need another tour tomorrow, and I still need to explain the reasoning behind each remodel. "Wait."

I take the remote from the wall, keep the lights out, and open the ceiling to reveal a clear night sky twinkling with stars.

"You are full of surprises, Poppy." He stares up to the open air and smiles. "Leave it open."

"We can close it and just have the glass because the night air is still chilly."

"You'll be warm next to me." He pulls me onto the bed, I scream as I land, and he falls beside me. "What did you say about each piece of furniture?"

I kiss his lips and murmur, "You'll have to refresh my memory."

29

FRANKLIN

PENNY's dark hair fans out over the white linen. *A sleeping goddess.*

Last night, something changed between us. I felt it deep in my gut. I was out of sorts for part of the night, the whiskey and drugs partly to blame. Thoughts of Penny overwhelmed me. Either I drive people I care about away, or they get hurt. I ruin lives. It's accepted in my line of work, yet it's crossed over into my personal life now.

Lifting a finger to my cheek, the pain still stings.

Yesterday began as a disaster.

I certainly made a lasting impression—not my finest moment. I'm throwing everything I got to win Penny over. All because she doesn't need me. Penny doesn't need anyone.

My wealth means nothing to her and her family, and I've never found myself in this position, having to prove my worth in other ways.

At dawn, I walk through the house, checking the contractors' notes to make sure everything was properly signed off. Penny has exceeded my expectations. A ball of regret grows in my chest at the thought of eventually having to sell the property after all her hard work.

Her personal touch.

There are pieces of Penny everywhere I look.

Thoughtfulness.

The artwork she sourced locally, the reclaimed wood, the gardens, the light and constant airflow through the house—it all gives it the comfortable feeling of a *home*.

But it's not *my home*.

I never intended it to be, and now it's somewhere *we* could call *home*.

I go to stretch my back, jerk, and moan with the pain.

Penny sits up and wipes her eyes with a finger. "Hey, you're awake. How are you feeling?"

"I've seen better days."

"Come here. Let me check your cuts," she says, and I sit on the bed beside her. "I feel so bad," she whispers.

"My stupidity isn't your fault." I close my eyes, savoring the touch of her fingers trailing over my skin.

"These appear okay." She presses a gentle hand to my face. "Look at me." She assesses my cheek, her brow tight, her expression serious. "I'm worried about this one."

She touches it, and I pull away. "Still freaking sore." I stand up. "I'll get it checked out."

She presses her cell screen for the time. "I better get up. I'll message Hugh and tell him I'm going to be a little late as I have to get an Uber from here."

"I can drive you." The words slip out of my mouth before my brain catches up.

"I thought you had to fly back to New York."

My gut is being weird. It's doing the whole trying-to-talk-to-me bullshit. Gut instinct. And it has my chest hurting right along with it.

I rub a fist over my stomach. "Call in sick."

"What?" She gasps.

"Call in sick. I'll change my flight. Let's stay here all day and just be together."

It's official. I've lost my fucking mind.

The way she smiles at me sparks a small fire of desire that flows to every cell in my body. If this is insanity, I really like it.

I want Penny.

More than anything else.

More than being on the East Coast to save millions of dollars.

Penny pushes up onto her knees. She is naked and fucking perfect. She runs her fingers through my hair. Her simple touch soothes me in a way I struggle to explain. "I will if you do one thing for me."

I wrap my arms around her waist and pull her warm body against mine. "What?"

"We have brunch at the Barefoot Bar."

"That's it? You could have asked for anything, and I would have said yes."

She gives a light laugh. "It's something you said you'd never do."

I flip her on her stomach, pull her to her knees, and take a good look at her ass. "Perhaps you could convince me," I murmur.

She wiggles her ass. "Frankie, your challenge is the worst because it's something I want too."

I smack her ass. "Until you're incapable of walking into the bar."

It's almost ten by the time Penny and I make our way along the beach, shoes in our hands. It feels right doing this with her. My thoughts drift to having a life with Penny in this house—walking along the beach on weekends, raising a family in a coastal community. Our lives are mapping out before me—it feels right, yet a sinking sensation settles in my gut.

It would be a perfect scenario if I could be home with her.

Penny stops, bending over to collect shells. Fuck. Her ass is perfect with her rust-colored polka-dot dress clinging to her curves. I want to pull her against my dick. She straightens and hands the shells to me to put in my pocket. I do it without hesitation.

Sand in my pockets.

The material is bulging full of shells.

Who am I?

"These are my favorite. I used to collect them as a kid." She hands me a cylindrical-shaped shell. "Oh, look. Beach glass." She studies a piece of shiny green glass with smooth edges refracting the brilliant morning sun.

But it's freaking glass, not treasure. "No more, Pen. I have no room."

She smiles and takes my hand, the gritty particles of sand still on her fingertips. We leave the beach and take a path to the restaurant.

Before we get to the foyer, my cell buzzes. I check the screen—*Kimberley calling...*

"Pen, I need to take this call. Go in and get us a table."

I wait for Penny to head inside before answering, "Kimberley. Is everything okay?"

"Yes, Franklin. Damien has pneumonia, but he's being treated with antibiotics. Since you said you might visit this week, I wanted to give you the heads-up."

"Is he okay?"

"He usually pulls through, but there is a chance he might not. We have to accept that as his lungs are weakening."

"I'll be there in a few days. Thank you for the call."

I stand outside and reminisce about my years at college with Damien. We both had goals and dreams. He'd never back down from a challenge or a dare. Sometimes we had to recognize when we should let the challenge go, as winning could result in a negative outcome like it did for Damien.

His only company is nursing staff, along with his family caring for him. He told me it's like living his life in solitude, and I'll never forget the pain etched into his sad face.

I'm about to spend another four weeks on the other side of the country.

Is being alone for weeks on end the life I want for Penny? She'd be lonely in a big, empty house.

If I win Penny's heart, the outcome is not so good for her being with someone like me.

And the selfish side of me still wants to win.

PENNY POPS A PIECE OF CHICKEN IN MY MOUTH. WE HAVE spoken about the house and how much she loved creating something she believes is better for the environment. We laughed like teenagers in love with the sound of the ocean, creating a carefree environment.

"Why don't you have your own business?" I pop a piece of chicken in her mouth. We're feeding each other like lovesick teenagers. A voice of the old me questions my behavior in public. This new man has no fucks to give. The only thing I crave is being with her.

She wipes her mouth with a napkin. "I don't have the money."

"I could help. Set you up and be a silent partner."

She shakes her head. "You have to stop trying to save me. If it's meant to be, I'll find my way."

"I'm not trying to save you. I know a good business proposition when I see it."

"Perhaps you could recommend me to your friends." She shrugs. "Start from there."

"If there was an office in your home..." I tilt my head at her, "... it would be a start."

She gives me a side-eye. "I can't take that condo."

"Too late. It's in your name. It's a perfectly good residence sitting empty. Or you could move in with me."

"Franklin... don't say things you'll regret."

"I'm not." Premature, maybe, but why fight fate when I know she is the one I want to lie with at night?

She throws her napkin onto the plate. "What's wrong with where I live?"

"Everything." My face tightens. "Do I need to remind you of the other night when I exposed myself to strangers?" She covers her mouth with her hand. "I'm not okay with it."

"All right, all right. Maybe I'll take another look."

"Today?"

"Yes, today." She bats her lashes. "I'm a good girl."

A groan comes from my throat. "Careful, Penny, or I'll slide you onto my lap."

After we eat, I convince Penny to drive with me. I have forgotten how liberating it is to leave the pressures of work behind and focus on the road.

The freedom.

She is playing her Spotify list through the speakers, and with every song, I feel like I'm learning a little more about her. The lyrics. The acoustic sound. Heartfelt words telling a story with only us listening. Our story evolving around us. Time feels limitless. Being with her is more liberating than I'd anticipated.

Hiring Royce gave me extra time to work in the car without having to focus on the hectic traffic. Cell calls, emails, and appointments all could continue from the back seat.

After thirty minutes with Penny, I've realized I need to drive more.

Instead of traveling north, we head south along the Pacific Coast Highway. "Could you please find somewhere where we can get a coffee?"

She reaches for her cell. "I'll find a great place with good reviews. How soon do you want one?"

"We have all afternoon. You choose."

She flicks off her shoes and crosses her legs on the leather seat. "Do you want a view?"

I glance down at her thigh. "The view is pretty good from where I'm sitting."

"Keep your eyes on the road, Hendricks."

"Hendricks," I say, amused. "Okay, Gilbert. I see where I stand. As for views, we'll swing by the condo."

"I don't want to argue with you," she says softly. I feel her eyes on me.

"Not argue. Negotiate." I want to nail down what she needs. "It's closer to your work. It has an office space if you want to start your own business and plan your work week because I don't see how you can do all that in your tiny bedroom." I keep talking so she can't interrupt. "It has a guestroom if your parents want to visit. Most importantly, I can stay over without your roommates intruding when we're fucking."

"Fucking," she says under her breath and turns to the window. "I thought I was more to you than a fuck."

"You are," I say firmly. "You know what I mean."

There's a space of silence before she replies, "I'd love for my parents to stay over." Her voice is light, as if she is thinking about what that would be like.

"It's yours, Pen. Do what you want with it. Sell it to buy something you think is more suitable."

"Why do I feel like I don't deserve it?" she murmurs. "You're a generous man."

I take her hand and lay it on my lap. "Only to those I care about." I squeeze it. "And I care about you, Pen."

"I care about you too."

Jesus, I love the sound of her voice when she's like this. There's a sweet kindness radiating from her, and it penetrates deep into my soul. I feel her entire presence, and it makes me want to be a better man.

"I found somewhere I want to stop." She taps away on her cell. "It closes soon. We'll check out the condo later."

"Give me the directions."

"Said no man ever." She smirks. "I hope you like donuts."

"Is that even a question?"

"These are not ordinary donuts."

"Is the coffee good?"

She laughs. "I have no idea, but there is a coffee shop nearby, closer to the beach."

"What is it with you and the beach?"

She glances at me. "Doesn't the beach bring you happiness?"

It does now.

Somewhere near Huntington Beach, I pull over, and Penny dashes inside the donut shop. She returns with a box —it was worth the stop to see her broad smile.

"These are for later with our coffee."

"Can I plug in the directions?"

"Keep driving for another twenty minutes."

My girl is bossy—a side to her I rarely see.

Penny turns the music up and sings out of tune. I listen to her tone and how she sings as though the song was written for her. It's a song about love and the joy it brings, and I want to be the one to give it to her.

"Turn right at the lights."

We're headed to Crystal Cove.

"Good choice," I tell her.

"You've been before?"

"Years ago, when I bought some real estate on the beachfront for movies and photo shoots. The coffee is good."

She doesn't say anything.

"It's a great spot. I think you'll like it."

She peers up at me, her brows tight. "Do you still have the house?"

"I do." We pull into a parking space, and I point toward the left along a stretch of sand where a small wooden structure is located. "Can you see a shack on the beach?"

"Yes. Can I see inside it?"

"I don't have keys since it's being managed by a media company. We could look in the windows." She takes her box of donuts and is out of the car before I've unclicked my belt.

Penny strides ahead and then turns to me with a smile

that could make me agree to anything. "It's so quaint and gorgeous. I love it."

It's an old wooden shack with a maintenance bill that has had me consider selling it in the past. It's rundown, with the ocean pelting the exterior. I stride after her, inhaling the crisp, salted air stronger with the breeze from the ocean. She sits on one of the white wooden beach chairs on the porch and points to the other for me to join her.

"It could collapse beneath me." I grunt.

Penny giggles as she stares out at the ocean. "Are you ready for your surprise?"

It's just a donut. "What flavor did you get?"

The box lid lifts. *What in the world?* She hands me a stick.

"You have a pussy donut, and I have the dick donut."

I take the stick and stare at the flattened, squishy donut with pink icing. It's shaped like a woman's vulva with an opening.

Penny giggles again. "The look on your face." She holds her stomach as she laughs. "Take a bite."

"It's not going to taste as good as you." I take a bite. It's sugary and not the flavor I desire.

She raises one eyebrow and slides the dick donut into her mouth, and when she pulls it out, the chocolate sauce coats her lips. Between us is a table and the empty donut box. I drop my donut in there with a craving for Penny. Dropping to my knees, I take her face and lick her lips.

"Open your legs, Penny."

Her eyes widen. She does what I ask, and I help to slide her panties down her thighs. I stuff them into my pocket. I take her ass and tilt it off the chair, my head under her dress. *Fuck, she tastes good.* With the ocean behind me, Penny before me, I lick and taste, flick her clit while stopping her hips from wiggling.

"What if someone sees?" She groans.

"I own the place. I can do what I want."

Her breaths are fast.

Inserting two fingers, I rub and finger fuck her while my mouth claims her clit. It's not easy with her bucking in the seat.

"Franklin," she says with a groan of pleasure, and the wiggling stops as she comes.

I lift my head. Her dick donut is on the sandy wood beside her. Her arm hangs limply over the edge of the chair. I stand and say, "Sorry about your dick."

Her eyes are level with my cock. "Sorry about yours."

"Mine will be fine as long as it's the only cock to pass those beautiful lips." She lifts her gaze, and our eyes meet in understanding. "I expect exclusivity." I lean and kiss her. "And you taste better than any donut." My tongue sweeps over hers as I claim her lips.

Voices echo from the beach. In the distance, people congregate, erecting their navy and white umbrellas in the sand.

The café is a short walk away, so I take Penny's hand to help her stand.

"My panties?"

"I'm not finished yet," I state.

She stands and adjusts her dress. "Since all cocks are banned from that pretty mouth of yours..." I hand her the pussy donut. She takes a tiny bite, and I laugh.

Penny sets her eyes on me while her tongue licks the opening of the donut, her stare unwavering.

"Careful, Penny." The sound comes from deep in my throat. I pick up the dick donut, place it in the box, and throw it in a nearby trashcan. Penny's eyes are on me when I slide off my shoes and socks. She giggles and kicks off her wedge sandals.

I take her hand, and our bare feet hit the soft sand.

"I've changed my mind about coffee. I need something stronger to prepare me for the next surprise," she says.

I chuckle. "It's a nice change. For months, you've been the one surprising me."

She stops walking and lifts to her toes to kiss me. "It's always been you, since the day we met."

Her words hit me like a sharp broadhead arrow to the heart.

I will bleed for this woman.

Seeming oblivious to the effect her words have on me, Penny links her hand with mine ever so gently. She lifts it and kisses one of the scratches. Seconds later, we walk up toward the café on the beachfront. We find a table in the sun under an umbrella where we can leave our shoes off rather than sitting inside.

The server appears, and I order a coffee.

"I'll have a watermelon mojito, please." Her smile is contagious. She begins to talk about her love of the ocean, rock pools, and the tiny creatures she would search out as a kid.

I have handfuls of sandy shells in my car.

Who have I become?

I watch her animated face as she speaks.

Tentatively, I touch the cut on the side of my face—a battle wound of proving my love.

Her gaze meets mine in understanding. "It was quite a day for you."

"It was worth it."

She giggles. Then, her brow changes as though a cloud is hanging over her thoughts. "Mom's limp has worsened."

"I did notice."

"And you remembered?" She smirks. "I wasn't sure how

much you would retain from yesterday after the meds and your whiskey session with Dad."

"I remember everything," I tell her. "If you move into the condo, encourage them to take a holiday and stay with you."

Her shoulders rise and fall while her gaze goes to the ocean.

My cell vibrates in my pocket. I need to ignore it, only I know better. Holding the cell low, I curse under my breath.

Paul.

"What's happening?" My eyes are on Penny while I take the call.

"I know you said to call only if it's an emergency. Well, shit has gone down. We need to be in New York by tomorrow."

Penny stares at me, her lips thin with worry.

If my lawyer is anxious, I'm sure it's written all over my face.

30

PENNY

ELEVEN DAYS of barely talking to Franklin.

I miss him.

Every day, I receive a text before he falls asleep. It's usually along the lines of... *Wish I was there with you*.

Following our day in Crystal Cove, we drove back to the condominium after I agreed to it and declined any payment for the renovation and redecoration of his Malibu home. However, the cost of the condominium is triple the figures in the contract.

It still feels wrong to accept such a generous gift.

We sat on the balcony at twilight. For a few minutes, it was only the two of us before he had to rush away to pack prior to Royce driving him to his family's jet.

He gave me the codes and the number of a trusted mover. Not that I had much furniture to shift because my new residence is fully furnished so I donated my old bed to charity.

It has everything I need, for which I'm grateful. Franklin left the decorating to me to carry out in my own time. He said I could sell the couch and dining table or all of it if they're not to my liking. Franklin ordered what he thought would appeal to me, and he was spot-on.

It's Friday night, and the sun is low in the sky when I arrive back at *my* new condominium. Hugh, Sienna, and Zara will soon arrive to celebrate my move. The wine and food I ordered will be delivered shortly. A chime notifies me of visitors in the lobby.

After checking the screen, I wait by the glass doors for them to appear. Hugh exits the elevator, holding a wine bottle. Zara has a box with a ribbon, and Sienna is carrying more bags.

I press the button, and the glass doors part for my friends to enter my home.

"This is fancy," Sienna says, eyes wide as she turns, checking out the space.

"It is. Here, allow me to take those from you." I unpack the crackers, chocolate, and chips and giggle under my breath. "It looks like food for a movie night, not a celebration."

"Honey, we're celebrating all night with you, and it will probably turn into movies on that big-ass screen of yours."

I turn to the massive television. "Yeah. I'm developing a relationship with that thing lately. It's just the two of us."

"We're here to fix that." Hugh spins in the kitchen. "Where do I find glasses for the champagne?"

I barely remember myself, so I go in search of the crystal glasses and then pour the champagne. We head out onto the balcony to watch the orange glow of the sunset between the surrounding buildings. Standing by the railing, we clink our glasses. For a moment, I think about what it would be like sitting with Franklin every night at sunset at his Malibu Beach house.

Romantic evenings together, just the two of us.

Or will it be just me?

"This is a little something from the three of us." Zara hands me the large box with a pink ribbon. Hugh takes my drink so I can unwrap it, which I do, and lift the lid.

"Oh, it's beautiful, thank you." I raise the white ceramic curved vase from the box.

Zara smiles. "For when Franklin buys you flowers."

"Or if you buy your own flowers," Sienna adds.

"Either way, you'll be thinking of us and not just him," Hugh says, clinking his glass with mine.

I laugh at Hugh, always wanting the attention on himself but in a fun way.

When the sun disappears, automated lights turn on, creating an ambient glow over the balcony. We move to the chairs by the round, white concrete firepit. Matching sculpted white concrete chairs surround the fire with comfortable cushions wedged over them. One of my favorite things about this place is that the balcony is wide enough to entertain. I think it could be what sold Franklin on buying it. At this time of year, we don't need the warmth, but watching the flames flicker and dance emits a calmness I feel all the way to my core.

The delivery arrives, and I grab plates and cutlery for the Thai food, which we all serve ourselves, and return to the balcony.

"Hugh finally booked our honeymoon." Sienna's smile is broad as she eyeballs Hugh. "He was so undecided I thought we'd miss out."

Hugh shakes his head. "Babe, we were always going to find somewhere. I couldn't choose between Fiji, Hawaii, and the Bahamas."

"And where did you decide?" Zara asks.

Hugh taps his nose. "I have it under control, and it's going to be a surprise."

Zara and I groan. "Women need to know what to pack."

Hugh waves his fork at us. "Bikinis for the water, some casual clothes for day wear, and nothing at night."

We all groan.

"I guess you know by those three destinations," I remark.

Sienna nods. Her eyes are bright with excitement. "I can't wait, and if I don't have appropriate clothing, I'll buy it."

Zara reaches across and pats her shoulder. "Right on, girlfriend."

"The wedding is only a few months away," I exclaim. "Where has the time gone?"

"This is probably my last weekend free as I have much organizing to do," Sienna says before taking a bite of a spring roll. "How does Franklin feel about sitting with a table of strangers if you're sitting with the wedding party?"

"He's invited?"

"Of course," Hugh says. "Give me his email, and I'll send an invite."

The idea of Franklin coming to the wedding excites me. I can visualize it all. His eyes on me as I walk down the aisle as a bridesmaid. How great it would be to laugh with him and my friends.

But am I kidding myself? Because behind me is an empty condominium. He can't even make it back on weekends, so it's unlikely he'll get to their wedding.

"You know, maybe count him out. He's stressed with work at the moment, and the last thing he told me is he expects to be in New York for a few months. It's one of the reasons I took this place as I feel closer to him here as he picked out most of the things for me."

"Oh, honey." Zara sets her plate down and comes to wrap an arm around me. "You're missing him more than you're letting on."

I nod, not wanting to elaborate as our future scares me. My stomach has a permanent knot, and it doesn't take much for the knot to expand and make me nauseous.

"If you need me to stay, I can. Anytime," Zara continues, and we all chuckle, but I know Zara is sincere.

"Thanks. I might take you up on that." I look at Hugh. "I'll pass on Franklin's email, though I'm doubtful he'll attend."

Sienna regards Hugh. "If Franklin turns up on the day, that's great. If not, then a few no-show guests can't be helped."

"He'll miss out on the best wedding of the year." Hugh uses his hands for emphasis.

It will be good, but have my friends forgotten how Franklin and I met? Their wedding will be epic, and I won't forget my bridesmaid commitments to sneak off to receive the best orgasm of my life as I did at the previous wedding. It has gone down as one of my favorite weddings to date because of *everything Franklin*.

Hugh leaves to get another bottle of wine. I check my cell for a message from Franklin, secretly hoping he's tried to call and I've missed it. Of course, that's impossible when my cell phone is beside me and I'm glancing at the screen every few minutes.

Still, there is a new email, but nothing from Franklin.

I read the email.

"Oh my God," I mutter.

"What is it?" Zara asks.

"James Lyons from Elite Coastal Decorators has asked to meet with me to discuss ideas for an upcoming project. Franklin passed on my email as James saw my work in

Franklin's Malibu house and loved it." My heart races with excitement that someone, another interior decorator, no less, appreciates my design concept.

Hugh stands beside me with an opened bottle, ready to pour our drinks. "He saw your work?"

"Yeah," I murmur, confused.

"When?"

I glance up from my cell, taken back by Hugh's tone. Hugh respects my ideas and has no reason to doubt the validity of the email.

"You said Franklin saw it once before he left for New York."

I now see the point Hugh is making.

Hugh refills our glasses and takes a seat, then pulls out his cell and scrolls while taking sips of wine. "You're not going to like this, Pen." Hugh holds out his cell for Sienna to pass to me.

"Just say it," Zara says since she can't see the screen.

"Franklin's Malibu home is listed for sale."

What?

Hugh's expression is serious.

I take the phone from Sienna and read the screen. The marketing is spot on and has elaborated on the excellent remodeling and decorating by Penelope Gilbert, emphasizing sustainable choices and environmental values as a way of the future while maintaining class.

I stare at Hugh, lost for words.

Our eyes are locked as he portrays concern. "Did you know?"

I can't breathe.

Zara flies out of her seat and takes the phone from my hand.

The world slows as I ruminate over everything he has

said to me and what Jobe said when I asked questions about the renovation to suit Franklin's lifestyle.

The bedroom, for fuck's sake. I'd dreamed of lying beside him, gazing up at the starry sky, night after night.

"No." My voice rasps.

"The bastard," Zara says loud enough for the neighbors to hear and quickly places my cell on the table like it's too hot to touch.

"Maybe I missed something." I spring out of the chair, grab my cell from the table, and scroll through our messages. "I tried so freaking hard to impress him that I must have missed him telling me it was an investment."

Hugh is beside me. He places a hand over the cell phone and lowers it away from my face. "You spoke to me most days about it. Not once did you mention he might sell. You thought it was his forever home."

"If you consider the positives..." Sienna begins, "... he has mentioned you several times, your creative ideas, the importance of investing in sustainable remodeling choices and being environmentally conscious." She looks up at us. "You're going to receive a ton of work from this. It's so different from everything in LA being over the top when you are offering something unique and mindful to the buyer."

Zara wraps an arm around me. "While that's great, it's not helping Pen get through the hurt of Franklin not telling her his intention to list it after she finished pouring her heart and soul into making it a home suited to him."

My chest is so tight with devastation.

I'm insignificant to him.

I want to puke.

"I thought it was his dream home," I murmur.

Hugh steps into my line of vision. "You should listen to Sienna. She's right. She always is," he says and raises his eyebrows. "Her ability to see beyond emotions interfering with business decisions keeps me grounded. And you know me..." he squeezes my hands, "... I was an emotional fruit box in college."

"Right."

His eyes are wide, perhaps searching for understanding.

I try not to let the tears build. My thoughts go to the time when Daphne and Franklin were together and how she didn't like the décor. "Do you think he hates it and doesn't want to live there? Is it too... well, me?"

"Nooo," my friends say in tune.

"It's freaking amazing," Zara says.

While I work with wealthy people and take pride in my work, my ideas are not about the best and most expensive remodeling, and I don't pretend to think on the same level as a billionaire. What I offer is unique and thoughtful. I'm still working on my skill in reading people's body language to help me gauge their reactions to my remodeling ideas. The joy I witnessed in Franklin when he walked through his Malibu home wasn't fake. We talked about nights in his bed and days on the balcony, listening to the sound of the ocean.

"Pass me the bottle," I say to Hugh.

The listing has cemented how I don't know Franklin at all.

Why didn't he tell me?

"While we have come a long way since college, tonight I'm reverting to old ways." I chug down several mouthfuls of champagne straight from the bottle. I rub a circle over my chest. "Tonight, I don't want to feel any of this emotion."

My cell dings with a message.

Zara reaches for it and reads the screen. "It's Franklin," she says dryly. "He misses you." She rolls her eyes and hands me my cell.

I read the message to my friends, hoping for any hidden clue in his words.

"Miss you, Pen. I wish you were here with me. This could take another month to wind up, then I'll be home."

Home?

My friends wait for me to say something. "Why is he avoiding telling me about the house?" I tap on his digits. "I'm calling him..." I wait for the connection, only it rings and rings, then goes to his voice message. I don't finish listening to the whole message before I end the call and toss my cell onto the table.

Sienna stops the cell from sliding off the table. "May I?" I give her a nod. She scrolls through the messages. "Pen, he adores you. If he didn't, it's fair to say he could get any woman to his penthouse with one call. I can see all over your face you think he's with you for the sex, but it's not what the two of you are about."

Hugh stands beside Sienna, wraps an arm around her, and kisses her cheek.

I want to believe Sienna.

"We all know billionaires can get sex anywhere, anytime, and be discreet about it," Zara adds, and the truth in that statement kills me.

"How do I know he's not doing that? I get one short text every night."

"And he doesn't have to send it, does he?" Sienna's eyes plead with mine. "I'd be thinking what has happened for him to list the property, especially if he loved it and knew how much work you'd put into the renovation."

My mouth dries.

Has something happened that he's not telling me about?

"He could've warned Pen." Zara's words are lined with frustration. She picks up the bottle from the tiles and hands it to me, and I take a few more mouthfuls.

Sienna grabs her purse. "I need to go as I have an early start tomorrow." She comes over and kisses my cheek. "Give him time to explain, and in the meantime, don't beat yourself up."

Hugh hugs me. "I'll take Sienna home. If you need me to come back, I can." He looks to Zara. "Are you staying?"

Zara nods.

"I'll be okay," I tell my friends.

"I know you will be," Zara says in a reassuring way. "But tonight, you need a friend."

On Monday morning, I drag my ass into the office. My body aches, and I feel like I've been hit by a train. Before I have time to ready my desk, our boss's boss, Jody, storms into the room and closes the door. She is wearing a light pink suit, a white shirt, and I'm in love with her blazer.

"You have been working out of hours."

It's not a question.

"I have." My voice croaks because of the weekend abuse of my body. "A friend asked me to help with remodeling and decorating his home."

She places both hands on my desk and leans closer. "Word gets around fast. While I'm annoyed you didn't run this by me or even ask for my ideas, I'm proud of you." She straightens and folds her arms. "You have ethics, and the environment has always been important to you."

She's not angry? Holy cow. And she wishes I'd asked for her help? I nod, not thinking straight. "My whole family is... I have grown up respecting our earth."

"You didn't think to add your ideas to the table in business meetings?"

"I did talk about it once with Hugh. We didn't know whether it was in our client's best interests here."

"Harumph." Jody takes a few steps as though she's about to pace the length of my desk while she ponders what I've said. "Well, from now on, let me be the judge." She halts her step, a deep-set frown on her face. "Our clients don't just want class and impression." She walks to my side table and picks up my books on meaningful remodeling. "Many have the funds to stand out and be impressionable by doing everything you've advocated. Gray-water harvesting systems, a green roof and walls, smart home technology to reduce the environmental footprint."

She turns and stares at me. "Our company will implement this ASAP, and I want you to oversee this new direction. You and Hugh will liaise with client builders to remodel with environmental values. After I read about your work on a Malibu Beach listing, I asked clients the relevant questions on how your remodeling concept could be offered. Let's jump straight into this by creating contracts with companies who make furniture with organically, ethically sourced fabrics for upholstery, rugs, and drapes for the clients' homes to be sustainable and unique."

I'm gawking at my boss.

"I want this to start happening today, Penny. We have clients waiting for ideas."

"Yes, of course."

She stops at the door. "Whatever you are working on now can be passed to Jackie and Steph."

The door clicks closed behind her, and I raise my brows before falling back onto my seat to take a deep breath.

Is this really happening?

A leadership role is a step in the right direction to follow my dreams.

The door swings open as Hugh strolls in. "Jody said I needed to speak with you." His brow is tight. "Is everything okay?"

"More than okay. You'll need to sit down to hear this."

As of two weeks ago, the idea Jody had is now in the budget, and they're confident enough in its success that they can rent a new office. Hugh and I will be running Style Plus.

I have ignored the calls and texts from Franklin.

He broke my trust, and I'm not ready to have a conversation with him yet.

I am more than aware avoidance is not a cure, yet it helps keep my head straight when work is all I can currently think about.

Touché.

The last thing I need is to become distracted and spiral downward.

I'm not sorry it's Friday afternoon because all I want to do is sleep.

Hugh strolls into my office and slides his rear onto the corner of my desk like he does every Friday afternoon. He's wearing a geometric blazer in bright orange, pink, and green colors, and it suits him. "After that crazy week, what are your plans for the weekend?"

I slide my laptop into my handbag as I'm finishing early. "I thought about driving down to see my parents. What are yours?"

"Wedding things." He grins at me. "It's my life for a few more weeks. The most amazing honeymoon is set." He is bragging and wants a rise out of me.

"Where?"

"Good try, Pen. No one will get it out of me."

I giggle, and then a cough interrupts us.

Jody's standing only a few feet away and says in an authoritative voice, "Penny, you have a visitor."

Hugh springs off the table so fast. "I'll talk to you soon," he says quickly, leaving my tiny office before stopping and nodding to whoever is standing behind Jody. "My apologies."

I stand and lean my hands on my desk as Jody leads a woman into my office. She's wearing a classy navy dress and Christian Louboutin heels. A Louis Vuitton purse is slung over her arm. First, I notice the perfectly styled hair until the woman smiles, and I stop breathing for a second. Not in my wildest dreams did I expect a visit from Mrs. Hendricks herself.

Jody gives me a nod before closing the door.

Mrs. Hendricks rounds the table and hugs me. "It's good to see you, Penelope. Do you have a minute?"

"Of course." I point to the chair. "Please take a seat."

My thoughts are running wild with every second of silence.

Mrs. Hendricks takes a seat and crosses her legs. "When did you last see Franklin?"

I'm sitting so straight my back hurts. I swallow the nervous lump in my throat before I speak, "When he flew home for a brief stay a few weeks ago."

"Has he called you lately?"

What? "Yes, but I've been so busy, and with the time difference..." I reach for my cell. "I'll call him back tonight."

"Penelope."

My fingers freeze, and I meet her gaze. "Is he okay?"

"It depends on what you define as okay." Her eyes hold mine. "He thinks the world of you, and whatever you think of him, please know he is a good man." She pauses, and I have no idea where she is going with this. "He needs you...

in New York. This damn court case is dragging out—" She waves a hand at me.

"He'll explain everything to you. Right now, he is stressed and lonely. I've called some of his friends, and yes, they were ex-girlfriends, but I didn't call them for what you might think."

Her brow pinches. "He needs to talk to friends. Only when someone reaches out... he turns them away." She anchors her attention on me. "He'll never turn you away. You are the one person he *will* listen to."

"You want me to go to New York to speak to him?"

"I do. My guess is he called to ask you to come."

I shake my head. "Work is busy, and it's an impossible time to take days off."

"I have that covered. Arrangements have been made for the jet to take you tonight and have you back on Sunday evening. Royce is waiting downstairs to take you to your condo to grab a few things."

I'm speechless, so I say nothing.

"Franklin is exceptional at handling stress. Only he received a call informing him a friend's condition had deteriorated. A few weeks ago, he visited his friend, Damien, in New York. Every visit upsets him..." She pauses and glances down at her hands before meeting my gaze once more. This time, there is sadness in her eyes. "Both boys were in college and had traveled to Hawaii for spring break. Unfortunately, swallowing a slug while drunk at a party had dire consequences. Damien never backed down from a dare."

I shake my head. "Franklin never mentioned it."

"Franklin keeps most things close to his heart. Even you..." She tilts her head. "He attempted to keep you to himself for as long as possible. He tries to protect people. He blames himself for Damien's actions and believes if he wasn't drunk, he could have stopped him. Friends stop friends from doing stupid things. Franklin and Damien were as stubborn as each other. Damien swallowed it and won the dare before Franklin could stop him." She sighs loudly. "Most slugs are not poisonous. Only this one carried rat lungworm disease. He fell ill ten days later and showed deterioration on the flight home."

"He's still sick?" I stand and pour a glass of water from the dispenser in the corner and hand it to Mrs. Hendricks, then take the seat beside her.

"Thank you, dear." She takes a few mouthfuls and keeps hold of the glass. "Doctors are amazed how Damien has survived, but his quality of life is not great. He suffered meningoencephalitis. A brain hemorrhage left him paralyzed. Yearly bouts of pneumonia weakened his lungs. A month ago, his mother called Franklin and said he should come and see him as it might be his last chance. You can only imagine how it's affected Franklin. I tried to tell him it was an unfortunate accident, and no one was to blame. But..." she pauses and stares at me, "... with Damien taking a turn for the worst on top of the stress of the court case, Franklin is worried and... lonely."

My throat burns. "You think I can help?"

She offers a subtle smile. "I *know* you can help."

Her belief in me is encouraging, but Franklin not telling me about the house indicates he has less faith in me than she knows. For her to come here and tell me this—I blow out a long breath through pursed lips—I can tell she is desperate to help her son. But despite my heart wanting to go to him, I'm wary. Yet I can't stand the thought of him carrying this weight alone. I've seen him stressed about work, but adding personal worries to the mix would leave him crippled.

So I answer with my heart and not my head...

"What time do I leave?"

ROYCE STEERS THE CAR CLOSE TO THE PRIVATE JET.

On the tarmac, a woman and man dressed in pale blue and black uniforms stand straight, waiting for me.

Royce opens the door and says, "Have a safe flight, Penny."

"Thank you, Royce. Enjoy your weekend."

He takes my overnight bag.

"It's fine, I can manage." He gives me a questionable look, but I carry my bag toward the plane.

"Hi, I'm Penelope Gilbert."

Trent introduces himself as the pilot, and Heidi is the attendant. Trent apologizes for the wait and that the copilot will arrive shortly.

Heidi leads me aboard, and I'm struck by the lush interior designed for the utmost comfort. The height inside the cabin surprises me, along with the width. Each contoured chair is crafted from soft ivory leather where I could curl up and read a book. Four single lounge chairs sit at the front with wooden tables between them. Behind is a set of four chairs around a table. Behind those is a long couch and more single chairs. There are also two television screens.

"Make yourself comfortable wherever you please," Heidi says. "Before you settle in, I'll point out the restroom." She leads me to the back and opens a door. "The other door is if you need to refresh before landing." She opens the door to a beautiful shower with ivory tiles and marble benches over the vanity. "Do you care for a champagne before takeoff,

Penny?" She steps aside, and a galley kitchen comes into view.

"I would like that, thank you."

"Our meals are prepared at the front of the plane, and this is for refreshments."

Behind her is another door, and Heidi turns to see what I'm staring at. "Mr. Hendricks' bedroom is locked, though we were given instructions to make your flight comfortable, so if you need to sleep, I could unlock it for you."

A freaking bedroom.

"No, I'm fine, thank you. I'll just take a seat."

I walk along the soft carpeted floor and choose a seat, where I then check out the buttons to recline. One is to move the table, and the others? I have no clue.

Heidi arrives with my glass of champagne. "We'll be cleared for takeoff in fifteen minutes. All business services are offered during the flight." She places the glass beside me, along with a bowl of nuts. "There is a selection of hot food on offer. Give me a few minutes to check what we have today."

"It's fine. I understand how this was all last-minute."

"Can I help you with anything else?"

"No, thank you."

Once Heidi is out of sight, I kick off my heels, bring my feet up close, and hold my drink near my lips. The large round windows bathe the cabin in natural light, almost an orange glow with the sun setting behind us.

A man in dark trousers and a white shirt speaks to staff on the ground before dashing up the stairs. I catch a glimpse of him before he disappears into the cockpit.

I sip my champagne and hope I'm not making a big mistake.

31

FRANKLIN

Caleb walks to my cabinet and pours himself a whiskey.

"Make it two." I rub at the kinks in my neck and stand to give my back a rest. It's after seven on Friday night, and we've been waiting all day to hear from the lawyer representing PetroDepend.

I hold my whiskey glass toward Paul as I speak, "Firstly, I'm fed up with the destructive practice by PetroDepend that was hidden from us. My option is to make a public speech at a shareholders' meeting to make a stand against unethical practices."

Paul's expression implies he doesn't approve or disapprove. "It could work."

I throw the whiskey down my throat. "If the court case swings against PetroDepend, stock will plummet. The significant loss will infuriate our investors. Hendricks Capital Management as a hedge fund will be jeopardized."

"I'm building a case so that won't happen." Paul taps

away on his laptop. "We have time before the hearing on Monday."

The pain in my gut is like a rock grinding a hole. It's probably an ulcer. We have been talking in circles for months with investors and PetroDepend. "I could sell a significant portion of the PetroDepend stocks, putting my reputation and career at risk. Will it save our investors and my relationship, or will it backfire, making things even more complicated?"

Paul shakes his head. "I can't speak for George or Caleb but tell me what else you have in mind before I state my opinion."

"If I confront PetroDepend's leadership to protect both our investors and the environment, I could demand that they take accountability for their environmental damages and push for a more sustainable future. Or we—"

Caleb points a finger at me while he takes a call. "Right." He listens, his expression deadpan until he throws his cell on the table and cheers. "We have an offer from a more sustainable company looking to buy out PetroDepend. It's an opportunity that could save the hedge fund." George and Caleb high-five before Caleb turns to me. "But it involves risking your entire portfolio on a venture that is, while environmentally sound, not as financially proven as PetroDepend."

Paul and I stare at Caleb.

"And you've been transparent to our investors," George adds.

Thank fuck. "Which venture is it?" I ask.

"Cleanrgy."

We all exchange blank stares.

I sure as hell haven't heard of them.

"Hear me out," Caleb begins. "Think of us when we started. They have proper backing and are taking the right steps in becoming future leaders in the natural energy sector."

My cell buzzes. After a long day, I have ignored all calls unless it's related to this case.

Jobe.

I hold up a finger. "Give me a moment."

"Jobe. Everything okay?" I walk to the cabinet and pour another glass of whiskey.

"Your house is sold. I'll send through the paperwork."

"That was quick. Anyone I know?"

He laughs low. "Did you doubt me? A basketball player from the Sharks. He outbid everyone at the auction. A million more than the asking price."

"The fuck? How much are we paying these guys?"

Jobe laughs again. "I need to go. Wanted to give you the news to make your weekend."

"Nothing will make my weekend until this fuckery ends. Enjoy yours."

I toss my cell on the desk. Closing my eyes for a moment, I roll my shoulders to ease the stress. Paul is eyeballing me, so I tell them, "Finally, some good news. My house sold."

Paul closes his computer. "I'm calling it a day, gentlemen. If I hear anything, I'll let you know. Caleb, send me the details of Cleanrgy, and I'll get back to Franklin on the figures. Franklin, go celebrate."

CLOSING MY EYES, I PUSH ALL THOUGHTS OF PETRODEPEND out while I throw the last of the whiskey down my throat. I stand, head to the window, and stare out over the sprawling lights of New York. Endless police sirens wail in the distance. These walls block out most of the noise and... life...

I feel lonelier than I have in my life and want to call Penny and tell her the good news. I check my cell—she hasn't replied to a text all week, and my calls have been ignored.

My cell buzzes in my hand, and hope swells until I read my mother's name—*again*. I want to ignore it only five missed calls are excessive.

"Mom."

"Franklin. Where are you?"

"In New York."

"Don't act smart with me. Why didn't you answer my calls?"

"You can't blame me for being apprehensive after you've had certain women checking in on me. I'm dealing with something, as you know, that's requiring all of my time."

"And you can't blame me for being concerned. What's more important is I have spoken to Penny."

"Mom!" I growl. "What did you say?"

"The truth. You need her. She is on her way to you now."

"To New York? What flight?" Jesus, my head is in a spin.

"I organized the jet. Call it an intervention, but I know when my son is spiraling."

"She agreed to get on the jet?"

"Why wouldn't she? It's more comfortable than commercial."

"Penny is environmentally conscious." I close my eyes and imagine Penny's reaction to my mother.

"Meaning?"

"Penny is aware a private jet emits ten to twenty times more carbon pollution than a passenger plane. Just what did you say?"

"Oh, I see the connection with the Malibu house."

"Mom," I warn.

"I understand how much she means to you, so I mentioned how lonely you are in New York."

What?

"Damien's name came up, and I explained what happened."

I tug at my hair. "Next time, ask *me* what I need. By the way, Damien is finally improving."

"Franklin, that is wonderful news. Son, please understand whatever I do, it's out of love. I sat by and watched your father emotionally detach himself from the family all for the Hendricks' name, and I'm not about to let my eldest son do the same. Be honest with yourself and open your heart to this girl."

There is not enough air in the room when dealing with my mother. "Do you believe Penny will be happy living a life like yours?"

"Franklin. You can't help who your heart chooses. Embrace it and learn from our past. Be honest with Penny and allow her to decide if you both have a future. Pushing her away is *not* the answer."

Muted horns and sirens sound from below. Staring out over the lights, I dream of a world with Penny in it—a property by the beach or maybe in the country with a little hobby farm.

I shake my head to snap out of it.

"What time is the jet's scheduled arrival?"

"If you want to be there to greet her, you have an hour. Otherwise, I've arranged for a limousine transfer."

"Cancel it. I'll be there."

"You can thank me later."

I end the call and find Quinton's number. "I need a favor. Can you get me to the airport in an hour?"

"Yes, sir. I'll be there in fifteen minutes."

I bring up Penny's name in my cell and send her a text.

> Hey. I heard you are on your way to New York. I'm looking forward to seeing you.

I wait.

> I thought it was a surprise. I'm excited to see you too.

After one text, she has me smiling.

> The element of surprise eludes my mother.

> I like your mom. As much as I want to chat, I need to finish this movie because I know it's not your type.

> Try me.

> It's a rom-com.

> If it means cuddling then count me in.

> I'll hold you to it.

EACH STEP PENNY TAKES FROM THE PLANE IS WITH THE GRACE of royalty. She pauses and glances around, her eyes landing on the black sedan, where I take a few minutes to watch her. My heart is beating abnormally fast. Her long legs are masked in flared white pants. A delicate black blouse that ties around her neck ensures no skin is on show. Classy as always, though I have memorized every inch of her body hidden beneath the fabric.

I open the door.

She shoots me a smile before taking the last steps.

I stride toward her and wrap her in my arms. "I've missed you."

We kiss.

Her soft lips remind me of what I desire. Our tongues dance briefly before she pulls away. "I have one small bag."

Heidi is standing ten feet away so I make my way to her. "Thank you for taking care of Penny."

"Our pleasure, Mr. Hendricks."

Picking up her overnight bag, I place my other hand on the small of Penny's back and lead her to the car. Quinton takes her bag from me and places it in the trunk. I open the door and slide in after her, then take her hand and stare into those alluring green eyes.

"While I'm sorry my mother had you rush here as though I was sick, for once, I'm thankful for her interference." I pick up her hand and kiss her knuckles.

"How are you?" she murmurs.

"Better now you're here." I lean closer, take her chin between my thumb and finger, and kiss her again.

Her hands wrap around my neck, and this time, she relaxes into the kiss. *Hell, I've missed her.* Her scent hits me, jolting memories of us lying naked together in my bed. My dick reacts, wanting her now. It seems our time apart has made me want her more and not less, as I had hoped.

I can't breathe with the need.

Desire hits me hard.

She pulls back. "We need to talk, Franklin." Her eyes flick over my face. "But not here."

AFTER FAMILIARIZING PENNY WITH MY PENTHOUSE, I WATCH her expressions as she takes it all in.

"It's a lot for one person." She comes to join me by the floor-to-ceiling windows—the one feature I demand when buying residences.

All I can think about is her hands pressed against the glass...

"Can I get you something to eat or drink?"

"Water is fine. I ate on the plane."

Conversation about her flight and the jet is the furthest thing from my mind. We're past small talk.

"Do you have personal drivers in every city where you work?" Penny is deflecting what's really on her mind.

"I do, and they are paid well. Though, I did give Quintin the weekend off before I heard about your flight. I have a car here, so I don't need him for the remainder of your stay." She eyes the opened bottle of whiskey and turns to me. "Let's talk about what's on your mind."

"Or we could discuss honesty in relationships if this is what this is." Her eyes hold mine before she downs all the water in the glass. I take it from her, refill it, and pour myself another whiskey. Taking a seat on the couch, I pat the spot beside me. "You heard about the Malibu house."

"Home," she says bluntly and lowers herself on the couch with some space between us. "It was your beach home. Wasn't I hired to remodel around your tastes for a future?"

"Mine or yours, Pen?"

She glares at me.

"To clarify, I loved what you did. I gave you the reins, and you created a beautiful home for a family, though all those ideas are what *you* believe in. While I love it, and it is the way for the future, please don't infer it was *all* for me."

Her eyes narrow. "You bastard."

"I said I loved it."

She attempts to stand, and I gently grab her wrist to stop her. "If you loved it, then why did you list it before spending time there?" she asks. "You didn't even give it a chance."

Letting go of her hand, I swirl the whiskey in the glass and stare into the golden liquid. "I didn't have a choice."

"Everyone has a choice." Her expression has hardened. This woman is more pissed than I'd anticipated.

"We do. The reason I'm here is our company is heading to court. My investors could lose thousands, and for some, that's their pension, their life savings. It has environmental impacts, and you have opened my eyes to more than you realize. While I can't save many, I can sell something of mine that will help offset costs."

"You're not selling to profit?" Her voice is softer—this is the Penny I know.

Taking her hand in mine, I squeeze it again. "No. I figured, in time, you could build a home that *you* love. It was never going to be *my* forever home."

Her eyes widen.

"If it's what you want?" I ask.

Penny's gaze scares me. I sense the cogs turning behind her eyes. I don't blame her for being cautious.

"When the time comes, and you want me to remodel a new home, we can discuss—"

I kiss her before she finishes.

Slowly, I sense the tension leave her shoulders before she pulls away again. "Franklin. I'm tired. Can we finish talking in the morning?"

BEFORE MY ALARM SOUNDS, I SILENCE IT.

283

If I move, I'll disturb Penny, and right now, there is no better sight than watching her sleep. She's curled into a ball, her face mere inches from mine. Her warm breath tickles my cheek. Long, dark hair splays out over the pillowcase. It's as close to heaven as I've been in a month.

Last night, I promised her we'd chat. We spoke about her work and then about my friend, Damien, until she fell asleep in my arms. An invite to Hugh's wedding should be in my inbox since she asked him to send it last night. Unless it had to do with PetroDepend, Bill has sifted through emails unrelated to the mess in New York.

Minutes pass, maybe hours.

Time is irrelevant with Penny.

Peace surrounds me in a way I haven't felt for months. My heart is calm. My thoughts are about her, and there is no better distraction.

Dark lashes flicker, her eyes open, and a few seconds later, she smiles. "Morning, Franklin."

"Go back to sleep," I whisper. "It's only five o'clock in LA."

"Which means it's eight here." She pushes up onto one elbow. "Don't you have to be somewhere?"

"Right here with you." I kiss her cheek. "Now sleep."

"You're busy, and I don't want to get in the way of your work."

A smirk creeps across my lips. "Not today," I say firmly. "So where do you want to go today?"

She falls back onto the pillows and rolls into my arms. "Can we stay here a bit?" Her eyes search mine. "In bed?"

She doesn't have to ask twice.

I gently kiss her lips.

"Uh-huh..." Penny moans. "I'm happy not to leave for the entire weekend."

"Fine by me." My fingertips make a trail up her arm to

her breast. I caress each breast from her nipples to taking her mounds in my hand.

Penny groans.

My hand lowers to her panties, lifting the elastic edge, then I hesitate when her hand covers mine.

"No, Franklin."

Did I misread Penny?

She takes my face in her hands and guides my lips to hers. "I need you. *Now*."

"Are you ready?" This time, she allows my fingers to find her opening. She's not lying. "Were you dreaming about us having sex?" She smiles up at me with desire written on her face, but something has changed for me.

I want to feel all of her.

Feel every squeeze when I rock inside her.

I want to love her, every inch of her.

And she needs to know it.

"We're not having sex, Penny." I ease up and reach for a condom.

She stops me, then wiggles out of her panties. "I take contraception."

That's an invitation, so I watch her eyes as I push in. We both know our sex has shifted to something more meaningful. The arousal fog blurs my thoughts. I thrust into her, overwhelmed with an urge to simply fuck, but I get my shit under control and study her face to guide my movements. I pull out slower, wait, then push inside her again. I lean down and kiss her lips. "I've missed you so damn much."

Her hands are on my ass. "And I you." She gives me a little smack, and I thrust harder, deeper.

"Is this what you want, Penny?"

She gasps. "Yes." Her hips rise to meet mine with every thrust.

I'm blinded by lust, slipping into a rhythm, our hips smacking, my balls slapping her ass. I adjust my arms, fall onto my elbows, and come hard, emptying myself and a bucket full of emotions with it after I kiss her shoulders and slump onto the bed beside her.

While we're warming up to a day of sex, I want to keep my focus on making this about Penny and what we share. I trace a line along the side of her face. "For once, I'm happy to stay in for the entire day."

32

PENELOPE

LATE MONDAY MORNING, I sit in a café across from work and call Jobe. I imagine he is busy and probably in a meeting. I take a quick sip of my coffee and place the mug on the table.

"Well, if it's not the famous Penelope Gilbert." *Shit, he answered.* "Did your weekend go well with my brother?" His playful voice eases my nerves.

"It was fun. Though I think your mom exaggerated his stress levels."

"She didn't. It's that magical power you have on him. His world changes when you're by his side." I snort out some sort of noise. "While I might sound cheesy when Franklin and I chat, his voice changes as though he's equally calmed by you as he is excited. No one affects him the way you do."

I screw up my face. "I don't have any magical power over him. So many times, he's too busy to give me any time, so I know I'm not a priority to him."

He chuckles. "Penny, babe... you are *the priority* even if you don't see it."

"Thanks," I murmur because I don't know what to say. The problem is I don't feel what he's just said to me.

"This call isn't to discuss Franklin's commitment to you, is it?"

"No." I take the last bite of my chocolate chip muffin.

"You want to know about the sale of the house? Because I assume you're in demand after he emphasized your remodeling should be highlighted in the listing."

"It sold?" I croak.

"On Friday."

Friday. I was with him the entire weekend, and he never mentioned it. I crumple the serviette in my hand and take a deep breath. "Right. No. My call is about something else. The condo. I want to sell it."

Silence.

"This is between you and me." My heart races. I've thought about it for weeks and *I am doing this.*

"If that's what you want, but the listing will be public."

"What about private buyers? It will be furnished."

Jobe's silence is unnerving.

"I'm moving somewhere out of the city." He doesn't ask, but I sense he is thinking it.

"Do you need help finding another property?"

"Not yet. After the house sells, I'll consider my options." I unfold the brochure on the house in Crystal Cove. The beachside community filled me with happiness when Franklin and I visited, and I kept going back to why. Something about being close to the beach, in tune with nature, appeals to me.

"I do have potential buyers on file. Leave it with me, and I'll get back to you in a couple of days."

"Thanks, Jobe. And remember, this is between us."

"My brother is going to kill me."

"I doubt that."

My heart thumps in my chest as I end the call.

Yet it feels damn good to be in control of my life.

THREE WEEKS LATER...

IT'S FRIDAY NIGHT, AND I'M HEADING TO MY CONDOMINIUM for a quiet night.

I am not watching *The Proposal* again.

No more love stories...

But the scene when Andrew proposes to Margaret in front of their staff... oh, my heart. If only movies replicated life, and if I hadn't met Franklin at a time he wanted to propose for all the wrong reasons, we might have stood a chance.

With a rosé wine in my hand, I step outside on the balcony and lean against the railing, ready for the color show of the night sky at dusk.

My cell buzzes in my pocket.

Jobe.

My heart races with thoughts about why he's calling.

"Evening, Jobe."

"Evening, Penny," he says with that trademark Hendricks' drawl. "Want the good news to brighten your weekend?"

I close my eyes.

Is Franklin home?

"Yes, please make my day. It's been a crap week."

"The condo has an offer above the asking price."

My shoulders slump while I clear my throat. "That's great news. Thank you, Jobe." Tears well in my eyes.

Why does it feel like the beginning of the end?

"I now have something to celebrate." I raise my glass toward the building opposite me. Thirty years old and celebrating milestones in life alone.

"You should celebrate with your friends. Give them a night out because you'll make a massive profit."

I choke on my wine. "You forget it's all profit. I didn't buy the condo." I sound bitter, and yet I should be ecstatic. I want Franklin here to clink our glasses together since he's the one who made this all happen for me.

"Don't undersell your worth, Penny. The remodeling on the Malibu house has created a new buzz, and your name is on everyone's lips."

It's why I'm exhausted and had a week from hell. Though it's a great thing to be in demand, right now, there is only one person I want to whisper my name.

"Has everything settled for Franklin?" I didn't want to mention his name, only now I can't get him out of my head.

What will he say about the sale?

Does he know?

"Yes, he called my father and is headed to Singapore and then to Australia for business." There's an awkward silence. "I thought he would have told you."

I suck in a deep breath. "We haven't spoken much with him being busy." Our messages have dwindled, with no calls for two weeks. The silence correlates with the condominium being listed for sale.

"Yeah, he's barely spoken to us. But, Penny, you haven't asked about the offer."

"Sorry. What is it?"

"You'll get double the asking price. I'll let that settle in.

Call me tomorrow so we can finish the paperwork. Have a good night, Penny."

Fuck. I raise my glass again. I should be on top of the freaking world, but instead, I want to crawl into a corner and cry.

No. Pull yourself together.

I open my emails to an inquiry about a beachside house in Newport Beach, at Peninsula Point. It's not Crystal Cove, but it's a step closer to buying my dream house. And this house is on the waterfront.

I am ready to do what's right for me.

August...

On Monday evening, I can barely place one foot in front of the other. After moving into my new home, I partied hard with my friends into the early hours on Sunday. Spending time in the sun and swimming in the ocean helped dehydrate my body, along with the alcohol.

Guzzling down a bottle of water, I plop onto the couch and then let out a long sigh before reaching for the remote. Romantic movies are listed, and before I click out, an old one is suggested. *Sliding Doors.* I remember the storyline and am intrigued by the different paths to love.

Love will *find a way...*

Are Franklin and I destined to be together?

I reach for my cell.

It's been two weeks since I last sent a text.

He hasn't responded.

Let it be. It's what's best.

Franklin will only bring heartache with more loneliness. God, I'm tired.

And lonely.

I tap on his name and listen to the ringtone. If he's on the other side of the world, he should be asleep. As expected, it goes to his voicemail.

"Hey. I know it's been a while since we spoke, and I can't remember if it's because you've been busy or if I'm angry with you or you with me. But I'm assuming you heard I sold the condo. You did tell me I was free to do what I pleased, and it was mine to sell if it was what I wanted. So, I bought a house, an actual house by the ocean. It's not large and nothing like your Malibu home, but it's mine." I let out a long sigh before closing my eyes. "I miss you. I'm lonely without you."

I'm finding it harder to breathe.

"You said we needed to be honest. You also said I'd be lonely waiting for you to come home to me. I'm lonely now. So, so, I..." I swallow hard, "... I wanted to know if there is still a chance for us?" I end the call and groan loudly.

What the hell am I thinking, sounding so desperate for his love? It's not the answer, and neither is confusing great sex with love.

Pushing up from the couch, I go to the window and gaze out to the darkening ocean.

My cell dings on the table behind me.

I don't breathe when I see who it's from.

> Penny, it's nice to hear your voice. I'm between meetings. I'll try to get back for the wedding. We'll talk then.

I clutch the cell phone to my chest and let out a sigh filled with hope.

He said *try*...

Stop being an idiot.

Nothing will change.

I'll be lonely if I'm with Franklin or not.

There is someone out there who is right for me.

Hugh is right.

LA is *not* an aquarium.

33

PENELOPE

Mid-September...

Peeking through the drapes, I watch guests arrive and take their seats in the garden setting. We are minutes away from celebrating Hugh and Sienna's wedding. Briony, the maid of honor, adjusts Sienna's veil. The bride is stunning, her dark hair falling in waves over her shoulders, while the tight-fitting lace dress flares midthigh.

Zara adjusts the flowers in the back of my hair. "Is he here?" she whispers.

I shake my head. "I wasn't looking for him. I love watching people's expressions at weddings. Everyone is happy, most of the time."

Zara nods, yet she knows I hoped Franklin could make it.

Over these past four weeks, I understand how I'll always

come second to him. While my heart believes it's enough, it's not the person I see for future Penny.

Zara lifts the other side of the curtain. "Sienna has created a wow factor."

"Flowers and food are always memorable," I whisper.

"If guests don't drink too much booze and forget."

"It's going to be unforgettable."

A little girl rounds the flower arrangements near the wedding celebrant. Her mother chases her, and she only stops when Hugh and his groomsmen walk the aisle to take their places. Their white suits with a touch of pink accentuate our soft pink gowns. It's tame for Hugh, but Sienna was determined to have the wedding of her dreams.

I turn to Sienna. "Hugh has arrived," I say softly. I smile, knowing he is wearing his new Christian Louboutin shoes.

She joins us at the window and takes a deep breath.

"Time to pledge your endless love to each other." I take her hand and smile.

We follow Sienna down the stairs and wait inside before the wedding planner signals and the music begins. Zara leads the wedding party, and I follow with the background sound of a harp playing romantic music.

As we walk toward him, Hugh shoots us both a smile, excitement etched all over his face. There is no sign of nerves. His face changes—the moment he sees his bride. Hugh wipes his eyes and beams his big, beautiful smile as if Sienna is all he sees.

Sometimes, you meet people who make your world a better place just by being in it.

It's how Hugh described meeting Sienna. She made him feel like he belonged. She is his home—seen him at his worst and best. Knows what he deserves and laughs and cries with all the versions of him.

We all need a person of certainty who will comfort us at our worst. I would do that for Franklin.

The question is... *Would he do it for me?*

My heart tells me he would.

My brain tells me he would always be somewhere else. Working in *another* city. *Another* country. Meeting with *another* group of people.

He warned me...

Listening to my friends' declaration of love offers hope.

The crowd cheers when the bride and groom's lips meet, and in typical Hugh style, he dips Sienna and deepens the kiss.

"Let's get this party started," Zara whispers over my shoulder.

I take a moment to gaze over the crowd.

A girl needs hope in her heart when it's a wedding.

He's not here.

BY THE TIME THE SPEECHES HAVE FINISHED AND THE TABLES are cleared of plates, the guests have consumed enough champagne to want to dance the night away.

I watch Hugh and Sienna sway romantically to the music while they stare at each other. The warmth of love oozes from them, wafting around the room and romantically inspiring their guests. Oohs and aahs sound quietly as women place one hand on their chests.

Zara takes the bottle from the middle of our table and fills our crystal glasses. She clinks hers with mine. "To friendship."

I down my drink and stand. "I need the restroom."

"Same."

Scooping our long gowns in our fingers, we hurry off to the restroom. By the time we return, we're both giggling when we stumble into the marquee, the impact of one too many wines making everything hilarious.

I pluck a long pink rose from a vase and hand it to Zara. "To forever being friends."

She takes it and inhales the scent. "I do." She hip-bumps me and stops like she's seen a ghost. "Nine o'clock."

"What?"

"Nine. Oh. Clock."

I turn, and I lose all train of thought with Franklin Hendricks staring back at me. He stalks toward us, taking two champagne flutes from a waiter's tray as he passes. He wears a black tux and is so impossibly handsome that I can't look away.

"Remember, I said I do first." Zara kisses my cheek, glides past Franklin, and takes one of the glasses from his hand. "Thank you." She takes a mouthful. "Hurt her, and I'll make your life a living hell."

"Noted." He turns and hands me a glass.

I take it, yet my brain is scrambling to catch up. "You came." They're the first words that come to mind.

"Sorry I'm late." He wraps an arm around my waist and pulls me close. "You're a beautiful woman, Penny Gilbert." He leans and kisses my lips. "I've missed you."

My body melts into his. Longing creeps in and settles under my skin. I want this man more than he'll ever know. Only I decided to do what's right for me, and while I dream about a life with Franklin, the reality is not all dreams come true.

"You missed all the fun," I say.

He grins. "Depends on your viewpoint. The last wedding I attended, the fun happened at night."

My cheeks warm. "You missed a beautiful ceremony today."

His nose nuzzles my neck. "I would have missed it anyway, as my entire attention would have been on one particular bridesmaid."

I close my eyes and allow his words to sink in. "While you make it sound romantic, there is nothing chivalrous about arriving late to a wedding. It's disrespectful."

He pulls back, his brow pinches and his eyes search my face. "I'm sorry. The storms in Florida delayed the flights. We had to wait for hours."

My sober brain would have appreciated what he was telling me. Instead, feisty Penny is in the house. "Why did you wait until today? I thought you could snap your fingers and make shit happen."

Franklin clicks his fingers.

I frown at him. *Smartass.*

"Maybe my fingers are broken." He shrugs.

I have never witnessed a shrug from Franklin.

"You are not confessing your love for me, so no, I can't magically make shit happen."

My fists dig into my hips.

We're doing this now?

"You come here hoping I would confess my love for you? Maybe if you had called me late at night when I was all alone and told me you loved me, just maybe I would have told you that I loved you too."

Franklin pulls out his cell and dials my number. He has it on speaker but keeps it close to his ear. My voice sounds, asking the caller to leave a message.

I roll my eyes.

"Penny, it's Franklin. I'm sorry I haven't called because I'm an idiot. I was too scared to get close to you as I can't give you the attention you deserve. I didn't want you to be alone weeks at a time in an empty house waiting for me to come home."

What?

His eyes bore into mine. "I'm a boring man. Work all day... you know the gig. Only I can't imagine a life without you. Whenever I feel myself needing you, I tell myself a lie and push the coldness into my heart so I can't get close. I was lonely, but it felt safe to be alone. You deserve someone better than me."

My heartbeat sounds in my ears, and I'm breathing too fast when I shake my head. He places a finger over my lips before I can respond.

"The problem with the Hendricks' men is we are a selfish bunch and used to getting our own way. So forgive me while I spend the rest of my life proving to you we can have our own happily ever after."

Now he's playing on the fact we are at a wedding.

Goddammit! I storm out of the marquee.

Why did I drink so much?

Franklin is right behind me.

"I have a proposal."

I freeze, then turn slowly.

"I want to spend my years getting to know the beautiful woman who stole my heart the first time we met on the beach. I still remember watching you, then at Noah's wedding, thinking love is better at second sight than first sight, and believing we were destined to meet again."

I glance down at my feet, my heels sinking into the soft grass. I remember him being lost that night on the beach. He came to me like I was a beacon offering him a light home. I wondered about him too. Only I convinced myself the suited man's world was somewhere I didn't belong.

"Penny," he says, and I meet his gaze again. "I want you to trust me to be the one who protects you. Every morning, we'll wake up together, spend perfect days together, be each other's reason. You strengthen my weaknesses, and no matter where life leads us, I'll know that as long as you are there, it is where I'm meant to be. Falling in love with you has made it impossible to stand again. Please say tonight is the beginning of us."

I take one step forward. "You mean it?"

Franklin keeps the cell to his ear. "Every word. *I love you.*" He drops the cell into his suit coat pocket. "Now you have it in a voice message for evidence."

I laugh and shake my head. "Okay, Franklin Hendricks, you have one chance. Don't mess it up."

Franklin lifts me into his arms and kisses me as though I've said, *I do.* It wasn't a wedding proposal, more a promise to love and trust each other beginning tonight.

A perfect beginning to our own happy ever after—*for now.*

EPILOGUE

Five months later...

Showering in Franklin's huge marble bathroom is as surreal as the first day when he asked me to move into his penthouse. The marble has fine streaks of gold and black throughout the design, perfectly fitted with brass faucets and accessories. For the past two weeks, the bathroom feels ridiculously larger than it is with him not here to shower with me. Even though we both have our own showers, side by side, we spend more time together under one spray.

We have our own dressing rooms. Mine is only half-filled. After slipping into my business skirt and white blouse, I walk into his dressing room and run my fingers along the row of suits—Armani, Burberry, Brioni, Versace, Gucci, Ted Baker, Tom Ford. His hanging space is full of designer clothes. I get to the end and flick through his business shirts in an array of colors. Lifting one from the hook, I inhale a deep breath, holding the shirt close to my face. The crisp linen scent with a touch of citrus has my heart sinking. I miss him. At least this trip is short, and he calls me twice every day—in the morning when I wake and before bed to say good night.

After finishing my makeup, I head into the kitchen and grab some greens and a pineapple to make a smoothie. He has accepted that our cook has time off while he is away. It gives me time to make my own meals and be in touch with the old me. It also leaves time to dine out with my friends.

Though today is Valentine's Day.

Sienna and Hugh have a date night, and Zara has recently met a guy, so neither is free tonight.

Franklin said he'd be home by the end of the week and make it up to me.

Every day is special with him, and I don't need one day to make our relationship perfect. Though, I have woken up missing him more than I usually do, if that's even possible.

Pouring the smoothie into a glass, I walk to the massive windows and stare out at a sprawling city. I'm dwarfed by the expansive room, the mega-high ceilings, and the four-foot ceramic and crystal chandelier hanging above me.

Gazing out to Downtown LA, I feel even more insignificant.

I need to snap out of it.

My work has skyrocketed into one of the city's most talked-about designers. Franklin has transformed the fourth bedroom into his own study, which leads into the library. His penthouse is decorated with extravagant furnishings, and although he said I could decorate it as I wanted, I couldn't remove anything that beautiful and purposeful.

We have our Crystal Cove holiday home for me to design with my own touch. After selling the Newport Beach house, Franklin and I bought our dream beach house. The penthouse is all Franklin, stylish, and over-the-top. The beachside house is all me, environmentally friendly with a personal touch. It's where we stay on weekends. We caught the end of the warm weather and swam in the ocean most weekends. In these colder months, we sit by the fire, reading or simply being with each other. I have even taught Franklin how to cook. He's not great, but we have fun doing it together.

The buzzer alerts me to Royce waiting downstairs.

I grab my briefcase and head to the private elevator.

The moment I step out of the rotating doors, Royce is there to greet me.

"Morning, Penny." He opens the car door for me with a broad smile, and I wonder how his morning went with *his* wife.

"Morning, Royce. Happy Valentine's Day."

"Happy Valentine's Day to you too."

Inside the car, I check for any messages from Franklin— nothing since six this morning. I send Hugh a message regarding the first meeting of the day. We are both remodeling a Shark's player's home in Beverley Hills. Our third from the team. After one of the players bought Franklin's Malibu home, most of the team requested we remodel their homes.

> I have discovered a new artisan we need to visit on the weekend. Talk to you in the meeting.

I pop my cell into my purse as Royce pulls into the park in front of Style Plus Designs.

What the?

All the air leaves my lungs.

My boyfriend is waiting out front with a bunch of red roses so large they partially obscure his face and chest. Before Royce has time to get out of the driver's seat to open my door, I have pushed the door open and am running to Franklin. I jump and smother his face in kisses. He's laughing while attempting to keep his balance, his one free arm tight around my waist.

"Happy Valentine's Day, Penny." He releases me, takes my chin, and presses his lips against mine. "I wasn't going to miss our first Valentine's together."

Taking the flowers, I inhale their unique scent. "They're so beautiful. When did you arrive?"

"About an hour ago." He nods to Royce, standing behind him. "Thank you, Royce."

I spin to Royce. "You knew?"

Royce allows himself a grin.

"Royce met me at six when my flight landed, and we stopped to pick up the roses I ordered last week. I waited here for you. I'm sure some people thought I was handing out roses to people passing on the street."

I giggle, then push up and kiss him again. Then I hug Royce, and he laughs. "Thank you both for the surprise. My day is already brighter."

"Tonight, I've booked us a private dinner." Before I ask where, he winks at me. "Call me when you finish work."

"Should I go out dressed like this?"

Franklin beams his big, beautiful smile at me. "Yes, Penny, like that. You look gorgeous."

My heart expands with every word Franklin says to me. "Okay. I'll see you tonight, but Royce needs to go home to his wife, and we'll find our own way home. He also needs to enjoy Valentine's Day."

Franklin pulls me into his side. "We are one step ahead of you. I anticipated you'd say that."

"Really?"

"Yes, Penny."

I kiss him again. "I love you."

"And I love you."

FRANKLIN AND I WALK INTO THE STADIUM, FLANKED BY security, and we are led to our corporate seats to watch the Sharks. Scanning the crowd near us, I recognize Hollywood film stars and musicians. We are stopped by VIPs to shake Franklin's hand. I take a seat beside Charlotte and Franklin sits beside Jobe. His father and mother sit in front, along with the important club staff.

"We Will Rock You" sounds from the speakers. Strobe lighting flashes over the court. A huge spotlight angles toward an opening where the players will appear. Every player's name is announced. When Byron Hendricks's name sounds, we stand and applaud. I glance at Franklin and Jobe, both of their expressions are of pride.

Brandon Johns is announced, and I sneak a peek at Charlotte's face. Her chin lifts ever so slightly, and there is a hint of a smile. The night I met them at the gala ball, I suspected they were attracted to each other. Nothing has been mentioned since, yet the clues are there. They joke around with each other less than what I witnessed that night. Plus, I have seen the way Charlotte stares at Brandon. She is in love with him because it's the same way I stare at Franklin.

I have never said anything to her as I don't want her to think her secret is threatened. She is the sister I never had, so I'm not going to ruin any trust with assumptions.

"Hopefully, the boys have a good game," I whisper to her.

She nods while staring at the court. "We need this win. It will keep us in good standing with the top teams."

"If Byron and BJ play like they did in the last game, we'll get the win," I say with confidence because they both played their hearts out and well together. I'm beginning to understand basketball better, especially since it's a topic often discussed at the Hendricks' dinners. Though Franklin said his father wasn't as passionate about basketball as he is now.

Halfway through the first quarter, Byron and Brandon play as though they have been part of the team for years, not like it's their first season playing in the NBA. Byron has six points, and Brandon has four and another four assists.

Brandon steals the ball and throws it to Byron.

Charlotte leans forward in her seat.

Byron dribbles past one player, then another, and sends the ball into the air. We don't notice Brandon zipping behind the defense. He leaps into the air, grabs the ball, and, in the same action, slams it into the basket.

The crowd roars.

Charlotte jumps to her feet and woo-hoos, clapping excitedly. Her face tells me everything as she watches Brandon sprint to stand beside his opposing player, ready to defend him. Charlotte cheers for the team, and her brother, but mostly for the guy who has her heart.

The Hendricks family applauds passionately.

"That was awesome," I yell at Franklin.

Franklin's smile is broad. "BJ and Byron know what the other is thinking."

Oh shit.

I bet Byron doesn't know what Brandon is *thinking* about his sister...

NOVEMBER...

THANKSGIVING THIS YEAR IS AT THE HENDRICKS. MY PARENTS are also invited.

Mom and Dad spent the night at our Crystal Cove beach house because I'm not sure they're ready to witness how we live in Franklin's penthouse. Small steps, and hopefully, they'll appreciate how hard he works and not that he is surrounded by extravagance in a place he only lives part-time.

It's been seven months since Mom's hip replacement, and she is moving as though she is ten years younger, handling the staircase in our beach house with ease.

Franklin drives us in his Bentley after giving Royce the day off. Dad and Franklin take the front seats while Mom and I are in the back. The men are talking about the upcoming game on Friday night.

Mom fidgets with the sleeve of her blouse. It's new, and the material is riding up her arm.

"It's pretty, Mom." I reach for her hand and squeeze it.

"I don't feel pretty."

"Hey." I squeeze her hand. "To me, you're always beautiful. I've grown to respect our bodies and love the skin we're in."

Mom's lips turn up into a smile, only it doesn't reach her eyes. My words are the same words she used to say to me.

"I've listened to all your advice over the years, though I've found something you said to be different for me."

Her brow furrows. "What's that?"

"No one person makes someone happy." I set my gaze on

Franklin. "He is my world, and everyone before him is insignificant." I stare at him with so much love in my heart.

"I understand, though you have happiness through other streams... your work, friends, and love of the beach."

"All true, although I'm happier if I'm doing those things with Franklin. I'm happiest when I'm with just him. He completes me."

She lifts my hand and gives it a little bounce as though she understands. "I'm glad you've found your soulmate."

I'm still grinning when we pull into the circular driveway of Carson and Sophia's grand home. A gentleman greets us, and once we are out of the car, he drives Franklin's Bentley to a special parking area beneath the house.

Franklin leads the way, nodding to the staff as we pass.

"This is..." Mom looks around, eyes round and mouth open. She has met Franklin's parents before, but it's their first time in their home.

"I know," I whisper.

We pass some framed pictures hanging on the wall, and Mom stops to peruse each one. She points to one of Franklin as a teenager, his siblings much younger. "Even then, he was a handsome young man."

I giggle. "He probably knew it," I say so only Mom can hear.

Sophia greets us and hugs Franklin and me, then Mom and Dad.

"Happy Thanksgiving. I'm so happy you could join us." Sophia is wearing a white chiffon blouse and a flared skirt to her ankles. She is not overdressed, and my heart swells knowing she didn't wear all her jewels in front of Mom.

Carson is right behind her, wearing a white shirt and black trousers. No tie. "Happy Thanksgiving."

Sophia chats to Mom as we move into the dining room. "I love your pearls, Lacey."

"Thank you. They were my mother's."

Sophia touches the nape of her neck and lifts a fine gold chain with a single pearl. "This was my grandmother's. We have kept it in the family."

Mom's smile widens. She reaches for Sophia's arm in appreciation. "It's gorgeous."

We are seated at the dining table like one large family. Minutes later, Jobe, Byron, and Charlotte stroll into the room. So does Brandon.

Once everyone is seated, the conversation shifts to basketball.

"How long do you intend to stay in the US?" Mom asks Brandon.

"As long as the mother country will have me." He gets a few chuckles. "Nah, as long as I'm playing basketball, I'll stay."

"You'll return to Australia?" Mom asks innocently.

Charlotte stiffens beside him.

Am I the only one who notices?

"My family is in Adelaide, ma'am. I think my mum is hoping I'll come home soon."

My mom is staring at Brandon, and I sense her empathy. "I bet she does. It must be hard."

"It is. Some days are harder than others. Technology today is great, and we FaceTime a few times a week."

"He's a mommy's boy," Byron jokes.

"And there's nothing wrong with that," Sophia adds.

The turkey is set on the table, and everyone is silenced by the amount of food presented.

Sophia asks us to join hands. "God, thank you for bringing us together today. Thanksgiving is a special time to share with family and friends, and we are blessed to have this time together. Today is about relationships, not just a meal, as our family appreciates the beautiful people who are joining us today. We are grateful every day for what we have and blessed with our health."

"Amen."

Franklin slides onto his knee beside me, pulls out a folded piece of paper, and hands it to me.

"What are you doing?" I whisper. I'm shaking my head because his family is staring at me. *My mother* is watching me, and all of them are smiling and not at all surprised.

"I have surprised you with a trip to Australia. We leave this weekend."

What?

"BJ has told me all the best places to visit. I even found the perfect tropical paradise for us and intended to ask you then."

"Ask me what?" I croak.

He takes my hand and lifts the paper closer for me to read.

My hands are shaking, so he takes the note and clears his throat. "Every love story starts with a first meeting. Our paths crossed in an unexpected way.

"Our story was even better at second sight.

"You once said sometimes you meet people who make the world a better place. On our second-chance night, you were determined to make me smile. A stranger sitting alone at a bar."

"At a wedding," I rasp out and shake my head.

"Pen," Franklin says gently. "Being sad worked in my favor. In a short time, you understood me better than I did myself. You knew what I needed and reminded me of what I deserved." He stops reading and stares into my eyes. "I don't deserve you, Penny, but you have convinced me that we are right together. More than anything, I want our love to be endless."

I swipe a tear and blink several times to stop my mascara from running.

"In an ever-changing world, you are my certainty. My home team. The love of my life."

I look at Franklin, the tears blurring my sight. He is holding a red velvet box, the lid flipped open. A whooping solitaire diamond ring sparkles under the lights.

"Penelope Gilbert, will you marry me?"

My hand covers my mouth. I'm stunned he's doing this here. Now.

"I planned to ask you when we were alone in one of the most exotic locations in the world. Only I considered your thoughtfulness and sharing our special day with our families."

My beautiful man thought to include my parents. My heart is so full of love for him.

"I thought about what you would like, and some might think it's arrogance to ask you to spend the rest of your life with me in front of family in case you said no. Except this time, I thought long and hard, and since I know how I feel about you, and I already know how you feel about me..." He winks. "I want to spend forever with you."

I fall from my chair into his arms and onto his bent knee. My arms wrap around Franklin in a bear hug. "Yes," I cry. "It will always be yes." I smother his face with kisses until he takes my cheeks in his hands and holds me still.

Franklin gazes into my eyes, and I feel the love pouring from him.

"I love you," he whispers before he kisses me long and hard. Cheering and applause sound around us.

I pull back, and Franklin slides the ring on my finger. I giggle with the emotion swirling through me. I kiss him, then hold his gaze and say, "You are *my person* who brings me happiness."

"And it's my priority to make *you* happy *every single day*."

THANK YOU FOR READING PENNY AND FRANKLIN'S STORY

If you want to read more you can download the Bonus Epilogue at https://BookHip.com/BGDLAKX.

THE WRONG MOVE Book #2 in the series is Byron Hendricks story and out now. Buy on Amazon.

THE WRONG PROMISE Book #3 is Jobe Hendricks story.
THE WRONG TIME Book #4 is Charlotte Hendricks story.

Want more of the characters in this book?
Brandon Johns (BJ) is originally from my Australian sports series.
You can read about Brandon in Winning the Player.

If you want more of my books please follow me on Amazon, and be notified about my next book release.

If you are on Facebook please join my Reader group. We have a lot of fun talking about books.

Please join my <u>mailing list</u> to be notified of my next release.

You can learn more about me on my <u>website</u>

ALSO BY LEESA BOW

www.leesabow.com

ACKNOWLEDGMENTS

First and foremost, to my husband. Thank you for your encouragement, love, and support of my writing journey.

My gratitude extends to my amazing editors. To Kaylene Osborn at Swish Design and Editing. Thank you for all your expertise, for answering endless questions, and for making my book shine. You are my rock! And a big thank you to Nicki!

To Lauren at Creating Ink, you always point me in the right direction so early in writing my story. I appreciate you!

To Virginia Tesi Carey for proofreading, and helping to eliminate all the Aussie terms in my writing. I thank you all from the bottom of my heart!

To Letitia Hasser at RBA Designs, thank you for my beautiful cover.

My appreciation extends to my Facebook reader group, and all the blogging community for helping to get my book out to the world. You all make the book world a much better place. A special thanks to Jenn at Social Butterfly for all the talks and guidance!

To my author friends, I can't express enough gratitude for all your advice and inspiration. Especially to Nina, and Beth who are always ready to offer any advice and support.

To my beta readers, Carol and Robyn. Thank you for reading on short notice and finding the little things to help my story be the best it can.

To my readers. Thank you for your endless support, and most of all, for loving my stories. Some of you have been with me from the start of my author journey, and to others, I'm a new author. What I love most is you all embrace my characters and stories and love them as much as I do. Thank you for reading, reviewing, and talking about my books to your families and friends in book clubs and blogs.

I appreciate everything you do for me.

ABOUT THE AUTHOR

Best selling Australian author, Leesa Bow lives in sunny Queensland, Australia. She spends her spare time with her family, and catching up with girlfriends for coffee or a wine.

Leesa loves to keep fit at the gym, in the pool, and walking surrounded by nature. Importantly, Leesa keeps it fun with laughter in her life.

She loves nothing more than to curl up with a good book, and a glass of South Australian wine. Or if its by a pool then a cocktail is preferable.

Leesa's love of travel inspires the next story. She hopes her books transport the reader around the world by the words on the page.

www.leesabow.com